The Watchers' War

BOOK ONE OF THE SWORD OF THE WATCH

THE WATCHERS' WAR

JOHN MONTGOMERY

imc
STUDIOS
INCORPORATED

THE WATCHERS' WAR
BOOK ONE OF THE SWORD OF THE WATCH

Second Edition

Copyright © 2025 John Montgomery.

Sword of the Watch series books may be ordered through booksellers or by contacting:

IMC Studios Incorporated
901 Deerfield Court, Russellville AR 72801
www.imcstudios.com
1 (479) 880-8802

Because of the dynamic nature of the Internet, any web addresses or links contained in this book may have changed since publication and may no longer be valid.

The views expressed in this work are solely those of the author and do not necessarily reflect the views of the publisher, and the publisher hereby disclaims any responsibility for them.

This is a work of fiction. All of the characters, names, incidents, places, organizations, and dialogue in this novel are either the products of the author's imagination or are used fictitiously.

Chapter artwork by John Montgomery, Copyright © 2025

ISBN: 979-8-9999009-0-6 (sc)
ISBN: 979-8-9999009-1-3 (hc)
ISBN: 979-8-9999009-2-0 (e)

Print information available on the last page.

IMC Studios Incorporated rev. date: 03/14/2026

For Asia, Matthew, and Mia

CONTENTS

ILLUSTRATION

FOREWORD

In the spring semester of 1981, a sweet, generous-spirited young man walked into my classroom and my life. He was—and is—John Montgomery, the author of a trilogy of novels, the first of which you are on the verge of reading.

The class of mine John walked into was called Advanced Composition. A mythopoetic frenzy was upon John, and he spent his time in my class building a world he peopled and animated with all manner of arresting denizens and events. I read him for proof and with pleasure.

John used to wear an army coat to class. He wished to have lived in the '60s and seemed a bit in awe of me for my having merely come into manhood during that dizzy decade.

For better reasons, I was more than a bit in awe of John, owing to his boundless energies in the service of his narratological project and to his sheer goodness—his profound decency.

And then one day he was gone out of the orbit of Ouachita Baptist University and, it seemed, my life. I lost touch with John and that stirring world he'd been making.

A quarter of a century passed.

John reappeared. By then life had overtaken him: he'd become an explorer of nuclear worlds and a writer about them, had gotten married and had children, had established his own business. Surely his mythopoetic dream had disappeared under the weight of the thing we call real life. *Mais non!* And John was still building the books to prove the contrary. *The Fall of Daoradh* emerged in 2007. *The Rise of the Western Kingdom* made the scene in 2012. And now, behold *The Watchers' War*.

A brief note about a stylistic tic of John's that I observed when first reading him back in the '80s. Whereas Generic Writer A might say, "'The sedge has withered from the lake,' he said,'" John was inclined to do something rather like this: "'The sedge has withered from the lake,' he lamented, remembering gray Rebecca's gentle embraces, her sadness in the embers of their time together, her ebon tresses, the sheer glory of her figure as she mounted her palfrey in Rion's brutal dawn."

I was fascinated by the numerous occasions on which John, in the process of simply exiting from quoted material, began making a new story.

Such digressive behavior of course had to be curbed for the sake of the story at hand, and John, always a tireless honer of his craft, did indeed curb it.

That stylistic "weakness" of John, however, bespoke a great strength, emblematic as it was, of John's mythmaking energies. John knew then— and goes on knowing—that everything's tied together, that way leads on to way, that roads go ever, ever on.

I wish you joy and shivers of this book and the two that follow it as you make your way into the enchanting and enchanted labyrinth that is John's imagination: the bubbling eye of the Land of Mires; wise Mategaladh, who informs us that revenge poisons the well from which all must drink; the Mourner's Fault; the Faceless Mountains; the ghastly Syrae; ghostly Ardidhus (J. M.'s Banquo); the hilt of the sword; Aphlarin (J. M.'s Gollum); the sadness in the brown eyes of the Witch of Southwood; the vile, vial-engendered Angrodha; Rendaya's Captus; splendid Galbard (J. M.'s Everyman); Bellows, the black cat who helps restore the sword; the nightmarish weaving worm; the fierce Huntress and the bizarre "arms trade"; and a Soru bush, the modest botanical contraption that putatively gets the whole glorious narrative ball rolling. Enjoy!

Johnny Wink

Acknowledgments

To my wife, Bobbi, for the countless hours of listening to my reads, looking at my artwork, reading my proofs, and discussing the plots. You have the patience of a saint.

To Johnny Wink, for your kind words in the foreword to this book and for many years of encouragement well above and beyond the call.

To Brenda Ringhardt and Kevin Wiser, for their uncanny ability to see the world and ways of Erathe and its characters, and for guidance when I'd lost the path.

To the fans of the Sword of the Watch series, for the sheer joy you bring me when you quote a character or relish a plotline. Those are the moments for which writers live.

Calarph Wood
Fortress of Durageim
Calarph
The Faceless Mountains
The Known Continent of
Etharath
28 A.F.
MoonLedge Peak
The Upland Plains
The Northern Plains
The Black Mountains
Candra Mountains
Highborne Falls
Harot
Highwood
Highborne River
Arch of the Patriarchs
Monastery of Ardidhus
The Western Frontier
Southwood
Northern Fields
Blue Water
Rion

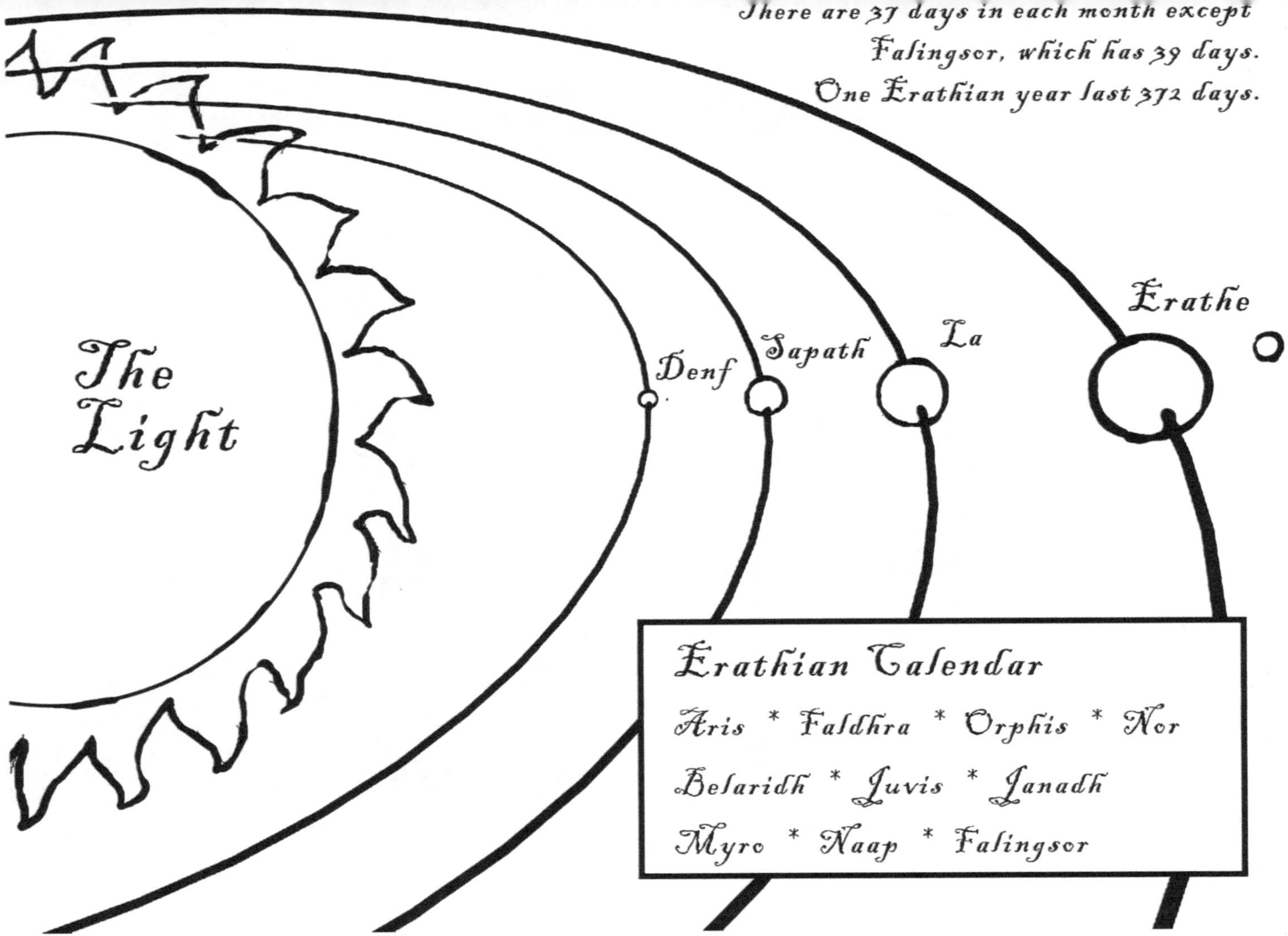

There are 37 days in each month except
Falingsor, which has 39 days.
One Erathian year last 372 days.

The
Light

Denf
Sapath
La
Erathe

Erathian Calendar
Aris * Faldhra * Orphis * Nor
Belaridh * Juvis * Janadh
Myro * Naap * Falingsor

Spellmaking Glyphs

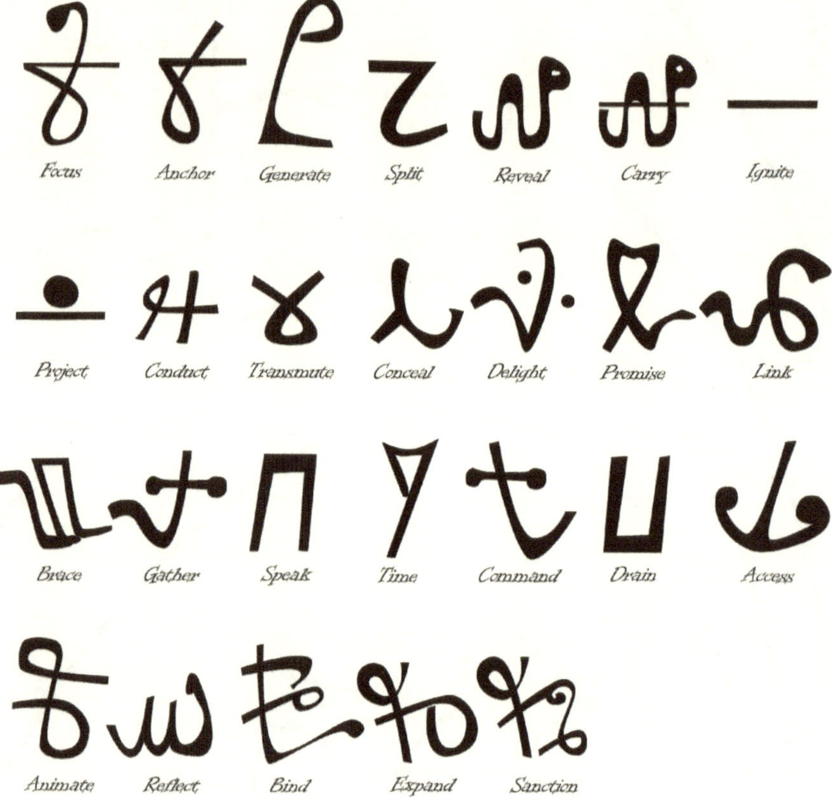

Prologue

Seventeen summers before, in Mura-Et, east of the Black Mountains

Rendaya sat perfectly still, clutching her rag doll as if shielding it from the strange creature perched on a lilac branch behind her parents' home. The black strokes on the butterfly's wings were hypnotic, like a cat's eye awash in autumn hues of burnt orange and brown.

It didn't seem to mind her presence as she squatted close, watching it slowly open and close its wings against the backdrop of swaying wildflowers. Time rested in the gentle breeze of late summer.

Suddenly a voice echoed through the field. 'Rendaya!' Her mother's tone was the same as the day Rendaya stepped in front of her father's plow horse.

"Rendaya!"

A bit of panic took hold. "I'm here!" Rendaya yelled, popping up from her squatted position. She looked for her mother but didn't see her—only the butterfly fluttering away at the edge of her vision.

She ran toward her mother's voice. There was a sudden ache in the pit of her stomach, and when she saw her mother's worried face, Rendaya threw out her arms. "Mama!" she cried.

"Come inside, Rendaya! Hurry!" her mother said. She grabbed Rendaya up, and the moment she had her, she rushed the frightened four-year-old into their one-room house.

Her father was on his hands and knees, pulling at a floorboard.

"What's wrong, Mama?" she asked. She fought back tears without knowing why, but her mother's alarmed look made Rendaya's heart pound. "Mama!" she cried.

Her mother turned back to her and drew a sharp breath. "Oh, no, it's okay, sweetheart! It's going to be okay!" But the look on her mother's face screamed to Rendaya that indeed it wasn't. Rendaya couldn't hold back her tears any longer and tucked her head into her mother's neck.

Her mother snapped back around to her father. "They can't do this. They wouldn't do this!" she said. They can't do this. They wouldn't do this!' she said, shifting Rendaya to her hip and rocking her.

He nodded toward the table. "Grab that bread, and let's go!" he said. Rendaya's father rarely shouted at her mother, and it made her jerk her head up. "They've already done it, Mera! There's …" He stopped. "Quiet! Quiet!" he shouted, waving his hand.

Rendaya's tears stopped. A cold, unfamiliar terror tightened around her heart.

His eyes widened, and then he looked sternly at them. A faint rumble rose, like distant thunder. "They're coming!" Her father pulled up the floorboard he'd been struggling with in one motion, nails and all. He reached under it and removed a leather pouch that jingled with coins.

Her mother set Rendaya down and grabbed a cloth sack from a hook on the kitchen cabinet. She grabbed the bread from the table and stuffed it into the bag.

"We have to go, Mera!" he said.

"Come here, Rendaya!" her mother exclaimed, scooping her up and settling her on her hip. She scanned the room. Rendaya held on tightly. She could feel her mother's heart pounding in her chest. "Yes, we're ready."

"All right, then!" her father said, jumping to his feet. He reached out his hand, and her mother took it in her own. He cracked open the door to look outside, but gasped and quickly shut it again. He turned back to them, stopping just short of their faces. "No! No! No!" he said. He had gone pale. "They're on the ridge! They're already here!"

He backed into the wall and slid down, sitting beside the door. Her mother quickly sat down beside him. She never took her eyes off the door.

"Terrin," she began, her voice shaking. "Terrin, what are we going to do?"

Rendaya would never forget the broken look on her father's face. "I don't know," he said.

The distant rumble grew louder, shaking the little house and sending dust drifting down from between the wooden slats of the ceiling. Rendaya's insides quivered with the force. "Mommy!" she screamed, causing her mother to jump. Rendaya climbed onto her until she was nestled under her mother's arm. "Quiet, Rendaya, please!" her mother said, shifting to sit beside her father. Rendaya clutched her little rag doll tightly, and thankfully, the rumble outside slowed to a stop.

The silence didn't change the look on her father's face. He peered into her eyes. "Rendaya," he said, and then he gently stroked her hair and kissed her head. He stared at her mother then, and Rendaya thought he looked very sad.

"Run. Hide. I'll give you as much time as possible," her father said. Rendaya's parents kissed for what seemed a long while until her father pulled away and jumped to his feet.

Her mother cried out, but he opened the door and swung it closed behind him, catching his heel as he exited. The door didn't close all the way, and a thin strip of daylight shone through the opening. Her father started shouting something outside.

"Rendaya, go to your hiding place, quickly now," her mother said. She was sniffling now, desperately trying to hold back more tears.

The panic returned, and Rendaya began crying again. "No, Mama, no!" she cried.

Outside, her father yelled—and then came abrupt silence. Her mother gasped and jumped to her feet, causing Rendaya to fall to the floor. "Mama!" she protested.

Her mother turned to look at her, her face wild and fierce. "Go now, Rendaya! Hide!"

A sudden hot trickle of urine ran down her legs. She screamed and pulled back her father's wolf-fur chair to hide behind it, glancing back once to see her mother peer out the doorway before disappearing outside.

Rendaya slipped into a crawl space behind the cabinets. The spiderwebs usually scared her, but she slid back as far as she could against the wall without any regard for them. She pulled her dolly close, went still, and waited, her breath the only sound she could hear. *Could she stop breathing to make no noise at all?* She tried to hold her breath, but she couldn't do it. Her heart was racing.

Suddenly the house door crashed open, followed by the thud of heavy feet. A gravelly voice called out, followed by claws ticking on the floorboards, furniture scooting around or falling over, and panting and huffing. The panting grew closer and louder, then turned to sniffing that abruptly became a loud howl. Rendaya wanted desperately to scream, but she put her hand over her mouth.

Without warning, the entire cabinet tore away from the wall, and over her crouched a manlike creature twice her father's size, holding the cabinet in one hand and reaching for her with the other. Though his red eyes looked more annoyed than angry, her scream burst out involuntarily.

Behind the creature stood a black dog the size of a cow. It started barking savagely at the sight of her. Its fur stood up around its neck, and it lunged for her, teeth bared. The manlike creature snatched her up just in time, but when he tried to stand, he struck his head on a ceiling rafter. The dog snapped at her dangling feet, and the creature let out a sound between a yell and a bark. He squared his shoulders to the beast and waited, almost daring it to attack.

Rendaya had dropped her dolly and was screaming at the top of her lungs. When the hound cowered down and turned its head away from him, the creature huffed, and then he turned and snatched the dolly off the floor. He crouched through the doorway and went outside.

Swinging in his hand, Rendaya caught a glimpse of her parents on their knees outside their house. The man-creatures had hurt them. She wanted to yell out to them, but her voice was gone.

More of the man-creatures appeared to go on forever in every direction, encircling a sedan chair carried by eight of their kind. Rendaya's captor stopped at the sedan's enclosed carriage, and then his deep voice bellowed forth again.

From within, there was another voice. It terrified Rendaya, but the soldier opened the door, abruptly dropped her and her dolly on the floor inside, and closed the door behind her. She flung herself on the door, trying to figure out how to open it and escape, but unable to do so, she parted the curtain and looked for her mother and father. "Mommy!" she screamed.

A voice from within the darkness of the carriage cabin said, "Kill them!" The man-creature took a spear from one of the others standing by and walked toward them.

"Rendaya! Don't look, Rendaya! Turn your head, baby!"

She did as her mother said and hid her head in her arms, but fingers suddenly wrapped around her head, lifted it up, and forced her to watch the man-creature kill them.

At that moment, something broke inside of her. She knew it was so because she *felt* it. She felt it snap, and then she felt nothing more.

The fingers released her head, pushed her into the opposite seat, and then grabbed her firmly around her waist, pinning her there. Another hand of slender fingers pinched the little dolly from the floor and placed it in her arms. She clutched it but couldn't feel it. She couldn't speak. She couldn't even cry. There were no tears left.

A sallow-skinned bearded man leaned his face in close to hers. He was big like the man-creature, but his appearance was more human. His eyes began to glow red within his hooded cloak.

"I am Broeden. You belong to me now."

CHAPTER 1

HAROT

In the years of Rion's Foundation

A Soru bush, that's what started this—all because Evliit wanted to rescue a girl who lived in a little village just southwest of Harot, the latter being the place he'd called home since leaving his father's farm in the northeast at seventeen years young.

He'd met her standing in ankle-deep mud in an alley next to the Marker, a tavern in the darker heart of Harot. Dusk was falling, as was an unusually chilly rain for early spring.

She was shaking, and her steamy breath rippled outward between her chattering teeth. "Hello," Evliit said in a quiet voice, though he'd still managed to startle her when he'd emerged from the shadow of the tavern roof's overhang.

"Oh!" she exclaimed, taking a step back. "I didn't see you there!"

"Sorry!" he offered sheepishly. "I didn't mean to scare you."

She gathered her composure, her widened eyes narrowing as if measuring up his intentions.

He had the sudden urge to speak up. "I'm Evliit—Evliit of Arentis. Arentis is northeast of here."

"I know where Arentis is." She relaxed her narrowed eyes but held her stare.

"Nice to meet you." He paused, extending his hand. She looked at his outreached hand but didn't take it. He quickly returned it to his side.

"Sorry to have scared you. I'll be on my way." He turned to leave.

"I'm Jenna," she said. He stopped and turned back to her.

"No place attached? Like 'Jenna of Harot' or 'Jenna of—'"

"No, just Jenna," she said. She glanced at the side exit of the tavern.

"You here for the scraps?"

He noticed then that her blouse was torn as she fumbled with pulling the wet, drooping fabric back up over her bare shoulder. "No, I know nothing of that. I was just trying to get in the dry." He made a quick glance up and down the alley. "Hey, uh, are you okay?"

She made another quick effort to fix her blouse. "Yes," she answered, but Evliit saw that tears were brimming in her brown eyes. She looked away and wiped her forearm across her face. "I work in the tavern. Some drunk ass thought the ale I was serving him was a little too watered down. He wanted me to make it up to him—in other ways. I hit him on the side of the head with a full mug. He let go of me, but not before ripping my one good blouse."

Evliit broke eye contact. "Oh," he said. "An ass indeed."

Behind them, the tavern side door opened. A burly man stood in silhouette against the lantern light coming from the tavern kitchen. He wiped his hands on his apron and took a long drag on the stub of a cigar. The reddish orange glow highlighted his blocky, stubbled jawline and baggy, squinted eyes. His barrel chest heaved, and a hint of Soru smoke suddenly infused the alleyway air. He flicked the last of the cigar end over end into the alleyway and reached back inside the kitchen, producing a large bowl that he placed under one arm.

Jenna quickly approached him, but when she reached toward the bowl, he grabbed her wrist with his free hand. "You owe me for that mug, Jenna!" the man shouted. "You learn to please customers rather than breaking my mugs, or this will be the last food you get! Don't think I won't throw you to the streets. I can get ten more just like you!"

"Hey!" Evliit cried. "What are you doing?" He stepped toward the two of them, but before he could say anything else, the burly man released Jenna's arm, took one step toward Evliit, and grabbed Evliit's entire face in his large, rough hand. He pulled Evliit's head toward him and then pushed backward with enough force to put Evliit squarely on his back in the mud. Evliit sat up just in time to see the man turn away, shaking his head. He thrust the bowl into Jenna's arms and went back inside, slamming the door behind him.

"I guess it's my turn," said Jenna. She hunched over the bowl to shield the pieces of day-old bread and half-eaten meat from the rain, and then she reached out her hand to Evliit.

He took her hand. "Your turn for what?" he said. His pride was stinging.

"My turn to say, 'Are *you* okay?'"

She smiled, and something about it was magical. Evliit felt his anger drain away, and with a tug, she helped him to his feet. "I hate wet bread," she said. "Come on. Let's eat this over there, out of the rain." She pointed to the nearest shelter—an empty covered stall that the farmers used during the day to sell their goods along the main thoroughfare. "Come on!" she yelled, and she darted toward it. She giggled as she ran, the sound of which stretched a broad smile across Evliit's face.

They ate the scraps in the leaky old structure and talked well into the night after the discussion turned to surviving Harot's treacheries. They both admitted that the lure of "wild" Harot had brought them to her streets from their peaceful farmlands, but that the enticement had diminished with the harsh reality of the conditions there.

"Harot's the most lawless town in all of Erathe," said Jenna.

Evliit smirked. "Oh, there's a law all right. One thing still rules over Harot—one thing and one thing alone."

"And what is that?" she asked.

"Soru," answered Evliit. "All will pay for Soru."

Jenna's face changed. She looked a little worried. "You have Soru?"

"I can get it."

She worked to swallow the piece of bread she was chewing, shrinking from him against the stall slats. "I'm not stealing Soru. That's a good way to get killed."

"No, no, no, that's not what I mean. I mean I know where Soru grows wild. I'm not talking about trying to steal anything."

"Oh," she said, nodding. "You mean the Black Mountains?" She pinched some mold from another piece of bread she was about to eat and pitched the moldy piece over the side of the stall. She gave the bite another once-over before eating it.

"Yes, the Black Mountains."

"*High* in the Black Mountains. You're that brave, are you?"

"I can climb them."

He sat down beside her, and he was suddenly struck by the miraculous scent her wet hair was giving off. He drank it in, and his heart beat a little faster. "I could sell it in the market, and we could have a real meal."

Her eyes met his, and Evliit thought he saw her face light up. "Pork loin and a big loaf of bread, hot out of the oven? With butter! I'd have to have butter."

"Of course," he answered. "You shared your bread with me, right?" He chuckled, and their eyes met again. Their common joy was miraculous. Everything about her connected with him deeply, and in the heat of the moment, he blurted out, "I find enough Soru, we could even get a place to stay."

Her smile faded. "You can't buy *me* with Soru," she said. "I—" "Oh, I … I don't mean it that way," said Evliit. His face grew warm.

"I just meant someplace safe, that's all."

She looked at his face as if she was trying to determine his sincerity. "If I could just get out of that tavern," she began.

"It's settled then," he said. "First light, I'm off to the mountains. Harot hasn't beaten us yet."

Much to his delight, her smile returned, but then she rubbed her arms. "I don't know; is it getting colder?"

"Here, take my coat," he said. He took it off and draped it over her shoulders before she had time to answer.

Jenna seemed pleasantly surprised by his gesture. "Why, I—" Thinking it the perfect end to the night, Evliit interrupted. "Well, it's getting really late, and it's quite the little hike to the mountains. I should get some rest." They met eyes for another moment, and Evliit resisted the urge to lean over and attempt a kiss. "Good night, Jenna. I have to say that meeting you has been the best thing Harot's ever done for me."

"Good night, Evliit of Arentis," she answered with a slight chuckle. He lay down on the gapped wooden slats forming the floor of the structure. It wasn't much, but lying just a little above the mud made all the difference.

A moment later, Jenna lay down beside him and huddled close. She opened the coat and threw the lapel over his shoulder and tucked her head and hands into his back and her thighs to the backs of his legs. Her body heat made him melt inside.

They slept until a vendor arrived early the following morning. He was carrying chickens in cages, and the sunrise had an old rooster crowing loudly and flapping madly in his cage. "Hey! Get out of there!" the man shouted.

"We're leaving! We're leaving!" Evliit shouted back, but he couldn't help but laugh.

They were both tired and a little giddy. Jenna rose slowly and pushed her hair out of her face. Her sleepy eyes were barely open, but when she saw him, she smiled. Evliit felt intoxicated by it. He pulled her to her feet, and laughing, they crossed to the tavern side of the street, back to the alley where they'd first met. They each stumbled on their goodbyes, promising the other to meet again at the tavern in ten days, and then he kissed her on the cheek and set out for the mountains. He had to stop twice to look back at her as he left.

To bring back Soru leaves would net them room and board, he was sure, for Soru was a prized herb among healers, soothsayers, and even wizards. It could command a hefty price in Harot's markets.

The Black Mountains were only about a day's ride southwest, but young men in Harot only dreamed of owning horses. Young men in Harot were lucky just to walk someone else's horse. So, for Evliit, it had taken four days on foot to reach them, and only a few pieces of the dried bread he'd shared with Jenna remained in his shoulder pouch. It's was going to be a long, hungry trip back to Harot.

He'd climbed the better part of a day before finding the elusive plant. To make matters worse, the small Soru bush was on a tricky ledge below him, the path to which was a sharp descent covered with loose shale. The footing was dicey at best.

He made his way down slowly, sliding twice, barely able to maintain his balance on the shifting grey stone. At the base of the ledge, he stopped on all fours and then scurried over and grasped the Soru by the stalk and pulled it from the clay. He lifted the plant to his nose; its musky aroma confirmed its freshness. He placed it in his pouch and threw it over his shoulder, and then he started back up the mountainside, unable to stop smiling.

He was just two steps from the path above when the shale shifted. He started to fall backward, but he managed to turn so he was sliding on his rear. As he approached the cliff's edge, he flipped around and began clawing at the stone pouring past him.

When his feet slipped over the edge, Evliit started to cry out, but then he stopped suddenly as the leather strap of his shoulder pouch caught on a sharp outcropping of stone. He just managed to keep hold of the pouch with one arm, kicking his legs instinctively as he did, as if to get away from the drop below him.

Still holding on to his pouch with one hand, Evliit swung around and pushed against the ledge with one foot and then pulled himself up until he grasped the ledge with his free hand. Now if only he could pull both arms over!

His arms were shaking. The stress of trying to pull himself up to the ledge and the thought of falling made him panic. A rush of adrenaline raced through his body. He pushed against the pouch to gain more leverage, and there was a popping sound. The strap gave way.

He watched the ledge moving out of his grasp, farther and farther away. The mountainside blurred past him, and then everything went black.

Evliit's fall had left the tibia of his right leg jutting out of the skin just below the knee. His right arm was crumpled up beneath him like a purplish red sock. Just before he'd struck the ledge below him, he'd reflexively stuck both appendages out to catch himself, as if the fifty- foot fall were something he might stop with a mere extension of one arm and one leg.

He tried to yell for help, but his throat only gurgled. In his head, the exertion made a wet, crunchy sound. He was blind in his right eye, but with his left, he could see his blood flowing in what looked like a dry, brownish red river. A brighter, fresher red flowed down its center, sometimes forming a random distributary as it spilled across the stones upon which he lay.

There was so much blood.

A tear formed in Evliit's one good eye, and a whimper of sorts dribbled down what was left of his chin. Then, thankfully, his sight blurred and everything went black again.

Evliit wasn't sure how long he'd lain there unconscious, but when he opened his eyes again, the sun was setting. He thought he saw the trail of blood next to him shifting in the dirt, but when Evliit focused, he saw that it was a line of ants. They were moving to and from the feast they'd discovered on the stone just in front of him.

Suddenly a drop of water struck the stone. The ants carried on, seemingly oblivious until there was another. And another. Evliit glanced upward and saw a line of thunderclouds moving toward the mountainside.

The wind gusted. One raindrop landed directly on the stream of ants, and their tiny bodies scattered from the impact. Evliit watched them break in all directions, disappearing beneath the stone through almost invisible cracks.

The rain picked up steadily.

The wall of approaching thunderclouds captivated Evliit. He watched the dark clouds rolling upon themselves, the lightning dancing in the turbulence. The sheer power of Erathe's nature made his mind wander, struggling to understand the workings of it all. He remembered the Elders preaching in the streets about one creator who had the power to stir the winds. Maybe the spirit of the sky was close now, traveling in the billowing storm clouds? Perhaps he would hear Evliit's cry and see the agony he was in?

Evliit tried to cry out, but he made no words. He tried repeatedly, but his face was paralyzed from his fall. Defeat besieged him, but then he remembered the words of the Elders, who said, "The Creator sees everything." Surely the Creator would see Evliit's broken body and take pity on him.

Evliit heard a stirring on the ledge below him. There was a snorting sound and then, suddenly, growling. A wolf's howl cut through the white noise of the rain, and Evliit's heart rate shot up. He felt as if he wasn't getting enough air. A clawing sound made him look down toward his feet: two large paws were on the lip of the ledge, and then they disappeared back over the side. A short silence followed, and then the growling came again.

There was another ledge that rose beside Evliit from below, and a movement there caught his eye. The wolf had made its way up this rising ledge to see Evliit, and it was glancing about the trails, working out how best to get to its prey. Moving toward Evliit on the descending ridge only increased the height of the jump the predator would have to make to reach his broken body—a predicament that agitated the wolf into another howl, followed by repeated, ferocious barking.

The thought of being eaten alive loosened Evliit's bowels. He was terrified.

Spirit of the sky, grant me life! Do not let me die like this!

Evliit's mind raced. His pouch was gone. He couldn't move to find it. He couldn't even bow in homage. He had nothing to offer this god of the sky.

The wolf's head suddenly appeared over his paws on the ledge. It was winning the struggle now to climb to Evliit. It pulled itself over the ledge and stopped instantly, taking stock of Evliit's ability to defend himself. Its lips stretched wide with another growl, baring its greyish gums and sharp white teeth. Saliva flew from its mouth as it barked again. Its fur was standing on end.

Suddenly he pictured Jenna's face in his mind. She was smiling the way she had on that fateful early morning in the market just a few days before.

With his whole being, he prayed one last time to his creator: *Please do not let me die like this! I can serve you!*

A roar of thunder made the wolf lower its ears. Lightning burst in the sky, and the wolf turned with a jerk to look at it. Evliit just managed to move his left leg, and the wolf instantly turned back and snapped its jaws onto his pants leg, thrashing its head this way and that until it tore a piece of cloth away. It chewed feverishly, savoring the bloody fabric.

Evliit closed his eyes. His ears were ringing. Then the sound changed; he thought he heard a buzzing noise. He opened his eyes to see the luminescent body of what looked like a knee-high winged man coming to rest on the ground between him and the wolf. The wolf lunged at the angelic figure, but the small creature drew a glowing blade. Lightning burst in the sky with a roaring clap of thunder, and the wolf cried out in pain and tumbled over the side of the ledge.

The figure's luminescence faded as it quickly moved close to Evliit's face. "You have been given a second chance, Evliit. Use it well," he said. "The Creator calls upon you to watch over the people of Erathe as we have watched over you."

Evliit was in shock. His mind was reeling with a million questions. His crumpled body lay still, but then the angelic creature reached out and touched his shoulder, and he felt the bones of his face shifting. A terrible pain shot through his entire body as his insides began to move back into place.

"I am Aleris, leader of the Bhre-Nora, craftsmen to the Creator himself."

Evliit's racing mind stopped, focused on the clarity of Aleris's voice. It seemed to block out everything else.

Aleris's face grew brighter and brighter until its intensity blinded Evliit. He began to feel weightless, like that of a child topping a hill at a dead run. His insides floated in his body, and the fear of death melted away as a great peace came over him.

"Come with me, Evliit. I will show you your destiny," said Aleris.

Evliit gasped. His surroundings blurred as they suddenly jetted skyward. Just as quickly, it felt as if they were turning and then falling. For a moment, he saw a vast, barren landscape toward which he descended at incredible speed, and then he crashed into the dry, cracked earth with deadly force. A cloud of red dust marked his landing. It flowed outward in concussive rings around his impact. The dust settled, and he stood up from his crouching position, totally unharmed.

Aleris was gone, and Evliit stood behind two groups of men wearing gray hooded robes. They faced away from his impact, allowing the shock waves to pass before turning back toward him. From all appearances, they were alone in this lifeless, shadowy world.

The winds whipped the hooded men about as the air swirled past them, lifting the dusty soil into the air. Evliit cupped his hands around his eyes to look up at the sky. The rolling storm clouds overhead parted ever so slightly, allowing a thin beam of light to pierce them. The light struck the ground on the opposite side of the hooded men, and a golden flame sprung up from the red dirt at its touch. In this new light, Evliit saw that a straight path lay between the two groups.

He instinctively began walking toward the now waist-high golden flames that shot up from the point at which the beam touched the ground. The growing blaze drew a swirling wind into itself, and the dust caught up in it appeared to ignite, sending streams of golden flame outward from its origin.

Evliit flinched as the group abruptly chanted in unison: "A light was seen driving out the darkness!" He glanced to either side, and he realized then that the men were all facing that same point of light.

The murky heavens parted further, and the beam of light expanded. A roaring wind deafened him as the golden flames spread with the expanding base of the light. He instinctively threw up his hands as the fire passed over them, but in the wake of the wave of gilded flame, the winds calmed, and brightly colored flowers and lush grasses replaced the dark soil. When the light encompassed all the horizon, only beauty and stillness remained. Tall oak and silverbell surrounded the group, their high canopy gently dropping some of their white blossoms' petals to the soft breeze. In mere moments, the land of shadow was gone. It became utterly silent, save the whisper of that same cool breeze.

He heard the quiet voice again. "Sword bearer," it said. His vision blurred in time with the syllables of each word; the sound seemed to resonate through his every fiber. He closed his eyes and embraced the warm energy coursing through him. When he opened his eyes, he was in a beautiful garden. A deep sense of joy filled him, as did a feeling of oneness with everything.

There was an older gentleman there, seated at a short table in the center of the garden. He was pouring tea. A sword lay across the table. "Come," he said. "Sit."

Evliit did so, seating himself on a plush cushion and accepting a cup of tea. "What's happening to me?"

The old man set the teapot down, toying with the lid as he spoke. "Peace be with you, Evliit. Worry not, for all is well." When he turned to look at Evliit, his blue eyes were piercing, but his weathered countenance gave Evliit great ease. "You called for me from the mountain."

"I called?" Evliit asked. He rubbed his forehead, trying to remember the mountainside and his fall. It seemed so long ago. "You are the Creator?"

He smiled and wiped his hand down his trimmed white beard. "I have taken this form to talk with you."

"But why?" Evliit asked.

The old sage sipped his tea, and then he placed the cup gently on the table. Evliit thought his face suddenly showed a hint of sadness. He offered up his right hand, which Evliit reached out and touched.

A great pain ached in Evliit—despair like he had never known. "Ah!" he said, drawing back his hand as if he'd touched something hot. Evliit put both hands on the table to catch himself. He felt sick to his stomach. "What was that?"

"But a sample of the pain," lamented the Creator. "The pain of the innocents."

Evliit tried to get his bearings back as he watched the Creator pick up his cup and drink again. There were lasting images that he worked in vain to push back out of his mind.

"I'm sorry, Evliit. It will fade," the Creator assured him. Much to Evliit's relief, the memories and emotions did fade at his speaking of them.

"There are those who have sought me out through prayer and alchemy. They possess great skills to set right that which is wrong in the Second Domain," he said. "But they require a leader." He gestured to the sword on the table. "Will you be its bearer, Evliit? Will you lead them? To do so would invite many trials, for evil knows no end to its lust for the freedom of men."

"You've saved me," Evliit answered. "Anything you ask of me, my lord, I will do."

"So be it," declared the Creator. "When darkness threatens to consume all light, you will be my champion."

The sword was beautiful, and yet Evliit was sure its edge was as sharp, as its lines were clean.

"Let it be so, Lord." He reached out and took the sword in his hand, and a strange energy coursed through his veins. He felt his body lifting weightlessly again. The garden drifted away below him, and his eyes were drawn upward.

Time seemed to rush by as day and night blurred across the sky. A cold breeze displaced the soothing warmth of the garden, and he felt the gentle brush of snowfall against his face.

Evliit found himself back among the oaks and silverbells, now laid barren of their greenery by the deep of winter. When he lifted his hand to his cheek to brush away the tickle of a snowflake, he felt the coarse hair of a full beard.

Before him in the snow-covered field, the two groups of men stood motionless save the occasional burst of warm breath escaping their hooded robes.

Their gathering felt familiar, like something he'd done a thousand times before, but he felt a strange tension in the air. He shook it off and spoke to them with authority.

"We must stand strong, all that have been called by the Creator to protect the Second Domain, for it is in that land of men that evil festers. It is the Watchers' charge—our charge—to maintain the delicate balance between the free will of men and their ultimate destiny, so that at the end of this age, when we take our eternal rest in the ethereal world of the Creator, we will be judged righteous and faithful!"

He intended to carry on, but the name "Jenna" popped into his head. He struggled to decipher its meaning and the odd sensation that it left in its wake. He tried to recapture his thoughts. "You will be a great force for good throughout Erathe," he told them, but then words failed him entirely.

Her face, her smile, came rushing back to him. The memory of Jenna seemed to pierce through it all, and sadness overcame him. In all he'd seen, in all that this new life offered, Jenna was not there. Evliit somehow knew then that if he stayed in this place, he might never see her again.

In that instant, everything changed. The Third Domain was gone, like a dream that fades in one's first waking moment. He was back on the mountainside, and Evliit saw Aleris's face once again. The wrenching pain had returned. It coursed through Evliit's convulsing body until he could take it no more. His vision darkened and blurred into nothingness.

Evliit woke to icy rain falling upon his face.

He remembered falling, and the wolf, but then—nothing. He moved his arm and leg; he ran his hand over his jaw. His body was completely healed. Were it not for the bloodstains on his clothing or the torn leg of his trousers, he might have thought it all a dream.

He dropped to his knees and looked up into the light rain. The low clouds were barreling up the mountainside. He could almost touch the crackling lightning. He raised his palms to the heavens.

The Creator smiles upon me!

He couldn't contain his overwhelming joy, his intense sense of victory over some mighty foe; bubbling laughter sprang forth from deep within him.

When he chanced to look down, he saw it lying there on the stone ledge in front of him: an ornate wooden case. The golden tiger's-eye maple bore a mother-of-pearl inlay of a sword. He leaned forward, and a closer inspection revealed that ruby-red ringlets of flame had been skillfully painted around the length of the blade.

He watched the raindrops bead on its polished surface. It looked strangely familiar, as if he'd seen it someplace before, but he couldn't remember where.

Evliit picked up the case and opened it. Within a bed of red velvet was the most magnificent sword he'd ever seen. Its craftsmanship was like that of no sword ever made by human hands. Its mirrored blade bore delicately etched inscriptions, but Evliit's reading skills left much to be desired. He had no idea what they meant, but he did know one thing: a sword of this quality would command enough money with Harot's smithies to afford a little piece of land south of Harot, and he and Jenna would even have enough left over to cover many months of supplies!

His heart was racing at the thought of it. He quickly put it back in its case and, dropping down onto the rising ledge that rounded the cliff, began his climb down. The rain soon died down, and he made good time on his winding descent to the mountain basin.

He knew the worst of the climb was over when he saw the sediment-filled paths where erosion had cut deep into the foothills. He made his way down into one of the troughs in the alluvial fan, enjoying that the soft sands were surely more comfortable on his feet.

When he emerged from the trough at the foot of the mountain, he stopped in his tracks. There stood a robust white horse bearing a saddle and tack, including a scabbard that appeared to be perfectly matched to his new sword's design. He looked all around, but there was not another soul anywhere.

He walked up to the horse, opened the case, and removed the sword. It fit perfectly in the scabbard.

"How can this be?" Evliit inquired. He looked around again. He could see for miles, but there was no one anywhere around him.

The horse stood still, eyeing him, and then it shook its head, almost motioning him to get on.

The Creator smiles upon me again!

Evliit tied the case over the horse's saddlebags, placed a foot in the stirrup, and threw his leg over. The horse remained motionless. "You're a good horse, aren't you?" he asked, adjusting his seat in the saddle. He patted the horse's muscular neck. "A magnificent horse."

The horse turned its head and looked back at him.

"You know, a good horse needs a name," he said. "How about Torli?"

The horse looked at him with disinterest.

"No? Then Merek maybe?" Still nothing. Evliit turned his head to the side and looked up at the clear, blue skies overhead. "How 'bout Angwen?"

The horse tossed its mane and neighed.

Evliit had to laugh. "Angwen it is, then!" He adjusted his seat in the saddle again. "This is all just unbelievable, Angwen."

He couldn't wait to show these treasures to Jenna. This was so much better than the Soru. The money from this sword would change their lives forever. He'd go straight back to the tavern where Jenna worked. *She'll never believe me*, he thought, smiling to himself. *She'll never believe me.*

"On to Harot, Angwen!" Evliit said, and the horse broke into a trot down the path.

ZɣᏕᠵ.

Late in the afternoon, Evliit approached Harot from the west, and he could see smoke rising—more smoke than any fireplace or blacksmith's forge might generate. Something was wrong.

He slowed Angwen and surveyed the road that ran down the valley toward Harot. He could just make out banners of some type at the town entrance, and what looked like hundreds of black tents just beyond the city's northeastern gate. Harot looked empty, but there was movement among the tents.

Angwen appeared spooked, nervous.

"What's up, boy?" Evliit gently put a little tension on his reins and patted Angwen's neck, realigning him with the road. "Maybe time to wait out Harot's visitors, eh?"

He put a hand on the sword. "Be my luck, a few of those fellows would want this, and that'd be the end of my good fortune." He tried to make out the tavern, but he couldn't. It was just too far away. He exhaled in disgust. "Sorry, Jenna. I'll be a little later than I'd hoped."

Evliit dismounted and tied Angwen off on a little maple sapling, ever watchful of the city below.

Darkness was coming quickly, and he could see torches moving among the tents. He removed the bedroll that was tied across his saddlebags and looked over the sword's case, which was gleaming in the evening light. He untied it from the saddlebags and hid it under the long edge of the bedroll.

The sword he kept even closer, removing its scabbard and tying the belt around him. He lifted the sword out of the sheath one last time as if to verify its reality before letting it rest at his side. Almost giddy with the excitement over the idea of cashing in his wares, he stretched out on the hillside. He wouldn't dare a fire—not with strangers in Harot.

A brisk wind blew in that made him pull the bedroll close, and then he drifted off into a fitful sleep.

Dawn woke Evliit. He cleared the sleep from his eyes and immediately looked for the tents. *Gone.* The strangers had moved on during the night. He was starving, so he mounted Angwen and headed straight for Harot.

His appetite was short-lived, for when he got a little closer, he could see that there were not only banners swinging in the wind—there were bodies. Two dozen peasants were impaled or hanging on either side of the road leading into Harot.

As Evliit approached them, he saw that one was Jenna. "Please— please, no!" he screamed. He spurred Angwen toward her and leaped from his horse. Evliit gasped at the sight. A crudely painted nameplate bearing the name "Broeden" capped the sharp end of the wooden staff piercing her midsection.

"Oh, Jenna," he uttered.

Jenna' s head moved, and she let out a little moan. "Jenna!" he shouted. "Jenna! Hold on!"

He tried to figure out how to remove her from her impalement. He pushed against the staff, but it wouldn't budge. He ran to Angwen's side and drew the sword from its scabbard. With one stroke, the sword bisected the upright with ease. He dropped the sword and threw himself underneath Jenna, struggling to slow her as she fell over on her side. Her abdomen bulged with the weight of the upright as she lay on the ground. She tried to speak, but her first words were only a spray of blood.

"Don't move!" Evliit said, moving to lift her head.

She coughed. "Evliit? Is that you?" The desperate look in her eyes pierced his heart.

"It's me, Jenna! It's me! Don't try to talk!" He gently laid back her head, jumped to his feet, and grabbed the sword, intending to cleave the end of the upright so he might remove it from her limp body. "Keep your hands back!" he shouted, raising the sword above his head.

Jenna's eyes flew open, and she raised up her hands. "No, Evliit," she managed. "There's nothing you can do for me. Stop."

Evliit let the sword fall slowly to his side. "But—"

"Please stop," Jenna said. "I need to tell you …" But her voice trailed off, her head fell back, and her arms dropped.

"Jenna!" Evliit cried. He fell to his knees by her side and lifted her head. When he touched the skin of her face, she gasped, and her pale color instantly improved. She opened her eyes and grabbed Evliit's face with both hands. "Sentries remain, Evliit," she said, her voice stronger than he would have imagined possible. "You must go! Go now!"

Just as Jenna finished speaking, battle horns sounded at the southwest gate of the town. Evliit pulled back from her and looked over his shoulder: a group of two dozen riders bearing Broeden's black banner was moving toward him.

"Run!" Jenna said. She laid her head back down and looked toward the approaching riders, a single tear trickling down her face.

Evliit paced back and forth, looking at Jenna and then looking at the riders. "I'm so sorry, Jenna!" he said, and he kissed her cheek. Then he jumped onto his horse, and after looking at her one last time, he spurred the steed back toward the Black Mountains.

Angwen flew. If not for Evliit's mindless fear, the horse's speed would have been alarming.

He reined in the horse after they'd gone a good hundred yards from her and looked back. The riders had stopped where sweet Jenna lay upon the ground, and one of them had dismounted and pushed his sword through her. He used his foot to pin her body to the ground as he drew back his blade.

Taking in the whole scene, Evliit retched. It was all he could do to hang on to his mount. He was terrified to the point of feeling faint. He turned Angwen and goaded him forward again, flying toward the Black Mountains without regard for life or limb.

When he reached the foothills, he stopped, for the riders had not followed. He dismounted and burst into tears. "Creator!" he screamed to the heavens, but he stopped suddenly at an intense pain on the left side of his chest. Screaming in agony, he tore open his shirt and looked down. On his breast, just above his heart, was a single word, burned into his flesh as if by a brand:

Harot

CHAPTER 2

THE SWORD BEARER

In his shame, Evliit had hidden in the mountains for just over two days. Nothing eased the weight on his heart. He kept seeing Broeden's soldiers surrounding Jenna—the thrust of the blade, the careless kick that cast her lifeless body aside. The memory gnawed at him without mercy.

He was tormented—and starving.

He'd heard it said that even shame bows to hunger, and he found it true. On the third day after his escape, the burning in his belly overcame his remorse, and he made his way down the mountainside toward Harot in search of food.

When he reached the foot of the mountain, he saw a thin wisp of white smoke drifting along the road that led to town. Whatever remained of Harot's citizenry was tending to the dead by pyre.

It was grim work, but necessary. The dead outnumbered the living, and their decomposing bodies threatened the survivors as surely as Broeden's blades had. When he was younger, Evliit had seen battlefields northeast of Harot strewn with corpses as far as the eye could see—bodies that quickly became fodder for rats and the diseases they carried. If Harot's dead were left to rot, sickness would sweep through the survivors long before they could reckon with the aftermath of Broeden's savage attack.

What the pyre lacked in dignity, it made up for in efficiency. In the two days Evliit had been gone, the survivors had burned all the dead.

At the end of the road, just outside town, a rough circle of white ash lay six or eight inches deep in places. Layers of smoke rose from it, curling into the air from several of the larger grey mounds.

Life seemed fickle at that moment. The pyre's heat had taken everything they had been—everything they'd ever seen, said, or done—and reduced it all to fine white ash and a wisp of smoke. They were all merely drifting away in the slow-moving wind.

Evliit stopped Angwen and sat in respectful silence. He watched the smoke drift by against the backdrop of the Black Mountains, some of it catching a brief microburst and dissipating on an air current. Most continued westward, toward the mountain. There, eventually, it would press against the steep stone and rise. Jenna was somewhere in that smoke.

Evliit's brand ached upon his chest.

The mountain was peaceful. It wouldn't be long until the very last bit of Jenna rose to the colder air—perhaps to hang there for a few more hours before being washed away by the cold mountain rains.

A wave of shame poured across him again. *I should have buried Jenna properly! What kind of man hides in the mountains?*

Evliit pulled Angwen around. "Get away from me, evil! Leave me be!" he shouted. He turned his horse entirely around a second time. It was as if demons tormented him from all sides.

There was only silence on the road. And that smell—that awful smell.

He rode slowly into town. The silence made Angwen's shoes sound unusually loud on the cobblestone. Their clippity-clack echoed in differing tones off the adobe and wood guild establishments lining the thoroughfare.

He'd never seen the streets of Harot empty. At this time of day, the roads should have been teeming with every manner of people, from whores to preachers of piety. Their absence was eerie and lonely, and Evliit wrestled fitfully with his shame, his sadness, and his fear. These emotions ate a hole in his soul. If he let them win, he knew he would do what he'd always done when trouble came: run.

Never again.

A tiny spark of defiance flared within him. He could never watch something like that happen in front of him again. It would be better to die. Cowering before Broeden's soldiers had left him with a brand on his chest and a stain on his being. It was a wrong that could be righted only by blood.

"Jenna!" he cried out.

He hurt deep in his soul. There was a groaning for her within him.

"Creator, help me!" he cried. "Give me strength!" And in that instant, a calm came over him. His hands still shook, but his heart had changed. By the grace of the Creator, he had already defied death on two occasions.

He pulled the sword from its scabbard to look at it, and a brief reflection off the blade blinded him. He shut his eyes instinctively, and in the afterimage on his retinas he saw a winged being. He was trying to make sense of the image when he heard a voice: "I am Aleris, leader of the Bhre-Nora."

Evliit jerked around, but no one was there. Suddenly he remembered something more about the mountain—something of this being, Aleris. It was this angelic figure who had protected him from the wolf. He recognized the face of Aleris close to his own. "Protect the weak," he'd said. But as quickly as the pieces seemed to fit together, the memory ended, and there was nothing more.

He looked at the sword again. If it was indeed his calling to protect the weak, then he would start with the murderer of Jenna. Broeden himself would pay for taking the love of his life away.

Evliit replaced the sword in its scabbard and rode deeper into town, where thankfully the smell of burning wood permeated everything, finally pushing the stench of death from his nose.

Harot had been ransacked. Several buildings in the middle of town had been burned to the ground. The granary was still standing, but the wall facing the road was smashed open, and torn sacks of wheat and other goods lay strewn about a mostly emptied storeroom. A mangy-looking dog sniffed around the bags near the opening, but at the sight of Evliit it lowered its head and scampered across the road.

The farmer's market was mostly gone from either side of the road. Grey-and-black piles of smoldering debris lined the way. Evliit noticed that most had a scattering of objects around them, as though someone had carefully picked through what remained of the vendors' wares, tossing aside anything useless.

The market had probably been the first to go in the mayhem. The vendors sold from stalls that were little more than cloth-covered wooden frames, and that tightly packed tinder lined the main road through Harot— the route the attackers must have taken. Evliit was sure the stalls had lasted only moments at the wrong end of a torch.

Farther down the road, a child lay in the path, and near the child a man rummaged through what remained of his goods. A mile or so beyond, a small group of people also seemed to be searching through the wreckage.

"Hello!" Evliit shouted. There was a short delay as the sound traveled down the road. The man nearest him looked up, froze for a few seconds with a frown—as if Evliit had interrupted something important—then went back to whatever he was doing.

"All right," Evliit muttered. "There won't be trouble if you don't start any." He looked around once more, then dismounted. Tying Angwen outside, he ventured into the granary.

Inside, a mixture of pumpkin seeds, pine nuts, and dried cranberries lay scattered across the stone floor. Despite the blood on the floor beside them, he scooped up handfuls, filling his pockets, then poured a fistful into his mouth and chewed feverishly. He had never known nuts, seeds, and berries could taste *so* good.

He needed something to drink. It appeared all the water and whiskey were gone, though he did find a flask with a mouthful—nothing more—of red wine left in it. He was thankful it was enough to wash down the clump of seeds stuck in his throat. He had to find something to drink that didn't look like the wash off a butcher's block.

That left him two choices: a fountain on the road leading north through town, or a well on the eastern road. The eastern road led to the edge of town, where Broeden's black tents had stood just days before. At the thought of them, with what little spittle he could muster, Evliit spat on the ground. The fountain was a little closer.

He walked back out of the granary and emptied his pockets into Angwen's saddlebags. Then he made two more trips, leaving the bags practically full. On his way out, he grabbed a small sack of oats as a treat for the horse and tied it beside the sword's case; he would wait to feed Angwen until they reached the fountain. As he mounted up and guided the horse north through the devastation, it began to rain.

When Evliit came to the body of a child lying in the road, he stopped. A thin trail of blood twisted through the cobblestones, leaking into the gutter. The trickle came from the makeshift bandages tied around the boy's chest.

Evliit needed to move the body to get by. He leaned over to dismount, but something caught his eye. He looked closer. The boy's chest was moving. His breathing was shallow, but he was alive.

"Boy?" Evliit said.

"Help me!" a man shrieked to his right, startling him. Evliit's head snapped toward the voice. An elderly man stood there, shaking and wild-eyed, his palms held upward. "My grandson is dying! Help me!"

"Y-yes, yes," Evliit stuttered, dismounting. "We should take him inside." He reached down to lift the child.

"No, no! I'll do it! Follow me! Follow me!" the old man cried, scooping up the boy.

Evliit followed him through the wreckage lining the street. "Where has everyone gone?" he asked.

The old man didn't slow. "North around the mountain, then farther west—into the frontier, I suppose." He darted into a small room in one of the row houses behind the farmer's market and laid the boy on a cot. The roof had collapsed on one side, and rainwater was beginning to trickle onto the stone floor.

"We should pray to the Creator to help him," Evliit said.

"What good will that do?" the old man snapped. "Do you have Soru?"

Evliit's mind spun at the mention of the plant. "Listen! I know the Creator can help him."

"What are you now? A Watcher? A cleric of some kind?" the old man barked. He moved close enough that Evliit could smell his sour breath. "Where are the Watchers now, huh? Hiding in their holes? Broeden moves through the new world the same as the old—unimpeded by the god of the Watchers!" He kicked a chair aside, cursing. "Barodhma! I thought you had Soru."

The old man was unusually strong. The chair struck the wall and shattered on impact.

"No, I—" Evliit began.

"What do you know of the Creator, you imbecile?" the old man yelled. "Leave us alone." He turned toward the door.

"Where are you going?" Evliit asked.

"Outside to stand in the rain and wait for someone who can actually help us."

"You're going to just leave him here alone?"

"You're here. Do you think the boy would do any better lying in the streets?" Without another glance, the old man walked through the doorway.

Evliit pulled a wooden crate over and sat beside the cot. "Creator, I'm trying to do as You've asked. I'm here to help this little one. You said to protect the weak. Show me what to do." He leaned forward and brushed a piece of hair from the child's face. The boy didn't respond. Evliit couldn't even tell if he was still breathing. With one hand he felt for a pulse at the child's neck; with the other he opened the bandages and examined the wound.

It was an odd black puncture wound about the size of his thumb. Just beneath the skin, a web of dark purple veins radiated outward. Their color seemed to fade between the child's heartbeats—and from the look of things, Evliit feared those heartbeats wouldn't last much longer.

Evliit laid his left hand on the hilt of his sword, and as he did, a strange sensation washed over him. It was as though he could hear the voice of the Bhre-Nora's smithy again—the one who called himself Aleris—saying, *Heal him.* Filled with this thought, Evliit reached up with his right hand and placed two fingers into the child's wound.

The black web pulsed with the next heartbeat, and Evliit felt the skin closing around his fingers. The cluster of veins did not fade this time during the pause between beats; instead, they rose sharply to the surface, like blood vessels under strain. Evliit withdrew his fingers and leaned the boy over, allowing a black liquid to drain onto the floor. When the last of it had leaked from his body, the skin sealed shut—and the boy's eyes shot open. He gasped for air.

"Careful!" Evliit said. "You're in no danger now." He placed a hand on the child's forehead, and the boy immediately calmed.

"Evliit?" a voice said behind him.

Alarmed, Evliit spun and brought his right hand toward his sword. A man stood in the doorway. Evliit grasped the hilt to draw it but hesitated. The man looked to have seen thirty winters at least. He wore robes rather than armor and carried no visible weapon—only a bag slung over his shoulder. How does he know my name?

"Whoa! Slow down there!" the man said, raising his hands slowly. "The old man outside said the boy was injured. Just seeing what I could do to help, that's all." He smiled. "I knew you'd come back to Harot."

The boy whimpered. "Paw Paw?"

"What is happening?" the grandfather said, poking his head around the stranger and back into the room. When he saw the boy alert, he rushed past the man in the doorway, past Evliit, and knelt at the child's side. "Jora, let me look at you!" He pulled back the bandage and touched the skin where the wound had been. There was scar tissue in the shape of the web, but the puncture was healed.

"So you are a healer!" the grandfather said, spinning around. "My master knew the children would draw you out. Children are always the best bait!"

"What?" Evliit asked, intending to say more, but before he could continue, the grandfather backhanded him across the room.

Evliit slammed into the wall and slid to the floor. The boy began screaming. As Evliit managed to sit up, the child crawled into a corner beside the cot, still screaming at the top of his lungs. The man from the doorway had vanished.

"Shut up!" the grandfather bellowed, and the child fell silent instantly. His feet scraped against the floor as he pushed himself backward, trying to get away.

Never taking his eyes off Evliit, the grandfather crouched and slurped the black liquid from the floor—the same fluid that had drained from the boy. He wiped his mouth with his sleeve and exhaled as if savoring the taste. Then he shot across the room toward Evliit, drawing back his fist for another strike.

Evliit had just enough time to move his head. The old man's fist burst through the wall up to his elbow.

"Awake, are we?" the grandfather said.

"What?" Evliit muttered, still disoriented from hitting the wall. Everything was happening too fast. But one thing was clear: whatever this thing was, it wasn't human.

The grandfather pulled his arm free from the stone. The skin of his knuckles was gone, revealing a second, translucent layer beneath, slick with what looked like human blood.

"These frail coverings," the creature hissed, extending his fingers and examining them. He grabbed his wrist with his other hand and pulled downward. Rough black nails pierced through the ends of each fingertip. He tugged again, tearing away the damaged outer skin, then flexed the clawed hand beneath.

Evliit half-yelled and rolled to the side, scrambling away from the creature.

"Where do you think you're going?" it snarled, grabbing him by the calf. Its claws dug into the muscle of his leg.

Suddenly there was a crack of wood on bone and a spray of splinters. The creature's grip released. The man from the doorway stood behind it, holding what remained of a chair leg. His eyes were wide, as if he couldn't believe what he'd just done.

The grandfather's face was contorted, stretched unnaturally across the creature's head.

The man shouted and swung again, striking the creature's head and shoulder. The brute countered with wild, blind swings—missing twice, but catching the man in the chest with the third. Evliit watched his would-be savior skid across the floor and slam into the opposite wall.

The creature pulled at the skin on the crown of its head, stretching the grandfather's face until its right eye aligned with the creature's own socket.

Evliit's newfound ally staggered to his feet and braced himself against the wall opposite Evliit.

The creature's head darted back and forth, assessing its two foes. It reached up and adjusted the loose skin on the side of its head, but then, with an angry scream, it hooked a clawed hand over its scalp and tore it away as one might peel off a sweater.

Its true skin was silvery and translucent. As it stripped away the human covering, ridges of vertebrae became visible, and a soft fleshy lobe slipped free at the back of its neck. The lobe expanded as it filled with a dark red substance, thick as egg yolk. When the human face was fully removed, Evliit saw thin, pearly strings of cartilage crisscrossing the space where the grandfather's features had been. They writhed beneath the skin, recombining—forming cheekbones, a brow, and the framework of a new face. The translucent skin stretched over the shifting structure, and white orbs blinked at Evliit through the cloudy fluid that coated them.

As the creature hunched, its mouth formed and stretched open, and a set of canines hinged downward from its upper gum line. It hissed as it threw aside the handful of flesh it had been hiding behind. The discarded skin hit the floor with a wet slap.

The creature looked toward Evliit's dazed ally. "You will die first!" it bellowed, its profile revealing rows of small, hook-shaped teeth breaking through its gums at crooked angles. Spittle flew as it roared its piercing battle cry.

"No!" Evliit shouted. "Over here!"

But the creature ignored him and leaped toward the other man. While it was still in midair, Evliit's ally mumbled something and motioned upward with his right hand. A root burst through the stone floor, striking the creature in the chest and redirecting its momentum. It crashed through the wall into the alley, rolling onto all fours.

"We've no time! Come!" the man yelled.

Evliit tried to stand, but the puncture wounds in his calf made the leg useless. Seeing his struggle, the man started toward him—never noticing the creature scrambling up behind him.

The beast hauled itself back through the opening in the wall and swung. Its claws tore open the man's back like the tines of a pitchfork. He cried out and collapsed.

Evliit forced himself upright and drew his sword. The creature instantly turned its attention to him.

"Your turn," it hissed, leaping from the wall.

Evliit spun and swung. The creature crashed to the floor beside him, screaming with several overlapping voices. Its severed arm lay nearby. The fingers of the clawed hand relaxed, and for an instant Evliit thought they looked like the petals of a flower slowly opening.

The creature used its remaining arm to push itself into a kneeling position. Teetering on its haunches, it clutched the stump of its missing limb. Black blood ran down its thigh and pooled at its knee.

"You've won nothing here today!" it shrieked. "Nothing!"

Evliit approached slowly. The creature reached toward him, but he brushed its arm aside with the flat of his blade. Where the metal touched its skin, the flesh smoked and peeled away, clinging to the sword before turning to ash and falling off. The creature screamed.

"The Watchers are failing; the warriors are few!" it hissed. "The people scatter to the frontiers! It won't be long now!"

It laughed—and then lunged.

Evliit thrust his sword through its chest. The beast exhaled sharply and sagged to its knees. When Evliit pulled the blade free, it toppled forward and lay still.

Evliit returned his sword to its scabbard and turned to check on the boy. "Are you all right?" he asked, but the child didn't answer; he remained curled in a ball, staring blankly ahead. Evliit lifted him gently and placed him back on the cot. Then he turned to the injured man who had come to his aid.

The man was bleeding badly and groaning in agony.

"Creator, flow through me," Evliit said, placing his hand calmly upon the torn flesh. The man cried out as the tissue closed beneath Evliit's palm. His cry became a moan—and then silence.

"Ah!" he yelled suddenly. His eyes shot open. "The possessor?" he asked, looking around.

Evliit pointed to the prone creature. "This thing? Dead. It's over."

The man stared at him with a strange expression. "You don't remember me, do you?"

"No, I'm sorry," Evliit replied. He studied the man again. Maybe it was the shoulder-length brown hair? The beard? Something about him was familiar, but Evliit couldn't place it.

"I'm Mategaladh," he said, pushing himself upright. With a groan, he pulled his shirt over his head, then stopped to gape at the slashes and bloodstains across the back of it. He reached around to touch the wounds but couldn't reach high enough, so he flipped his arm over his shoulder. His fingers brushed the uppermost part of the injury. "Well, you haven't forgotten everything. You can still channel the Creator's power." He pulled his elbows inward to stretch the skin on his back, then hobbled to a bag he'd dropped near the doorway. He opened it, pulled out a tunic, sniffed it, and threw it on—hissing as the fabric touched his back. "I don't get it. The wound is completely closed; why does it sting like that?"

"I don't know, Mategaladh. Maybe it's not finished doing what it's doing?" Evliit shrugged. "There's so much I don't understand. It's like I remember two lives—two very different lives—and both feel real to me." He glanced at the creature on the floor. "Those were some nasty cuts. You should rest, Mategaladh."

Evliit examined his own calf, turning his leg and gingerly lifting the punctured cloth of his pants away from the wound.

Mategaladh twisted his back and grimaced. "There's no time for rest. That was one of Broeden's possessors—dark spirits that only take form when they enter the body of another. They're scouring these lands." He frowned. "I've never seen one up close before." He pointed at the scabbard at Evliit's side. "I'm thankful to the Creator that you carry the Sword of the Watch!"

Evliit stepped back slightly. "I don't know what you're talking about."

"The Sword of the Watch?" Mategaladh repeated. "The holy weapon of the Bhre-Nora?" His concern deepened. "Do you remember nothing of the Third Domain?"

Evliit sensed Mategaladh was probing for something. He shook his head. The streets of Harot had taught him to keep his trust small. "No. I've not heard of such a thing."

"Right." Mategaladh chuckled—until he realized Evliit wasn't joking. His expression shifted to confusion. "Well then… let's just say that such a weapon Broeden himself would covet dearly—an artifact capable of restoring the ancient wizard. If that were such a sword, I would take it and run from here as fast as I could."

Evliit hesitated, trying to size up his new acquaintance. "I'm grateful for your advice, Mategaladh," he said. "But Broeden has taken everything from me. I mean to avenge my losses with this very sword. Take care." With a brief nod, he turned toward the door.

Mategaladh reached for him. "Evliit, wait! I don't know what's happened to you, but it's going to be all right."

"How can it be that I can do things I don't remember ever learning—healing people, swordplay?"

Mategaladh's expression shifted. "Let me think how to explain this," he began, but shouting echoed down the street through the gaping hole in the wall. He stopped and looked out into the alleyway, then stepped close to Evliit and lowered his voice. "There are others like us who stand against Broeden. If we go to them, they will help us."

"This is my home," Evliit said. "I'll find others here who will stand against the murderer who did this. There have always been fearless men in Harot."

"Listen to me," Mategaladh said. He pointed to the dead possessor. "Killing this one will only bring more. These creatures will soon roam all of Harot. If we leave, yes, they will follow us—but then the people of Harot might have a chance to rebuild, to move on."

Evliit looked at the slumped creature, then back at Mategaladh.

"You and your friends… you'll help me avenge Harot?"

Mategaladh nodded. "Yes."

"All right. I'll go with you. But what about the boy?" Evliit asked, glancing toward the cot.

"The boy is in greater danger with us than if he stays here. We leave him," Mategaladh said.

Evliit drew a deep breath and closed his eyes, exhaling slowly. "Agreed."

Mategaladh led the way through the gaping hole in the row house's wall. Evliit followed, taking one last look over his shoulder at the boy, still lying on the cot.

They climbed over the debris and returned to the main road. There, Mategaladh whistled, and a splendid white steed appeared from nowhere, galloping to his side and halting at his touch on the saddle horn. With a grunt, he pulled himself up.

Evliit mounted Angwen as well.

"To the mountain range in the north," Mategaladh said, pointing to the high, sheer peaks, their white caps gleaming in the evening sun. "I'll introduce you to the others." Without further explanation, he goaded his horse and bolted northward.

Evliit and Mategaladh rounded the northernmost fingers of the Black Mountains and crossed the plains in record time, reaching the foot of the northern range by the middle of the next morning.

As they crested a low rise, their horses stepping high through the tall grass of the foothills, Mategaladh shouted, "Whoa!" He slowed his horse from a full gallop to a walk, and Evliit followed suit. "It's just ahead," Mategaladh said. "Let's let them cool down a bit."

As they walked, Mategaladh patted his horse's neck and eyed Evliit's mount with interest. "I've never seen any horse in all of Erathe that could keep up with my Calarphian," he said. "Where did you get him?"

Evliit felt a twinge of guilt. "I didn't steal him, if that's what you're asking." Immediately embarrassed by his defensiveness, he added more quietly, "What I meant is… I found him in the Black Mountains."

Mategaladh gave him a peculiar look. "A story for another time, I suppose." He dismounted and pointed toward a doorway cut into the mountainside. "One of our brethren lives here."

"Brethren?"

"Yes," Mategaladh said. "Some are called wizards, others healers or monks. You're among friends, Evliit."

"And who has followed you here this time?" a voice said behind them.

Mategaladh and Evliit turned. A man stood in the doorway, arms crossed. His expression changed instantly when he saw Evliit's face.

"Tophian!" Mategaladh exclaimed. "Tophian, look!"

"In the name of the Creator!" Tophian cried. "Where did you find him?"

"In Harot," Mategaladh replied. "He remembers nothing."

Tophian's eyes dropped to the sword at Evliit's side. He straightened. "It cannot be," he whispered. Then, with urgency, he waved them inside. "Quickly! Come in!"

CHAPTER 3

A Glimpse of Darkness

Praedhos looked around, but the blinding white of the snow-covered north felt as though it had permanently burned his corneas. His vision blurred constantly now, and it was especially maddening in the dark. He closed his eyes for a moment to clear them, then looked once more at the elite warriors surrounding him, thinking of everything they had endured to reach this moment. They waited for the order to attack; the only movement Praedhos could see was the mist of perspiration rising from their heads into the freezing night air.

Pride swelled in him. They had beaten the arctic cold of Calarph's tundra, where the wind cut through his leather longcoat with ease and through the meat on his bones until it threatened to freeze the air in his lungs. He had seen more than one brother-in-arms succumb to the lure of cold comfort—seen them fall asleep and never wake again. He pushed the sadness aside and gave thanks to the Creator. There had been moments when he, too, had been tempted to close his eyes and surrender to the stillness, to let the endless freezing wind take him. Somehow, he had found the strength to resist.

Captain Graeson had done what they said could not be done: he had led their company across the tundra of northern Calarph and around Broeden's armies to the north side of the dark one's fortress—Durageim.

"It's unprotected, Captain, just as you said," Praedhos whispered.

"For no one in their right mind would have tried to cross the tundra of Calarph to reach it," Graeson replied with a smirk. "It's a good thing guardsmen aren't in their right minds."

His bravado brought the faintest smiles to their frost-cracked faces, but the road had been long and merciless. The bitter cold had killed nearly half their company. Now fewer than a hundred remained, huddled in secret in the undergrowth on the sorcerer's northern lawn, unseen by his armies.

Graeson took a knee in the center of the group. Wild, unnatural sounds filled the air in the land of the sorcerer, but the captain remained steady and focused. "You are the greatest warriors Rion has to offer—those the cold could not kill," he said. "Here you stand, together, ready to rob this sorcerer of his life."

The sky darkened further as castle patrols lit great bowls of oil along the walkways, each as wide as a tabletop, casting dancing firelight across the stone. Praedhos watched the flames reflected in the bloodshot eyes of his fellow warriors as they waited for their chance to bring the sorcerer his due.

Sometime after midnight, they descended from the high ground where they had been hiding and made their way down to a gorge at the foot of the castle's rear. When they reached the bottom of the moat, they found something—something terrible. Bodies—no, bodies and parts of bodies— filled the ravine.

Praedhos tried not to look as he stepped on them, but he couldn't ignore the rotting flesh mushing between his fingers as he clawed his way up the far side toward the castle. *Get it done, get it over, keep moving,* he told himself. He tried to think of anything else, but his senses screamed to vomit—to flee.

His breathing grew ragged. The acidic, blinding stench was like nothing he had ever known. Panic tingled in his toes and crept upward. *Where is the captain?*

Just as panic threatened to take him, he saw Graeson claw his way through the last of the carnage ahead, up the hill toward the rear entrance. Relief washed over him. *I'm almost there.* Glancing at his fellow soldiers, he saw they were fighting their own terrors—but they pressed on, eyes wide, faces drawn.

Graeson was undaunted. He said nothing, stoic and unyielding, leading them onward without mercy as though he had seen nothing at all—until they had passed through the gorge of death and reached the stairs carved into the hillside. There Graeson drew his sword and ascended the stairs, eyeing the castle entrance and beckoning his soldiers in close.

Praedhos's stomach twisted. *We made it. We're going into the dark one's lair.*

He looked to Kelae, the exceptionally skilled youth who had risen to Graeson's third in command. The muscles along Kelae's jaw rippled with tension. "Are you ready, brother?"

"Ready," Kelae answered, though his bloodshot eyes were wild with fear. "Praedhos, sir," he added quietly. "A word?"

Praedhos forced himself to stay calm. There wasn't time for this. He placed a hand on Kelae's shoulder and turned him away from the others. "What is it, Kelae?"

"If I don't make it—"

"Stop! Don't say another word," Praedhos hissed. He grabbed the top of Kelae's breastplate and pulled him close. "You will live to hear of this day in song. All the bards will sing of it. Now ready your men."

Graeson glanced back from the steps. "Is there a problem?"

"No, sir!" Praedhos answered.

Kelae swallowed. "No, sir!"

"Then make ready," Graeson commanded.

Praedhos dropped his fist on Kelae's shoulder plate and turned away, rejoining Graeson on the steps. Kelae and the forty soldiers assigned to him fanned out silently at the foot of the stairs. They would hold the exit.

The second group of twenty watched Graeson's every move, ready for his next command. These were the men he had handpicked to ascend the stairs into the castle itself. Praedhos was among them.

It was quiet. The castle windows were open to the night air, but inside was black as sin—no torches, no lanterns, no movement.

Before signaling his men forward, Graeson paused—as if something felt wrong. Praedhos saw the hesitation, but the captain blinked once, set his jaw, and without looking back, started up the steps. Praedhos and the others followed.

They had trained countless hours for this moment—drilled on how to deliver death to Broeden with ruthless precision—and nothing short of death itself would stop Graeson from achieving his objective. His warriors would follow him anywhere, even into the Underworld. This mission had brought them to the very steps of Broeden's stronghold, deep in enemy territory. They all knew their mettle was about to be tested. None expected to return.

The moment Graeson pushed against the massive doors and stepped inside, Praedhos's breath caught. Smooth, polished stone stretched in every direction, and the black stonework of the atrium arched upward across three floors. The craftsmanship was unlike anything he had ever seen—graceful, intricate, almost beautiful. But laced with webs and dust, it looked more like a tomb than the hall of their great enemy.

As they ventured farther in, Praedhos pulled a vial from his belt and drank the light green liquid inside. He grimaced at the aftertaste, but his heart rate spiked instantly. He offered silent thanks to the cackling old woman who had given it to him as they left Rion. She had told him, toothless grin and all, to drink it when they faced the evil one—to protect him from the venom of Broeden's creatures. He had thought her mad, and more than once he had nearly thrown the vial away. Drinking it now felt wise.

Suddenly, movement echoed across the atrium. It grew louder by the second. Enormous planters dotted the floor, filled with vegetation unlike anything Praedhos had seen in Rion or the northern fields. Graeson slipped behind one, and his soldiers followed suit.

From his hiding place, Praedhos watched as a group of Broeden's warriors entered through the southern door. A Camon was said to be a creation of the dark lord—a seven-foot-tall manlike creature clad in light armor and furs. Together they were called the *Camonra*. Layered kilts hung to the tops of their heavy knee-high boots, and each step thudded on the stone floor, emphasizing the three or four hundred pounds of muscle they carried. Praedhos noted their war dogs were absent tonight. *Perhaps—just perhaps—the Rion Guard could remain unseen.*

The Camonra clanked toward the eastern door and exited—all except one, who stopped, turned, and sniffed the air.

Graeson looked down at the bloody muck on his hands and frowned. He pointed to his nose, then slowly placed his hand on his sword.

Praedhos mirrored him, gripping his own hilt, bracing for the worst.

But a shout rang out from beyond the door, and the Camon, after one last sweep of the atrium, hurried to rejoin his company. The door closed behind him.

Praedhos exhaled in relief.

Graeson wasted no time; he darted to the western side of the atrium, where stairs wrapped around the wall heading upward, and—holding his sword's scabbard tightly, so as not to make a sound—started up the stairs.

They were just quick enough on the stairs to miss detection by another group of Camon warriors on the second floor. On the third floor, they came to an intersection of hallways; Graeson moved to one corner, and his men all followed suit, pushing their backs to the adjoining wall.

As they paused there, waiting for Graeson's next move, Praedhos noticed that the doors of the room across from them were standing open. The room was full of strange glass objects connected by glass tubing. At the room's center was a wooden table the size of a flatbed wagon. Upon it sat a lamp, its flame licking the blackened bottom of a glass flask. The green liquid within it percolated and foamed, belching forth small, mushroomed puffs of emerald gas at irregular intervals.

Praedhos was shocked when he realized that there was a man in a cage beyond the table holding the glass objects. He was just sitting there on the floor of the cage, looking directly at them. His right arm, which was grotesquely out of proportion to the rest of his body, lay across his crossed legs and on the floor in front of him. Sores covered the arm.

Praedhos slowly placed one hand on Graeson's shoulder. When Graeson looked at him, Praedhos nodded to the man, who was still motionless. Graeson shook his head. There was nothing they could do. Praedhos nodded, and Graeson turned his attention back to the hallway. Praedhos tried not to look at the man in the cage, but he caught himself glancing back. The man never moved. He was the very picture of despair.

Graeson crouched down and slowly rounded the corner, and the others did the same, staying to the outside of the hallway colonnade. From there Praedhos could see that there was another set of doors at the end of the hallway, these even heavier than all the rest. The doors had a golden crest over them, and statues of dragons, as big as trees, stood on either side, their heads raised to the sky as if screaming their defiance to the Creator. Reddish flames rose halfway to the ceiling from their open maws, blackening the ceiling with soot.

Even in the dead of night, two of the Camonra were posted just outside the door. *Ornate, protected*—Praedhos was sure they'd found the resting place of the sorcerer himself.

With all care, they moved toward the doors and hid behind the pedestal of the dragon statue closest to the colonnade. The two Camon warriors stood at attention on either side of the door, but Graeson and his men had prepared for such an eventuality. Six of the Rion Guard moved into position along the corner of the pedestal; then two of them moved to either side of the dragon statue's base. Each produced a small tube, into which they placed tiny glass ampules filled with a white powder. They counted off silently, raised the tubes to their mouths, and then they simultaneously launched the pellets into each of the Camon's faces. They burst into small clouds of dust on impact, and the two Camonra collapsed without a sound, caught by the six waiting guardsmen before they could hit the ground. As silently as possible, they dragged the bodies behind the colonnade. Then Graeson moved to the doors and opened them.

The creaking of the doors seemed excruciatingly loud, calling for anyone to answer their intrusion. The warriors stood perfectly still and waited, but there was no other sound or movement.

Praedhos peered in through the doors and saw it—across the narrow room, maybe twenty paces from him—a bed fit for a king. Great curtains hung all around the bedposts, made from a cloth the likes of which Praedhos had never seen before. *You can see through them like smoke,* he thought.

Graeson waved his men into the room and closed the door. As they neared the bed, the dim light revealed a person lying there. He easily was twice an ordinary man's size. His long white hair lay spread out across the tapestry of his ornate pillow and sheets; his hands were folded on his chest. He lay there pale and motionless, as if in death.

At Graeson's signal, the men spread out quietly, swords drawn, ready to end Broeden with the points of their blades.

Then, suddenly, Graeson hesitated. He held up one fist, and everyone stopped where they stood. Praedhos thought he had heard something—the sound of something scurrying—but before he could say anything, Graeson motioned for him. He was looking around at the ceiling and walls. When

Praedhos came to him, he pulled him near and whispered into his ear: "Go quickly. Bring everyone."

Praedhos stared at his captain in shock, but Graeson did not flinch. His face remained resigned, eyes scanning the darkness. His tension spread through the ranks; the others began listening, searching for whatever Graeson had sensed.

Praedhos didn't hesitate. He sprinted for the door, pulled it open, and bolted into the hallway, fear for their mission driving him. No one was there. He thought he heard Graeson shout something behind him just before the door slammed shut with a crash.

Praedhos tore down the colonnade and flew down the stairs. *Where are the Camonra?* They had been everywhere on the way in, but now the halls were empty.

He burst outside to the bottom of the stairs—but before he could speak, a gust of wind swept past him. It felt as though the castle itself had drawn a great breath.

In rapid succession, the shutters clattered shut, slamming against their frames. The noise echoed across the courtyard, surely alerting every creature within. But even that could not drown out the horrific sounds rising from inside. Red light flared around the edges of the third-floor shutters—long bursts, short bursts, pulsing like a heartbeat.

Before Praedhos could relay Graeson's command, something exploded through the shutters, clanged down the stone steps, and rolled to their feet.

It was Graeson's head, still strapped into his helmet.

Praedhos's horror broke free. "No!"

From within the castle, a long, chilling howl answered him.

He had to think. They had to regroup. A second howl rose, then a third, weaving together in an eerie, discordant harmony. Torchlight flickered through the castle's interior, moving toward them.

A shout came from the rear. Praedhos turned—and saw why. A thick, greenish liquid was bubbling up from a spot in the mass grave beside them.

Praedhos wiped his mouth with the back of his hand. A murmur rippled through the soldiers.

"What now, Praedhos?" someone asked.

He looked at his hand. It was shaking. He forced it down and stared at the bubbling green ooze.

At first, it seemed to dissolve the bodies—clean bones surfaced through the slime, rolling out like offerings from a wellspring. But then reddish veins shot upward through the corpses, threading through them like roots, pulling the bodies toward the opening that spewed the foul liquid.

Praedhos forced the word out. "Swords!"

They drew steel—and the veins reacted. They arced upward into a quivering mound six feet high. The interconnected bodies that still had eyes opened them all at once—and where there were mouths, they screamed together, a single, hideous chorus.

A torso near Praedhos lifted its one remaining arm. From its fingertips, veins—tentacles—shot outward. They pierced the soldiers to his left and right as easily as blades. The men screamed as the veins burst out of them and into others who swung wildly, trying to cut themselves free.

The tentacles yanked the entangled men into the air and dragged them toward the oozing pore.

The first two were already dead; their bodies slid into the mound without resistance, forced through a hole forming at its peak. The third and fourth were still alive. They clawed at the corpses around them, trying to escape. The third fell back against a shrieking carcass; it wrapped its arms around him and drove veins through his body. His scream joined the others, eyes wide and vacant.

The fourth was Kelae.

He locked eyes with Praedhos, kicking and screaming. "Help me! Praedhos! Help me!" Realizing the futility, he turned his sword toward his own throat—but before he could act, the vein jerked him upward and dragged him headfirst into the hole. His feet kicked once, twice—then stilled. Then vanished.

The company broke.

They fled through the carnage, across the ditch toward the opposite bank. They wanted nothing more than to escape—anywhere, as fast as possible. But the veins rippled through the corpses, shooting upward among the fleeing guardsmen, killing another and another as they scrambled across the grave.

Praedhos swung his sword wildly as he ran. Soldiers fell around him until only six remained. They reached the base of the opposite bank together and began climbing. Praedhos was nearly at the top when he heard his name.

"Help me, Praedhos!"

Kelae's last moments flashed through his mind.

"Wait!" he shouted to the others.

They turned. One of the creatures had latched onto a soldier's sword arm. The man had severed the tentacles but dropped his sword, his arm hanging limp. He fumbled for his knife with his left hand, but the delay allowed the creature to close. New tentacles burst from its palm, embedding in the soldier's shoulder.

He stabbed the monster repeatedly as Praedhos and the others stepped toward him. Without warning, the creature convulsed violently—and exploded in a spray of carnage.

The soldier turned toward them. Something slithered in the bloody paste covering his face. He screamed and clawed at the worms burrowing into his skin.

The others screamed as well. They had been splattered too, writhing in agony.

Then Praedhos felt it—a sharp pain in his side. A shard of the creature's skull had pierced his longcoat. He yanked it free, ignoring the burning sensation spreading from the wound.

"Run!" Praedhos roared.

They scrambled over the bank and fled into the darkness.

CHAPTER 4

New Allegiances

Mategaladh and Evliit tied off their horses at the entrance to Tophian's home in the Faceless Mountains and removed their gear.

Tophian led them through a doorway into a narrow hallway barely wider than a man's shoulders. Evliit marveled at the precision of the craftsmanship—the stone had been cut with exacting symmetry and polished to a glossy sheen. The passage sloped upward and inward, taking them deeper into the mountain.

Evliit's sword scabbard screeched as it scraped the smooth wall. "A tight fit," he muttered.

"Tight fits make it hard for the enemy to come at us more than one at a time," Tophian replied.

"Broeden?" Evliit asked.

"Anyone," Mategaladh answered.

"This stone must be fifty paces thick," Evliit said.

"That's right," Tophian replied. "And this is not the soft shale of the Black Mountains. The Faceless Mountains are five thousand feet of granite rising into the sky."

"Incredible," Evliit said.

After some fifty paces, the hallway widened, and other corridors branched off in multiple directions. Their footsteps echoed through the stone, making Evliit wonder at the sheer size of the structure hidden within the mountain.

"Tophian is the proctor of our library," Mategaladh said. "The collective knowledge of the known world is stored deep within this mountain. Rows of shelves filled top to bottom with books from across the ages."

"The monks of Rion have painstakingly copied entire volumes for us," Tophian added.

"What do you call this place?" Evliit asked.

"Moonledge," Tophian said. "Named for the peak above us. Even the dragons of old would struggle to pierce her walls."

Drawings covered the walls as they moved deeper. Near the intersection ahead, the torchlight was bright, and Evliit stepped closer to examine the art. The pictorials shimmered in the flickering light.

"What is this?" Evliit asked. "These etchings look very, very old."

"The history of our people," Tophian said. "It's as if someone took the Elders' Book of Time and carved its stories into the stone."

"That's Broeden," Mategaladh added, pointing to a towering figure tearing people in two.

"I've only heard bits and pieces of these tales," Evliit said.

"Well, allow me to fill in the gaps," Tophian offered.

"With all that's happened in Harot, perhaps now is not the best time," Mategaladh said, giving him a stern look.

Tophian paused and turned back to Evliit. "Yes, of course. I was sorry to hear of the tragedy in Harot. Another time, perhaps."

Evliit's chest tightened, but he shook his head. "It's best to know well the one with whom you make war. Go on."

"Very well," Tophian said. "Follow me."

They exited the long hallway and entered a chamber with doors on each of its ornate walls. Tophian pointed to an eight-foot-tall image on the arched ceiling to their left, where people knelt around a figure several times their size, dressed in black.

"As you can see," he said, "our people have a long history with Broeden. Long ago, after years of war, fearing their destruction, our ancestors succumbed and agreed to worship the wizard as a god."

"A dark time," Mategaladh said. "But even then the Creator was with us." He pointed to a row of figures in the clouds above the black-clad giant. "The Creator sent prophets, telling the people of a new day coming—of a time when they would prevail over Broeden."

"One day in the future," Tophian continued. "But meanwhile Broeden lived on beyond mortal years, ruling over them. Their towns grew in the shadow of his castle, and they toiled day and night for his pleasure. And as their numbers swelled, resources dwindled. They became dependent on Broeden's table scraps just to survive."

"I'm guessing Broeden wasn't a benevolent god," Evliit said.

"No," Mategaladh replied.

Tophian moved to the next panel above the adjacent doorway. "After many winters, the people were desperate and starving, powerless to change their fate. When things could not grow darker, the Creator sent the last prophet, Janus, who foretold of a free land called *Rion*—a place where Broeden would no longer rule, where mead and bread and wild game were abundant."

"Janus struck at Broeden's heart," Mategaladh said. "He called upon all who believed in the Creator to leave Broeden's service, to abandon the wicked city and flee into the frontier beyond the mountains. He prophesied that Broeden's city was doomed."

Evliit straightened. "Broeden's doom—yes, let us speak of *that*. Mategaladh said you could help me bring justice to Broeden."

Tophian and Mategaladh exchanged a glance.

"Yes," Mategaladh said. He crossed the chamber and lifted a torch, bringing its flame to the far side of the room. The light illuminated the image above him: a bearded man holding a burning sword. Nine men flanked him on each side—those on his right crowned with spheres of golden light, those on his left wreathed in red flame. Below the sword-bearer stood another man dressed in black, legs together, one arm behind him, the other holding a mask before his face.

Evliit stared at the mural, but it was the bearded man who held his attention. He blinked, looked again—yet his first impression remained.

The sword-bearer looked uncannily like *him*.

Mategaladh stepped beside him. "What is it, Evliit?"

Evliit hesitated. "Nothing," he said quickly. "Go on."

"See the men on either side of the sword-bearer?" Tophian asked.

"Yes," Evliit replied.

"Janus called them *Watchers*," Tophian said. "He prophesied that some among the people of Erathe would be given extraordinary gifts—healing, discernment, the ability to move objects with their minds." He pointed to the men crowned with globes of golden light. Then he gestured to the figures wreathed in red flame. "And others would wield great skill in alchemy and spellmaking."

"Janus said these Watchers would rise up and separate themselves from the people of Rion," Mategaladh added. "They would make their homes on the borders of the old world. Using their gifts, they would watch for the return of its evil, ensuring it did not creep unseen into the new." He lifted the torch toward the central figure. "But on the day evil rose again, one of the Watchers would bear a holy weapon—the Sword of the Watch. With that sword, Janus said, the Watchers would end Broeden's reign forever and guide the people back to the Creator."

"For a year, Janus preached that prophecy to anyone who would listen," Tophian said. "Until an assassin's blade caught him sleeping in his bed."

Evliit swallowed hard. Flashes flickered in his mind—hooded men, an old man in a garden—but they were still fragments, unanchored. They *felt* connected to what he was hearing, but he couldn't yet see how. "What happened after Janus was killed?"

"The murder of Janus ended an age," Mategaladh said. He pointed farther down the mural. "When Janus died, the Creator was filled with great sorrow. Tears rained upon the lands for two moons. When the tears ceased, the Creator unleashed three mighty winds from the north, east, and west. Sheets of ice fell from the sky, burying the northern lands."

"It is said the ice storm will last for all time," Tophian added. "Those who heeded Janus's warning survived—they had already fled south to warmer fields, never forgetting the Creator's promise of Rion. But Broeden, locked within his temple, was frozen in the sea of ice."

"But how did he escape?" Evliit asked. "The men who attacked Harot flew Broeden's banner."

"No one truly knows," Mategaladh said. "But it is believed Broeden dug down into the heart of Erathe—into the bowels of the Underworld. When the moon of Sapath aligned with the House of Naap, the gates of his castle belched molten rock, opening a pathway to the Underworld itself... and to Broeden's escape." He lowered the torch. "On the edge of the northern world, he built a new fortress—*Durageim*—and there he rebuilds his terrible army."

"It's been twenty-four winters since Sapath rested in Naap," Evliit said quietly. "I was born in that time." He studied the etchings again. "And you and Tophian—you believe this prophecy?"

"Yes," Mategaladh said. "Tophian and I—and others. We believe in the prophecy of Janus." He glanced at Tophian. "I told you. He remembers nothing."

"What could have happened?" Tophian asked.

"I'm not sure," Mategaladh replied.

Evliit rubbed his chin. "You think I am this sword-bearer?"

"Seek the Creator's face once more," Mategaladh said gently, "and all of this will make sense."

Evliit paced, trying to wrap his mind around it. Then he turned to them. "If I am this sword-bearer, then it is your calling to aid me in avenging Broeden's attack on Harot. Let us gather these Watchers and march on Durageim."

"Wait," Tophian said. "There are significant flaws in your logic, Evliit. First, it would take an army larger than the Rion Guard to assault Durageim. The idea that we could do it alone is madness." Mategaladh opened his mouth, but Tophian pressed on. "Second, you don't truly believe you're the sword-bearer—by Naap, I'm not sure you even know what it means. The Elders won't believe it either, not for a moment. And that is the heart of the matter."

He stepped closer.

"The survivors of the Forgotten Lands live on as our guiding fathers— our Elders. They alone govern Rion. They alone command the Rion Guard. And the people of Rion have always believed the leader of the Watchers will be called from within the ranks of the guard."

"The guard? The Elders?" Evliit asked. "Who are they to me?"

"Yes, yes," Mategaladh said. "That's exactly the point. What Tophian is trying to say is that some will take issue with your proclaiming that the Creator called you to save the people of Erathe—that the Creator gave you this sword. Some might even be offended. Deeply." He glanced at the mural, then back at Evliit. "You're treading on their religion."

"I don't really care what they think," Evliit said, heat rising in his voice. "I know that—"

"We are not those people," Mategaladh said, cutting him off. "We look at this image from our ancestors, and we see you. We remember our calling, Evliit."

"But for others," Tophian said, "the idea that some stranger from the East—especially one who clearly knows nothing about the faith he's invoking—would be given this sword? They won't just doubt it. They'll consider it an insult."

"An insult?" Evliit echoed.

"Sadly, yes," Mategaladh said. "The guard see themselves as the chosen few. You being given the sword threatens that status. And that could go badly for you."

"The guard won't simply let you strut into Rion calling yourself 'the people's warrior,' threatening to kill Broeden with this weapon," Tophian said. "That's not how this works. Their charge is to keep the peace and protect the people—and by that I mean peace and protection as interpreted *by the Elders*. Because the Elders have the right ear of the Creator—remember?"

An uneasy silence settled over them.

"So what do you propose?" Evliit asked, looking between them. "I assume you have some sort of plan."

"We do," Mategaladh said. "We think you should stay here and let us go to the Elders and tell them your story."

Evliit's eyebrows shot up. "Stay here?"

"Let us relay the news of the sword-bearer's existence with some delicacy," Tophian said. "Once we have others on our side, we'll return for you."

Evliit looked at each of them, his face flushing. "I realize you haven't seen what happened in Harot—"

"I know what Broeden is capable of," Tophian protested.

"He killed the woman I loved!" Evliit burst out. "A helpless, wounded—" His voice broke. He had to stop, catching his breath as Jenna's death washed over him again. "I'll go to them. I'll go to these Elders and demand justice for Jenna and Harot."

"You'll ride to the leaders of the most highly trained army in all of Erathe and demand they do what you say?" Tophian snapped. "You can't do that, you idiot."

"What did you call me?" Evliit said, blood pounding in his ears.

"Wait!" Mategaladh said—but too late.

Evliit lunged at Tophian, but before he'd taken two steps, Tophian raised a hand. A palm-sized rock shot up from the floor, striking Evliit under the chin and slamming him into the stone wall.

Evliit collapsed in a heap, momentarily stunned, vision swimming. Mategaladh and Tophian's voices sounded distant, muffled.

"Did you have to do that?" Mategaladh demanded.

"This one knows nothing," Tophian said flatly. "Sometimes I agree with Amphileph. How can he be the sword-bearer?"

"Who hit me?" Evliit groaned from the floor.

"I did," Tophian said. "You're not the only one with gifts."

He lifted his hand again, and another stone rose from the ground, hovering above his palm.

"Now you've done it," Mategaladh said, clearly agitated. "You would use the Creator's gift to strike down your brother—the one who bears the sword, no less?"

"Like what you were doing was getting us anywhere?" Tophian shot back. "Now he knows."

Evliit blinked hard, trying to steady himself. "Now I know what?"

"Do you really think you're the only one to whom the Creator has given power?" Tophian asked, a dangerous edge in his voice.

"That's enough, Tophian!" Mategaladh said, gripping his friend's arm.

"We are Watchers!" Tophian shouted, shaking him off. "Does he remember nothing?"

Using the wall for support, Evliit pushed himself to his feet and drew his sword. His legs were still unsteady, but he summoned enough strength to level the trembling blade at Tophian's face. The sword flared with sudden light, and the entire room began to tremble.

Evliit shouted over the rumbling stone. "Broeden can't just snuff out our lives and walk away!"

"Don't you point that thing at me!" Tophian barked. He raised his hands, and dozens of stones lifted from the floor, hovering at various heights around them.

Mategaladh stepped between them. "Wait! Listen to me! This is madness! The Rion Guard has no love for Broeden. They hunt down and destroy his hordes wherever they find them!" His voice rose above the shaking walls. "We can send word to them. Now stop it! Stop it, both of you!"

Evliit's sword dimmed.

"So the men who killed my friends—the creatures overrunning Harot…" Evliit said, breath ragged. "The Rion Guard will hunt them down?"

"Every one of them," Mategaladh said. "Tophian and I are not your enemies, Evliit."

Evliit lowered his sword. Tophian dropped his hands, and the stones clattered to the floor.

Evliit bowed his head. Tears welled in his eyes. "I confess these things—here and now, to both of you. The Creator saved me from an unspeakable death, and the Creator gave me this sword." He stared down its length. "But when the time came to defend the woman I loved, I was afraid. I ran. I left her there like a coward."

"You would have died there, Evliit," Tophian said. "Simple as that."

"There's more to living out your calling than throwing your life away," Mategaladh said gently. He stepped closer. "This power moving through you—it isn't from you. You're not the source. You're a conduit, meant to live out your destiny and serve the will of the Creator."

Evliit rubbed the back of his neck, trying to absorb it. His confusion must have shown, because Tophian burst out laughing.

"Yeah, I know, kid—he makes my head hurt with all that talk too," he said. "But Mategaladh can help you. We both can."

"We *want* to help you reclaim your destiny," Mategaladh said. "This pain, these regrets—they'll make you lead with your chin. And the Rion Guard are born fighters. Leading with your chin will get you killed."

Tophian crossed his arms, still chuckling. "This one. Thinking he's going to stroll into the middle of the guard's camp and say, 'I'm Evliit, and if one of you doesn't take me to the Elders, I'll kick every one of your asses.'"

"With this sword, I could do it," Evliit said.

"Are you hearing this, Mategaladh?" Tophian said.

Mategaladh rolled his eyes. "Yes."

"No clue," Tophian declared.

"None," Mategaladh agreed, rubbing his eyes with thumb and middle finger.

"If you're determined to go to Rion," Tophian said, "at least let us help you do it the right way. We're trying to keep you alive."

Evliit bristled. "I'll be fine."

"Very well," Tophian said. "So you don't need our help. Will you at least agree to let us tag along? If only to see the fireworks?"

"Please, Evliit," Mategaladh urged. "If we can't talk you out of going, at least let us go with you."

"Whatever suits you," Evliit said with a shrug. "But I'm going to meet with the Elders and demand they act. Broeden—this monster—must be stopped. He must pay for what he's done."

"It won't be boring, that's for sure," Tophian said with a smirk.

"Then we leave first thing in the morning," Evliit said.

"If you insist," Mategaladh sighed. He turned to Tophian. "I hope I haven't presumed too much in thinking you'd supply us with provisions for the journey?"

"To the cliffs of Blue Water, if necessary," Tophian said, clapping his hands together. He seemed oddly cheerful now. "Everyone happy?"

Evliit only scowled.

"Wonderful," Tophian said. "Now—can we eat?"

Evliit tried to stay angry, but the mention of food made his stomach growl. He and Mategaladh had ridden hard to the northern mountains without stopping. He gave a stiff nod.

"Follow me, then," Tophian said, heading down the arched hallway beneath the image of the Watchers, Mategaladh close behind.

The torchlight dimmed as they left, but Evliit paused, looking once more at the face of the sword-bearer before hurrying to catch up.

Evliit awoke to the faint echo of Mategaladh and Tophian's voices bouncing softly off the stone walls of a nearby room. He lay in a bed, still fully dressed from the previous day's ride. He didn't quite remember being shown to a room, but the mattress beneath him felt wonderful.

He allowed himself a few more moments of stillness before sitting up and stretching. Then he dropped to one knee beside the bed.

"Thank you for another day," he whispered.

As he stood, movement in his peripheral vision startled him. A full-length reflecting glass stood against the wall.

Evliit had never seen himself so clearly. The alchemists in Harot made small, cloudy mirrors, but this was flawless—eight feet tall and three feet wide.

He stepped closer. His dark hair was oily, his face rough from days in the saddle. His boots looked worn thin. In truth, everything about him looked worn thin. He looked away. Perhaps it was better not to know.

Someone had left clothing on the nightstand—new clothing. Evliit lifted the shirt from the top of the pile, letting it unfold. As he walked toward the voices, he pressed the fabric to his face. It smelled of jasmine.

He found Tophian and Mategaladh in the hallway near the mountain's exit. Both were clean and wearing fresh clothes.

"Well, decided to join us, did you, sunshine?" Tophian said. "How about some of Mategaladh's morning brew?"

Evliit ignored the jab and held up the shirt. "What is this?"

"Ah, you found the clothes!" Tophian said. "I can make a good trade now and then. They're for you. Thought you might want to get out of those rags. They looked about your size."

"I'm ready to leave," Evliit said, rubbing sleep from his eyes.

"Sure, absolutely," Mategaladh said. "Just get cleaned up, and we'll be on our way."

"Cleaned up?"

Tophian and Mategaladh exchanged a look.

"Oh, my friend," Mategaladh said, "you'd never forgive me if I didn't show you the bath."

"But—" Evliit began.

"Follow me," Mategaladh said, turning him back toward the rooms.

"We really should be going," Evliit tried again. "I don't need to wash."

Mategaladh laughed. "Oh yes, you do. We won't get to clean up for several days—that's how long it'll take to ride south. So do it now, and do it well enough to still look presentable for the Elders." He waved him onward.

"Go around the corner. You won't regret it."

Reluctantly, Evliit turned right—and the room opened into a hot-water bath. Steam rose from a beautifully carved basin where warm spring water bubbled up from a natural vent. At the far end, a three-foot-wide band of steaming water poured from an opening in the stone.

"The hot spring water's always the perfect temperature," Mategaladh said, peering around the corner. He pointed to a stack of soft white cloth. "Towels from southern traders are there."

He disappeared again, leaving Evliit alone with the warmth and the rising steam.

✳

It was midmorning by the time Evliit finally dragged himself out of the bath. He had never experienced anything like its luxury. Wrapping a towel around himself, he returned to the room where he'd slept and dressed in the new clothes—boots included. For what might have been the first time in his life, he felt completely refreshed. He felt *clean*.

He started toward the exit but stopped at the mirror, genuinely astonished at his reflection. He looked like a rich man he'd once seen riding in a carriage through Harot. He remembered how badly he had wanted to be like that man—someone respected, even envied—and now here he was, staring back at himself in the glass.

Evliit stepped closer, meeting his own eyes. That's when it struck him. The clothes would fray, the boots would wear, but something deeper had changed—something permanent. A spark of hope flickered in him, and for the first time since Jenna's death, he felt the faintest trace of happiness.

He went outside to rejoin Mategaladh and Tophian, but only Mategaladh was there.

"Where's Tophian?" Evliit asked. "I wanted to thank him for the bath and the clothes."

"He went ahead," Mategaladh said. "You can thank him when we reach Rion." He tightened a strap on his saddle and looked up. "Ready to go?"

"Ready," Evliit said.

They mounted their horses and rode south across what Mategaladh called the Northern Plains. As they neared the Black Mountains, they turned southwest—away from Harot in the east.

The western side of the mountains looked nothing like the harsh slopes Evliit had known. Flocks of sheep dotted the short green grasses, and clusters of trees and shrubs rose here and there. Lazy clouds drifted across the blue sky, casting slow-moving shadows over the rolling hills. Evliit drank it in. A sense of peace washed over him.

After riding most of the day, as the setting sun cast orange light across the valley, Evliit and Mategaladh slowed their horses to rest them.

"I've not been this way before," Evliit said, awestruck by the beauty before him.

"Few have," Mategaladh replied. "We go far south, to the edge of the earth, where Blue Water stretches farther than the eye can see. That is where the people fled during the first war with Broeden. That is Rion."

"And that's where the Elders are?" Evliit asked.

"Yes—and the great masons of the Forgotten Lands as well. They fled before the ice claimed them, and in Rion they build wonders, just as in the olden days. You're in for a treat," Mategaladh said.

ᘳᘯᕆᕉᕊ·

On the morning of the third day, they came upon grasses so tall they brushed the horses' bellies. The blades swayed in the warm breeze like an ocean of green. Far to the south, Evliit saw a stone temple rising from the flat plains, glowing gold in the morning sun. Construction bustled all around it—land cleared and leveled, foundations laid, new columns rising. The stories he'd heard in Jenna's tavern were true. The masons of Rion did build wonders.

The tall grasses gave way to vast fields of Soru. Harvesters moved through the stalks, filling wicker baskets to overflowing, while others loaded bushels into barrel-sized baskets strapped to mules. Dozens of dirt paths cut through the fields, all leading toward the temples of Rion.

"I had no idea this much Soru grew anywhere," Evliit said, eyes wide.

"The fields seem endless."

"The Elders harvest Soru for their rituals," Mategaladh said. "And they hold days of healing as well—any who come to their temples are cured of their ailments."

"Amazing," Evliit breathed.

They rode toward Rion for the rest of the day. As evening fell, the dirt paths gave way to cobblestone streets. Vendors lined the road, their stalls offering everything from bird sacrifices to prostitutes. Most of the stables and brothels had closed for the night.

At last they reached their destination: the central temple. An acolyte and several children hurried forward, offering to stable their horses. Mategaladh handed one of them a coin, and the group led the animals away.

Evliit and Mategaladh climbed the first set of steps into the temple courtyard—a long rectangular space with the temple occupying the far half. Tall palm trees swayed in planters at each corner.

The sun had just set, and stars were beginning to pierce the darkening sky. Four massive urns stood on stone pedestals before the temple entrance. Evliit watched a man touch a torch to the farthest vessel; a moment later, a flame roared upward with a loud poof. Soon all four urns blazed, sending towers of fire thirty feet into the night.

A line of enormous columns—each at least ten feet in diameter—ran behind the urns and along the temple's sides. Behind the front row of columns, an intricate facade of stone and glasswork shimmered in the firelight. Evliit glimpsed movement on staircases spiraling upward inside the structure. The entire temple rose nearly eighty feet into the air. The entrance teemed with people.

"They truly are the descendants of the Bhre-Nora," Evliit said. "I've never seen anything like it." He nodded toward the crowd. "How will we find Tophian?"

"He'll find us," Mategaladh replied.

Evliit looked up at the towering temple face. It seemed as high as a mountain.

"Tomorrow is a day of healing," Mategaladh said. "The temples will fill quickly. If you want an audience with the Elders, we'll need to reach their acolytes early."

A nervous pang tightened Evliit's stomach. "Yes. Of course."

"Follow me," Mategaladh said, crossing the carved stone tiles of the courtyard.

Evliit nearly collided with two different people as he followed, too distracted by the sculptures and fountains to watch where he was going. A statue of a Rion Guard stood at the center of the largest fountain, shield raised, sword ready. Evliit paused at the basin's edge, mesmerized by the reflection of the sculpture and the flickering urn-flames rippling across the water.

"Wait here," Mategaladh said.

He ascended the temple stairs and spoke with two men in ceremonial garb, gesturing back toward Evliit. They nodded, and Mategaladh returned.

"We're in, then?" Evliit asked.

"Yes."

They returned to the stable and bedded down beside their horses. Evliit expected his worries about the Elders to keep him awake, but he slept as soundly as he had in years.

ᘔ⅂⅄ᘜⅤ·

The morning sun woke them at dawn, and after Mategaladh bartered something with the stable keeper, they headed straight for the temple, weaving through the growing throng in the outer courtyards. Stonework was underway at every corner, and the ringing of hammers and chisels echoed across the grounds.

"The Elders hear petitioners in the early morning," Mategaladh said as they walked, raising his voice over the clamor. "By midmorning they turn to healing ceremonies, and by sundown their acolytes start turning people away."

"Can we still speak with them after the healing ceremony?"

"If tradition holds, they'll share a meal at someone's home after sundown. If we don't secure an audience this morning, we won't speak with them today."

They climbed the first set of stairs to the petitioners' area—a walled-in maze of waist-high stone partitions that reminded Evliit of the cattle chutes he'd seen in slaughterhouses. At least fifty people, mostly peasants, were already waiting.

"Stay in line," Mategaladh said, pointing to the maze. "This leads to the inner court. I'm going to see if we can bypass some of this."

Evliit nodded and took his place at the back. Mategaladh slipped through a doorway and vanished.

Evliit waited as patiently as he could, winding through the maze. At first the people around him were loud and hopeful, but as the sun rose and their chances dwindled, the chatter faded into quiet resignation.

He was halfway to the doorway when he heard Mategaladh shout his name.

"Evliit! Hurry!"

"Get out of line?" Evliit asked, reluctant to abandon his hard-won progress.

"Yes, yes!" Mategaladh called, urgency rising. "Come on!"

Evliit stepped awkwardly around the grumbling peasants and made his way back.

"With all speed, my friend," he said, jumping over one low wall and then another until he cleared the maze.

Mategaladh grabbed his hand and pulled him around the portico. On the far side of the temple, a man poked his head out of a doorway.

"Hurry!" he shouted, waving them inside before disappearing again.

Evliit and Mategaladh rushed after him into the ground level of the temple, through a torch-lit corridor and past a ramp leading toward an altar. The man skidded to a stop at the base of a staircase rising to what looked like a smaller temple—the inner sanctum, Evliit guessed.

Guards in plate armor stood everywhere. A crossed chisel and hammer were embossed on their gleaming breastplates, and gold trimmed their gauntlets. Beneath the armor, long mail shirts hung to their midthighs. As they moved, the riveted plates at their waists clinked against the mail, and with greaves and plated boots added in, their steps sounded like a beggar rattling coins in a tin cup.

The man who had led them there turned. "Stay here," he said, then approached one of the guards and whispered something.

The guard looked at Evliit and Mategaladh, then strode toward them. "No weapons."

"I've no weapons," Mategaladh said. "And my friend carries only a sheathed sword. The sword is what we've come to discuss with the Elders."

Mategaladh nodded to Evliit. Evliit pulled back his long coat to reveal the scabbard. The guard glanced at it—then did a double take. His eyes snapped to Evliit's face, and he shouted something in a language Evliit didn't recognize.

A flood of guards poured down from the portico of the inner sanctum.

"What did he say?" Evliit hissed.

"He said, 'How can this be?' in the language of Rion," Mategaladh murmured. "Stay calm."

The guards surrounded them, lowering their pikes. The man who had led them in vanished. The line of pikemen nearest the temple parted, and the guard they'd spoken with stepped through.

"Now we go," he said. "Elder Jonas will see you."

"I wouldn't alarm them with any sudden moves," Mategaladh whispered.

"I don't intend to," Evliit said, all fantasies of taking on the entire guard evaporating. He slowly covered the sword with his coat, and they followed the guard up the steps.

A man met them at the entrance of the inner sanctum. He pulled back the hood of his long white robe, revealing short gray hair and a goatee that framed a furrowed brow and a jaw set with authority. A red stole accented his robe, tucked into a wide silver belt. The crossed chisel and hammer were stitched in gold across the sleeveless shirt beneath, covering armor identical to the guards'.

"I am Jonas," he said. "What news have you of Harot?"

Evliit looked to Mategaladh, but Mategaladh looked back at him.

"Broeden attacked us," Evliit began.

A ripple passed through the guards at the name. Jonas's expression darkened.

"Never again use that name in this holy place," he commanded.

Evliit raised his hands and lowered his gaze. "I meant no insult."

"He's unfamiliar with our ways," Mategaladh said quickly.

Evliit looked up just in time to see Jonas's face twist with something like disgust.

"I ask you again, foreigner," Jonas said. "What news have you of Harot?"

"The evil one burned and pillaged our village," Evliit said. "I come to de—"

Mategaladh shot him a sharp look.

"Ahem," Evliit corrected. "I come to plead for justice."

"Justice from the guard," Mategaladh added.

"The guard will investigate Harot. Is there anything else?" Jonas asked.

"Anything else?" Evliit repeated, struggling to contain his rising anger.

"Evliit," Mategaladh warned.

But Evliit couldn't hold back.

"My friends are dead!" he cried. "If you're the authority—if you'll avenge them—then I swear allegiance to you! I raise my sword to you!"

Silence fell. Evliit's words echoed through the chamber. Mategaladh's face drained of color.

"My lord, I—"

"Silence!" Jonas thundered.

The alcoves along the walls stirred. Elders emerged from the shadows, stopping just within the dim light.

"I told you," Jonas said to his brothers. "This one is no sword-bearer. The sword-bearer would swear allegiance to no one. The sword-bearer would demand allegiance from all."

A murmur rippled through the hall.

Mategaladh leaned close to Evliit. "Be quiet. Let me speak."

"My lords," Mategaladh began.

"We'll accept your fealty," Jonas interrupted, slapping Evliit on the shoulder.

Mategaladh stared, stunned.

Was that a smile on Jonas's face?

If it was, Evliit wasn't sure he liked what it meant.

"But before the commanders of the Rion Guard will allow you among their ranks," Elder Jonas continued, "you must prove yourself."

"My lord," Mategaladh finally managed, "this man is unfamiliar with your ways. I owe him my life; I cannot let him do this alone."

"Then you will stand with him," Jonas said.

Mategaladh's expression darkened. "Yes, my lord."

Tophian suddenly stepped out from behind a column. "May I stand with them as well?"

The guardsmen snapped their spears toward him, startled.

"These are my friends—my companions," Tophian said, unfazed. "I could not possibly let them go into the arena alone."

"As you wish, sorcerer. Come out from the shadows," Jonas commanded.

"The arena?" Evliit asked.

"You have no idea what you've gotten yourself into," Mategaladh muttered under his breath. Then he turned and smiled at Tophian. "I was worried you wouldn't come, old friend."

Tophian raised his hands slowly and walked through the ring of guards to stand beside Mategaladh. "I'd not miss it for the world, dear brother. He'll get to test his mettle now, eh?"

Elder Jonas led Evliit and his companions down a stairway and through a long corridor, stopping before two more sets of steps—one leading up, the other down. Jonas stepped onto the first step of the upward stair, then turned back to them.

"You go that way," he said, pointing to the stairs descending. "Through the doorway at the bottom."

The doorway opened into a circular arena. Evliit hadn't expected anything so imposing. Nearly a hundred feet across, the arena floor was enclosed beneath a massive dome of iron bars. A twenty-foot retaining wall circled the floor, and beyond it rose tier after tier of amphitheater seating— twenty, maybe thirty rows high. Above the outer wall, masts held great sheets of canvas stretched taut by cables and pulleys. The coverings flapped in the wind, their rolling motion punctuated by the occasional sharp pop of stressed fabric. The arena floor itself was open to the sky, and the noonday sun cast a lattice of shadows through the iron dome.

As Evliit, Mategaladh, and Tophian stepped toward the center, the Elders filed into the staggered seating around the dome. The spacing between the iron bars gave them a clear view of the floor below. Voices rose in a swelling cacophony as the seats filled.

Jonas stood and took a spear from a fellow Elder. He slammed the butt of it against the stone steps again and again until silence fell.

"Welcome, brothers!" he called. "These three have asked to join you in your battle with the evil one. We will test them. You be the judge of their worth!"

The roar of voices surged again.

"Stand ready, foreigners!" Jonas shouted.

Tophian tilted his head. "Did you hear that?"

"Yes," Mategaladh said.

"No, I didn't hear anything," Evliit said.

Tophian pointed across the arena. "Doors there—and there. Nothing behind us."

"Backs to the wall, quickly," Mategaladh said, retreating toward the nearest section of stone.

"What is it? What do you hear?" Evliit asked. He still heard nothing over the crowd.

"Rakmuut," Tophian said. "War dogs twisted by possessors. More than one."

Evliit drew his sword. "Like the creature in Harot?"

"The same—or worse," Mategaladh said.

A horn bellowed—so loud Evliit felt it in his bones. The blast rolled through the arena long after the horn fell silent. Then came the grinding of stone on stone. Across from them, two ten-foot granite doors slid open, revealing torchlit halls.

For a heartbeat, there was only silence.

Then came the faint sound of screams and howling—growing louder.

"Stand closer!" Mategaladh shouted.

Evliit and Tophian moved to flank him, ten paces apart.

Long shadows flickered in the hallways. The pounding of running feet filled the arena like a war drum. Evliit glanced up—the Elders sat motionless, watching.

"Creator of everything, protect us!" Mategaladh cried.

Roots erupted from the floor around them. Some shoved aside four-foot slabs of stone; others punched straight through the tiles. Gasps rippled through the audience.

The sound of their astonishment bolstered Evliit's courage. "Yes, Mategaladh!"

The roots climbed eight feet high, then twisted inward, weaving into a rough sphere around the three men. The final knots tightened with a crackling crescendo.

Just as the shield finished forming, the first rakmuut burst through both doorways at once.

Tophian raised his hand. A six-foot chunk of stone—dislodged by Mategaladh's roots—shot across the arena and obliterated a cluster of four feral dogs against the far wall.

"They keep coming!" Evliit gasped. Fifteen, maybe twenty of the beasts now flooded the arena floor. "There are too many!"

"Steady!" Tophian shouted.

He swept up shards of stone and hurled them with terrifying force. Smaller fragments punched through three rakmuut, dropping them instantly. But the rest leapt onto the root-cage, biting and clawing, tearing away chunks of wood even as Mategaladh strained to reinforce it with new growth.

"Hold them off, Mategaladh!" Tophian shouted.

He hurled another slab of stone across the arena. It sheared the head off one rakmuut and smashed into a second as it tried to dodge, bursting stone and flesh against the wall.

Suddenly a sound like thunder boomed from the left doorway.

At the noise, the rakmuut recoiled from Mategaladh's barrier. With each successive boom, they crouched lower, whining.

Evliit saw Mategaladh and Tophian exchange a loaded glance. Whatever was coming frightened the rakmuut — and that alone made Evliit's stomach twist.

A roar exploded down the left hallway.

The rakmuut, still crouched, moved as a pack toward the opposite entrance. They huddled there, some glancing back as if deciding whether to flee.

Then the creature appeared — clawed fingers gripping either side of the doorway, struggling to pull its massive body through the hall.

"What now?" Evliit cried.

"From the size of it, a rhama," Tophian shouted. "A Camon consumed by a possessor!"

When the rhama forced its monstrous head through the opening, several Elders rose to their feet. Gasps and murmurs rained down from above.

The mutated Camon remained hunched, its thick neck and powerful shoulders rippling with bulging veins. Evliit thought the creature looked almost annoyed at the inconvenience of killing them. Its small, bloodshot eyes blinked and narrowed.

The rhama grunted and pushed. The top of the stone doorframe scraped white streaks across its thick gray hide. It stretched its neck, baring yellowed stumps of teeth the size of Evliit's fist.

Its fingernails gouged half-inch ruts in the stone as it dragged itself through. One shoulder, then the other, forced its way out. Cracks spiderwebbed through the surrounding wall, and a massive chunk of stone broke free and crashed to the ground.

When the rhama stepped onto the arena floor, it looked up through the iron dome and screamed at the Elders. Then it bent, reached back into the hallway, and dragged out a war hammer — the head nearly two-thirds Evliit's height.

It swung the hammer into the wall beside it. The concussion shook the arena's foundations. More Elders stood, visibly unsettled — and they weren't the ones trapped inside with the beast.

"Okay, this is serious," Tophian said.

"*Now* you think it's serious?" Mategaladh snapped.

The rhama turned toward the root-cage and lumbered forward. Evliit's breath caught as it roared at them.

He still held his sword, but his hands trembled so violently he nearly dropped it. He sank to one knee, planting the sword's tip against the stone. He prayed silently, eyes wide, watching the creature raise its hammer.

"Mategaladh!" Tophian shouted.

The rhama's hammer crashed down on the roots, smashing a gaping hole in the barrier. The creature thrust its other hand through, thick fingers groping for Mategaladh.

"Keep an eye on the rakmuut!" Mategaladh yelled. "I can't hold him off for long!"

The hounds, reassured the rhama wasn't focused on them, closed in again.

The rhama couldn't reach Mategaladh. It screamed in frustration and tore at the opening, ripping away a section the size of its chest. It hurled the chunk aside — striking a rakmuut square in the face. The injured beast shook its head, shrieked, and leapt onto the rhama, biting its shoulder and raking claws across its back.

The giant reached over with its free hand and seized the mongrel. The rakmuut went limp instantly. The rhama jerked once to free its claws from its hide, then lifted the beast overhead, glared at the others, bellowed, and squeezed.

Leather stretched. Bones popped. The lower half of the rakmuut dangled from its fist. It quivered once, then a black paste oozed between the rhama's fingers.

The rhama flung the carcass aside, shook the paste from its hand, and turned back toward Evliit and his companions. It gripped its hammer with both hands, raised it high, and slammed it into the arena floor.

The impact shattered the stone, leaving a web-shaped crater. The entire arena shook.

"That's my chance!" Tophian shouted.

A three-foot-thick slab of broken stone rose into the air and slammed into the rhama's face. The creature staggered, dropping to its haunches.

"Ha!" Tophian crowed.

But his triumph lasted only seconds. The rhama lurched back to its feet, angrier than before, and swung its hammer at the slab that had struck him. Stone exploded in every direction.

"No!" Tophian cried.

Evliit saw a fist-sized chunk of rock stop inches from his forehead and fall harmlessly away. But even as it clattered to the ground, he heard Mategaladh and Tophian cry out.

He spun to see Mategaladh doubled over, clutching his ribs, and Tophian on the floor, gripping his left thigh.

"I couldn't stop them all," Tophian hissed through clenched teeth. He moved his hand, revealing a jagged shard of stone protruding from his leg. "I think it's broken!"

"My ribs as well," Mategaladh gasped. "Help me up, Evliit!"

Evliit's pulse spiked. He sheathed his sword and rushed to Mategaladh's side.

The rhama barreled forward, swinging its hammer wildly, sending more stone flying.

Mategaladh's arms trembled. Evliit saw the agony etched across his face. New roots had already sealed the opening the rhama had smashed earlier, but the creature's relentless hammer blows were tearing through the barrier again. Behind him, the rakmuut spread out, waiting for their moment.

"It falls to you now, Evliit," Mategaladh whispered—and collapsed.

With a final, devastating strike, the rhama's hammer shattered the entire front of the root-cage. With a satisfied grunt, the behemoth lumbered forward, crushing roots beneath its feet.

Evliit looked at his fallen companions. Tophian had managed to rise to one knee, but Mategaladh lay helpless. There was no time to heal them. If he didn't act, they would die. Just like Jenna.

He should have been terrified.

But something shifted inside him.

He saw the old man pouring tea. The sword on the table. The peace he'd felt when he first touched it. And the quiet voice:

"Sword bearer."

The rhama's roar snapped him back to the arena.

Courage surged through him—pure, fearless. *He was the sword bearer. This was his calling.*

Evliit stepped directly into the path of the oncoming giant.

The rhama's hammer crashed down, pulverizing the stone floor and hurling Evliit backward. He rolled to his feet and drew his sword. Out of the corner of his eye, he saw the rakmuut closing in.

"That hammer has to go!" Evliit commanded.

At his words, the hammer ripped from the rhama's grip and flew toward the arena wall. The creature tried to hold on—its arm jerked with a sickening tear—before it released the weapon and screamed in pain.

The hammer smashed into the wall in an eruption of stone. Several rakmuut bolted for the opening.

But the rhama cared only for Evliit now.

It lunged, swiping with its massive left hand. Evliit ducked, pivoted, and swung his sword through the creature's knee. The blade parted flesh and bone as if slicing water.

The rhama staggered backward on the stump of its leg, catching itself with its uninjured arm. It drew a great breath and began a second scream—

Evliit cut it short.

His blade thrust upward, piercing the rhama's throat and driving through the top of its skull. A collective gasp rippled through the arena. In the stunned silence that followed, Evliit pulled the sword free in a single downward motion.

The rhama collapsed, lifeless.

For a heartbeat, everything was still.

Then two rakmuut leapt through the hole in the arena wall, and the stadium erupted in terror. Elders scrambled. Guards ran for the exits.

Evliit positioned himself between the six remaining rakmuut and the shattered barrier.

Two charged.

Evliit's battle cry drowned out the chaos. The sword blazed in his hand, and the world slowed to a crawl. The rakmuut drifted toward him, suspended in mid-air, mouths frozen in snarls.

The sword felt weightless.

Evliit moved like water.

His blade sliced through the ribs of the rakmuut on his right, then swept upward in a single fluid motion, cleaving the second beast in half.

"Behind you!" Tophian screamed.

Evliit spun. Four rakmuut charged at once.

"Back!" he commanded.

A pulse of energy blasted outward, hurling them into the arena wall with a sickening crunch. They slid to the floor, writhing.

Evliit strode forward and slew three of them. The fourth dragged itself into the hallway and vanished.

When he was certain no threats remained, he sheathed his sword and ran to Tophian. He placed his hands over the break in his friend's leg.

"It's coming back to him, Mateg—" Tophian began, but stopped as the bones shifted. "Grrr!"

Mategaladh watched from the ground. "I told you it would."

Evliit moved to heal Mategaladh's ribs. Out of the corner of his eye, he saw Elder Jonas enter through the hole in the wall, followed by Rion Guards and other Elders. Jonas stepped into the center of the arena, folded his hands, and stared at Evliit.

"We are seeking the Creator's will about you," he said, perplexed. "Wait here, please."

The Elders and guardsmen looked equally bewildered. They walked the arena floor, inspecting the carnage. Several couldn't stop staring at the sword at Evliit's side.

"My lord, the two rakmuut that escaped…" one guard said.

"Yes?" Jonas replied.

"With your permission, my men and I will dispatch them."

"Of course," Jonas said, waving vaguely toward Evliit. "We will deal with this."

The guards bowed and hurried out.

Evliit helped Mategaladh to his feet.

"My lord," Evliit said, "let us join the hunt. Let us avenge Harot."

Jonas set his jaw. "We will speak of this. Give us a moment."

He and the Elders gathered on the far side of the arena. A heated but hushed debate followed.

Evliit's patience thinned. "What takes so long?"

"I suspect they discuss the sword and the legend," Mategaladh said. "Patience. We'll know soon."

Tophian stood, testing his leg. "The bones are healed," he said, wincing.

Evliit's chest throbbed. He rubbed the brand.

"Something troubles you?" Mategaladh asked.

"All I can think is that I could have healed Jenna," Evliit said. "It haunts me."

"Oh, Evliit," Mategaladh said softly. "Some things are beyond even the sword bearer."

Elder Jonas broke from the group, shaking his head. He looked dissatisfied.

"They come," Tophian murmured.

Jonas approached.

"The Elders believe another will come to bear the sword," he said. "We wish you well, Evliit. Go in peace."

Evliit looked from Mategaladh back to Jonas. "Go in peace? What do you mean by that? Are you telling me you won't help us?"

Jonas stood impassive.

"But we did what you asked," Evliit cried. "We defeated the unnamed one's spawn. You saw it with your own eyes!"

"Pray for us, brother Evliit," Jonas said. "Pray for the victory of the guard and the Elders over this treacherous enemy."

"I will pray for you," Evliit said. "But I beg you—reconsider."

"Evliit," Mategaladh warned.

Jonas looked momentarily speechless.

"Elder Jonas," another Elder called, beckoning him over.

"Forgive me," Jonas said, raising a finger. He returned to the group to confer.

Mategaladh leaned close. "What are you doing? The sword bearer doesn't bow to the Elders."

"If only the Elders' soldiers can avenge Harot," Evliit said, "then I guess I have no choice. I don't see another way."

The Elders' whispers ceased. Jonas returned.

"My brother Elders have a request, Evliit. They accept your fealty and acknowledge that this sword is indeed powerful." Jonas sighed. "But we cannot accept that the sword you carry is of the Creator's making. It contradicts too much of what we believe. Let us investigate your claim. Turn the sword over to the guard so we may verify its origin."

Evliit stiffened. "My sword?"

"Yes," Tophian said. "A holy weapon should be kept here, protected by the guard."

Evliit was certain the Elders missed the sarcasm in Tophian's tone. Tophian glanced at Mategaladh, who remained silent.

"Such a weapon could do great damage to our enemy—in the right hands," Jonas said. "In the hands of the guard."

Evliit looked at his companions. Their downcast eyes told him everything. They were disappointed. They had known this was coming. The Elders were never going to follow him. They hadn't expected him to survive the arena.

He looked at the sword at his side for what felt like minutes.

"Forgive me, my lord," Evliit said at last. His hands trembled, but his voice was steady. "This weapon was given to me by the Creator. To part with it would be to deny my calling—to insult the Creator himself, and my friends who stood by my side."

Jonas frowned, then smoothed his expression. "Very well, Evliit. Let it never be said that the Elders caused a brother to sin."

He paced a moment, then clasped his hands.

"As for your fealty: By order of the Elders of Rion, you will return to the western foothills of the Black Mountains. You are assigned the position of protector of the Monastery of Ardidhus. You will live out your days there in service to the Creator. Brother Ulbrech will relay the details."

Evliit felt a sharp pang in his stomach. *Live out my days in a monastery? That can't be right.*

"May the Creator bless you and strengthen you in your service," Jonas said. He bowed, turned, and rejoined the Elders. All but one departed the arena floor.

The one who remained approached Evliit. A frail, emaciated man, swallowed by his monk's robe.

He bowed with effort. "I am Ulbrech."

Evliit returned the gesture. "Elder Ulbrech."

"I will prepare a letter for you to carry to our brothers at the monastery. It will explain your assignment. They will welcome you, Evliit." He surveyed the carnage. "May the Creator forgive us for such destruction." He leaned closer. "I am glad you and your friends survived this madness."

"Thank you, Elder Ulbrech," Evliit said.

Ulbrech cleared his throat. "Come; we have food. Join us and eat."

"Notice they don't ask until after the arena challenge," Tophian muttered.

"I need a moment with my friends," Mategaladh said. "Elder Ulbrech, will you excuse us?"

"Of course. When you're ready, help yourselves to our baths, food, drink, and a pillow for your head."

"Thank you, Elder Ulbrech," Evliit said. "We'll be along shortly."

Ulbrech bowed and exited.

The moment he was gone, Mategaladh rounded on Evliit.

"Have you lost your mind?"

Evliit felt the tips of his ears burn. "I—"

"I thought you were coming here to ask for help, not swear fealty to the Elders!" Mategaladh snapped, not letting him finish.

"I— it just came out of my mouth," Evliit muttered.

"Good lord, kid, you've got to get control of that," Tophian said. "Come on, Mategaladh. What can we do for him now? Let's go home."

Evliit lifted a hand. "You two have done more than I could have asked. Thank you both."

"Oh, Evliit," Mategaladh said. "You've committed your life—your entire life."

"I'm sorry if I let you down," Evliit said. "When you showed me the sword bearer's image on Tophian's walls, I didn't see a monastery painted around him. It appears I'm not who you thought I was." He looked from Tophian to Mategaladh. "And even I was beginning to believe it. I'm sorry."

Mategaladh exhaled heavily. "We all must choose our own path. This, it seems, is yours."

"Then please—let us remain friends," Evliit said. "Will you not ride with me to the Black Mountains? What can it hurt? It's on your way, isn't it?"

"Surely," Mategaladh said.

Tophian eyed him for a moment, then nodded. "Why not."

ᒣᚹᚍᚷᚍ·

The following morning, they left for the western foothills of the Black Mountains. The air was crisp, and the campfires scattered across the foothills filled Evliit's nostrils with a scent found only in the open wild—burning wood mingled with cooking bacon and fish, undercut by the sweetness of tall grasses and wildflowers.

They rode through the entire first day, and when night fell, the moonlight was bright enough that they pressed on. By midnight, the monastery came into view—flames burning atop each column along the high outer walls.

Evliit stopped Angwen and stared.

The Monastery of Ardidhus was far more impressive than anything he had imagined. Three massive towers were connected by walls at least forty feet high. The eastern tower was built directly into the foothills; the western tower stood on a small peninsula jutting into the Lake of Aertos, the largest of the five lakes north of Rion. The lawn sloped gently down to the water, where a small dock held two or three boats. Nets hung drying on racks. A larger flat-bottomed ferry was tied beside a stone tower at the water's edge.

Up the slope from the lake, they found a gateway in the outer wall. The great iron bars were closed.

"Who goes there?" a voice demanded from one of the two small towers flanking the gate.

"I am Evliit, sent with papers by the Elders of Rion. These are my friends, Mategaladh and Tophian."

A dirty-faced man in patinated bronze armor stepped from behind the left tower. He examined them through the bars, securing his helmet with a frayed leather strap. "One of you come down and pass the papers through. The other two stay back."

"Of course," Evliit said, dismounting. He approached the gate. "I have them here," he said, reaching into his coat.

"Keep your other hand where I can see it," the man said, lowering his pike. "Nothing done too quickly, right?"

"I wouldn't dream of it," Evliit said. "No trouble here."

"Reach through the bars and hold out the papers."

Evliit complied. "Here you go."

The man snatched them and stepped back. "Now move away. The gates aren't opened at night. You'll have to make yourselves comfortable until morning."

"What about the papers?" Evliit asked.

"It's only a few hours until daylight. The monks rise before dawn. After prayers, I'll request an audience with the head monk and give him the papers. Whether he sees you is not for me to say."

Without waiting for a reply, he vanished into the tower.

Evliit turned to his friends and shrugged.

"Not to worry," Tophian said. "We'll get some shut-eye and be off in the morning."

The full moon lit the night, its reflection nearly perfect on the still lake. "I've never been on this side of Aertos," Mategaladh said. "I've only seen the monastery from the western shore. It's actually quite nice."

"Yes, it is," Evliit said.

He tried to sound agreeable, but despair gnawed at him. He had listened with reverence to Tophian and Mategaladh's stories of the sword bearer. He remembered flashes—another place, another time—and the idea of an entire other life unsettled him deeply. Something had happened on that mountainside. More than he had first recalled. He had begun to believe he was meant for something greater than a guard post at an old monastery.

Evliit turned away and walked to the gate. He wrapped his hands around the bars and lowered his head. He could only shake it in disgust. He stepped forward and rested his forehead against the cold steel.

Silence hung between them until Tophian finally spoke. "Time for bed then."

He dismounted, pulled his bedroll from his saddle, and flicked a nod their way. "Good night, all."

Mategaladh dismounted and unrolled his bedding.

At a loss for anything else to do, Evliit followed suit.

In the morning, the loud clanking of metal on metal woke Evliit as the iron gate ratcheted open. He groaned and rolled over; he had slept little. Tophian, meanwhile, seemed to be sleeping like a baby.

"Tophian!" Mategaladh said. "Tophian! Wake up! They're coming."

Tophian rolled over. "All right, I'm up." He sat up, pulled one knee to his chest, and yawned. "What's the occasion?"

"It may be the head monk," Mategaladh said. "And if it is, I don't think you want to be lying down when he gets here."

"Yeah, okay," Tophian muttered. He stood and dusted off his clothes just as a monk in plain brown robes and sandals appeared at the gate.

"I think it's just one of the monks," Evliit said.

"There, see?" Tophian grumbled. "I could've slept through this."

"Hello!" the monk called, waving enthusiastically. "Welcome, all!"

"Chipper, that one," Tophian said.

Evliit shot him a look and raised a hand in greeting.

"I'm Ebert," the monk said, extending his hand as he approached.

"Evliit," he replied, shaking it.

"It's very nice to meet you," Ebert said. "Welcome to the Monastery of Ardidhus." He turned to Tophian and Mategaladh. "You're welcome to stay and rest, friends. I'm sorry about the gate rules. Abbot Jaros is adamant about the monastery's safety."

"We were just leaving," Tophian said.

Mategaladh glanced at him, and Evliit hoped he might say they'd stay a bit longer. But Mategaladh only smiled politely. "Another time, perhaps?"

"Of course," Ebert said. "Friends of Evliit are friends of ours."

"Be well, Evliit," Mategaladh said, extending his arm.

"Be strong," Tophian added, offering his own.

"Thank you both," Evliit said, clasping their arms in turn.

"You're headed south?" Ebert asked.

"North, actually," Mategaladh said.

"You'll save time using the ferry," Ebert said. "Abbot Jaros has arranged it, if you wish."

"That would be much appreciated," Mategaladh said. "Take care, Evliit."

He and Tophian mounted up and rode down the hill toward the lakeshore.

Evliit watched them go. In the morning light, he noticed the countryside for the first time. The Lake of Aertos shimmered blue in the valley of lush green grasses. Wind rippled across the meadows and trees, then swept over the lake's surface. Beyond a line of trees descending the slope of the Black Mountains, he saw the Faceless Mountains rising from the northern side of the valley—sheer, snow-topped, forbidding stone stretching as far as he could see.

It was breathtaking.

"Good friends?" Ebert asked, breaking Evliit's trance.

Evliit's eyes followed Tophian and Mategaladh again. "The kind of friends you trust with your life."

He watched them ride onto the ferry and dismount. The ferryman set his pole and pushed off from the shore.

"That's rare in this world," Ebert said. "I hope you see them again soon."

"Me too, Ebert. Me too."

Evliit watched the ferry one last time, then turned and walked with Ebert toward the monastery gate.

CHAPTER 5

HUNTRESS

Rendaya needed the peace of moonlight.

The balcony overlooking the western castle grounds offered her a brief chance to bask in it. She closed her eyes and let the chilly night breeze swirl her long, jet-black hair around her face.

Moonlight always drew the tension out of her. She could feel it rising from her body like steam.

Broeden had been beside himself—infuriated by the Rion Guard's attack. The gall of those men, thinking they could murder him in his bed as they had done to their holy man, Janus. She had seen Broeden tear men apart for far less. His anger tonight was terrifying, and she had excused herself from his inner court at the first opportunity.

The sound of barking on the lawn made her open her eyes.

The war dogs of the Camonra romped across the fields, playing as if they had not a care in the world. Below them, several Camon sat around a campfire, nearly motionless, watching the dogs as she did. For a moment, Broeden's servants—these oversized men he had shaped for his personal army—reminded Rendaya of children entranced by street performers in her village. The memory brought her a flicker of joy.

Good memories were rare. Her village had given her up to Broeden as a sacrifice, hoping to appease his wrath when their offering of crops had fallen short.

Two of the dogs chased each other, teeth bared, eyes wide, nipping at legs and ears, their growls rising with each clash. Rendaya smiled. It was rare to think of these chest-high beasts as pets, but tonight they reminded her of just that.

Then one dog broke off and howled at the moon. Instantly, several others joined in, their lone cry becoming a wild chorus. A Camon rose from the fire, strode among them, and backhanded the instigator mid-howl, sending it flying with a yelp. The symphony died at once.

So much for peace.

Rendaya turned and walked back into the castle, heading down the long corridor toward the court. The flames of the oil urns hanging high along the stilted hall cast a reddish-orange glow, their dancing shadows tricking the eye. It would have been a foreboding place for any human—familiars and other spirits roamed Broeden's halls—but Rendaya was no mere human.

Broeden had taken her under his wing. His affection for her was the closest thing to love he had ever shown in his long life. Under his tutelage, she had become the most powerful sorceress in the world. Darkness and light, flesh and blood—even spirit things—feared Rendaya.

"Enter!" Broeden's voice boomed as she neared his court.

The thick-timbered doors swung open at his command, releasing a wave of brimstone. Rendaya stepped through just far enough to clear the doors with her train, which flowed across the red-and-gold carpet beneath her.

The doors closed behind her with a heavy thud.

"My lord," Rendaya said, bowing.

The court attendants glided to her sides, their pale exoskeletons creaking as they reached out with long, bony fingers to lift her train with the hooked tips of their claws.

"*Huntresssss*," they hissed. A deep red flame burned behind their eyes, and thin trails of sulfurous smoke followed the bow of their heads. Rendaya smiled faintly. The curled, calcified extrusions on their skulls always made them look as if their hair were standing on end.

"Come closer," Broeden said. "Stand here, beside me."

He looked tired—worn thin and frail—but his voice remained loud and commanding.

"Yes, my lord." Rendaya took her place at his right hand.

Broeden drew a deep breath, and the courtroom full of dark creatures fell silent. They retreated into the shadows until only their glowing eyes and the spell-marks on their skin remained visible.

"You will find and punish those who have violated the sanctity of my home!" he thundered. "Rain down my vengeance on any who stand in your way!"

"*Punissshhhh*," the creatures chanted.

Rendaya bowed. "As you command, my lord."

"Who do they think they are, challenging me?" he roared.

Rendaya had never heard him go on like this. She couldn't stop herself from looking up at him. Something was different.

"They are but fleas to me!" he shouted. "Fleas I could brush away with a single stroke of my hand!"

Broeden coughed—a wet, rattling cough—and steadied himself on his chair.

"*Fleeeaaasssss*," the creatures echoed, agitation rising.

Rendaya kept silent, but when Broeden turned to her, she was certain she saw fear in his eyes—something she had never seen before.

As if realizing she had noticed, he broke the stare, stood, and slammed his staff against the stone floor. The impact echoed through the chamber, sending many of the creatures into cowering postures.

"Never again!" he bellowed. "Assemble my armies!"

The room erupted. Creatures scrambled over one another to reach the exits, giddy with anticipation as they clogged the doorways in their haste to obey. In moments, they were gone.

Broeden eased himself back into his throne.

"What do you know of them?" he asked.

"They came from the southwest," Rendaya said. "Over the Black Mountains, near the coast. They called their home 'Rion.'"

"You're sure of this?"

"Their tolerance for pain is limited. It was verified by several captives."

"Bring me a monk!" Broeden roared.

Immediately, two demons lurched in from the left, dragging a frail white-haired man by poles attached to his neck shackle. Their long, muscular arms yanked him forward in jerking spurts as their awkward, rocking gait alternated with low squats. They stopped before Broeden's throne, their hunched torsos rising and falling with labored breaths. Their mouths had been stitched shut after they once bit a captive.

The monk's clothes hung in tatters. His beard and hair were matted, his left eye swollen shut. He looked barely strong enough to hold up the shackles around his wrists.

"What of it, monk?" Broeden demanded. "What kind of army can this Rion field against me?"

The monk didn't answer. He looked confused, dazed. The demons jerked the collar violently, nearly snapping his neck. Their nostril flaps fluttered with exertion, and drool seeped through their bindings.

"Enough!" Broeden barked.

The demons froze.

"You will tell me what I want to know!"

The monk's right eye opened wide. He trembled. "L-Lord Broeden," he stammered, "I am but a monk. What would I know of armies?"

"Search this one," Broeden growled to Rendaya.

He leaned back into his throne with a long exhalation and closed his eyes.

Rendaya hesitated. She had used her gifts to battle the greatest warriors of their age, absorbing their spirits, their knowledge, their life force. But this man was no warrior—only a broken monk.

"This one is no threat, master," she said. "What would I gain from him? Let the torturer have his way."

Broeden's eyes snapped open. His gaze pinned her.

"You will do as I command!" he screamed. "No more and no less!"

Rendaya lowered her eyes. His words stung. He had never spoken to her like this—not once. Whatever had happened during the assassins' attack had changed him. But she betrayed none of this.

"As you command," she said quickly.

"Search him!"

"Wait!" the monk cried, struggling. "Please, no!"

The demons forced him to his knees before her. Rendaya removed her glove and raised her hand before his face. She would uncover whatever her master required.

She willed the monk's spirit toward her.

It began immediately.

He arched his back, fighting the pull, but within seconds he collapsed, limp. The demons dragged his lifeless body away by the neck restraint.

Rendaya swayed. Light-headed. *Something was wrong. Very wrong.*

A strange stirring moved inside her.

She turned back to Broeden—and flinched. He sat tall, watching her intently.

"What is it?" he asked. "What do you see?"

The monk's being unfolded in her mind, but the thoughts made her uneasy. This was no hardened warrior with memories of slaughter. This gentle soul tore through her with waves of emotion she had never known.

Service. Sacrifice. Compassion.

Sadness overwhelmed her, settling like a stone in her stomach.

Broeden's eyes narrowed. "What's wrong?"

"There are many memories, my lord," she said—though it wasn't true. It was the same memory, over and over: compassion. It rattled her.

She felt faint. Her knees buckled.

"Sit!" Broeden commanded. "Sit before you fall!"

Rendaya sank onto the steps before his throne. She closed her eyes. The ringing in her ears drowned out the court. Nausea rolled through her. She was certain she would vomit.

Then, finally, she managed to separate the monk's being from her own.

Her insides stopped quivering.

With control restored, she saw the monk's memories drifting around her like fireflies. She moved among them, sensing their brightness, until she found one unusually luminous—something precious to him.

She stepped into it.

Her eyes flew open.

"It is the same as the others, my lord," she said. "This monk believed with all his being that their deity—the one the men of Rion call 'the Creator'— would give unto man a holy relic. A sword whose bearer is made immortal."

"I will have this trinket," Broeden said, eyes gleaming. "And I will bend its power to my will. Where will I find this sword?"

"The monk called its bearer a 'Watcher,'" she said. "A warrior. A protector."

"We must know more!" Broeden thundered. "Have the last raids yielded any more monks?"

"No, my lord. That was the last of them."

"Go!" he commanded. "Raid the outposts of Rion! Bring me more Rionese monks! I will have this sword!"

"Yes, my lord!"

Broeden tapped his staff twice. Insects poured from a corroded floor grate, swarming around the throne. They ducked into channels carved beneath the throne's legs and lifted it. The ribbon-bodied creatures scuttled away, carrying Broeden—throne and all—toward his quarters.

Rendaya bowed until he was gone.

Then she hurried to the nearest balcony, where she knew a crystal service of elixirs waited. She pulled a packet from her breast pocket, dumped it into a stiff drink, and swallowed it. Then another.

Her heart pounded like a drum.

Within seconds, the agony inside her dulled to numbness.

Rendaya walked to the balcony ledge and looked over the gathering army below. A thunderous roar rose when she appeared. She didn't flinch. She didn't blink.

She raised her hands.

Another roar—twice as loud.

Rendaya forced all thoughts of the monk from her mind.

She would command the dark hordes to march southwest on Rion.

This was her path.

CHAPTER 6

THE MONASTERY OF ARDIDHUS

Evliit tried not to think of Mategaladh and Tophian, but their absence left an ache in him. He would miss them dearly.

He followed the young monk, Ebert, through the gates of the monastery's curtain wall. Inside, the place was alive with activity. Peasants tended overflowing plots of crops. Women fed chickens, goats, and sheep in small fenced lots. Children darted between the pens, chasing each other in wild loops.

And there was laughter.

Evliit realized he hadn't heard laughter in a long time.

"Do you see how we moved the mountain?" Ebert asked proudly, pointing to the far side of the courtyard.

It truly looked as though the builders had carved the mountain away. Nearly a third of the yard was cut directly into the rock. At the farthest point, a twisting stone walkway climbed the sheer wall to a doorway at the base of the eastern tower—built straight into the mountainside.

"Where we cut into the mountain, the yard is solid stone," Ebert said eagerly. "You'll have to see the pools we made there."

"For the monks?" Evliit asked.

"No, no," Ebert laughed. "For the people. A small town has grown within the outer walls of the old monastery. We are a community."

He pointed toward the women and children splashing in rectangular pools ahead. "On the southern side, the pools are for public baths and washing dishes and clothes. The northern pools store drinking water."

Evliit stopped and stared. Everything here felt different. So many people smiling, so much joy—it felt like stepping into a fairy tale. And it was contagious. He found himself smiling at a group of children watching him with wide eyes. They shrieked with delight and ran off.

The monastery was nothing like Harot. Happiness had never been a hallmark of life on those streets.

"Come; follow me!" Ebert called. "Let me show you the main entrance of the monastery itself!"

Toward the rear of the outer court stood the monastery proper—a rectangular structure built of stones three hands high. Small windows dotted the second floor. The facade's stone, wood, and iron were ornate, but the design was unmistakably defensive.

"Now this is the work of the ancient masters," Evliit said, running his fingers along the stone.

"Incredible, eh?" Ebert said.

"Absolutely."

"Let me show you inside." Ebert practically danced with excitement. "You may have noticed the main entrance faces south, toward Rion."

"No, I hadn't thought of it," Evliit said, his attention fixed on the towering entrance.

The massive oak doors rose ten feet high, each beam two hands wide. The mushroomed rivets—nearly two inches across—bulged like iron knuckles hammered flat by giants.

Ebert stopped at the hinges—each as large as a man's chest, coated in a thin layer of red oxidation. "Hard to imagine building such things, eh? Feel this."

He slapped the hinge.

Evliit stepped forward and struck the hinge with the flat of his hand. The metal was so dense it barely made a sound.

"Impressive," Evliit said.

Ebert beamed, bouncing on the balls of his feet. "Let me show you the garden!"

Without waiting, he wove through the people entering and exiting the main doors. Evliit followed him through the entrance, along a rectangular colonnade that wrapped the inner court, and down a few steps into a grassy courtyard.

Ebert turned slowly, sweeping a hand across the scene. "Incredible, isn't it?"

"Yes, it is," Evliit said.

The courtyard was filled with white flowers. At its center lay a pristine pool, twenty feet across. Rising from the water was a white marble statue of the Creator, surrounded by smaller sculptures of the Bhre-Nora—most depicted as blacksmiths. Their marble anvils sprayed arcs of water that crisscrossed the pool around the central figure. It was one of the most impressive works of art Evliit had ever seen.

Above the colonnade, monks watched from behind a waist-high retaining wall on the second story. And above them, an arched iron framework filled with stained glass spanned the courtyard. Morning sunlight filtered through it, washing the white flowers in brilliant colors and scattering rainbows across the fountain.

"Welcome to our monastery," said a voice behind Evliit.

Ebert was already bowing. "Your Excellency."

Evliit turned to find an older man with a long grey beard peppered with white. His face was pleasant—peaceful.

"Your Excellency," Evliit said, mimicking Ebert's bow.

Ebert shook his head and gestured for Evliit to rise. "Warriors don't bow to monks," he whispered.

Evliit rose quickly and extended a hand, but Ebert shook his head.

"His Excellency doesn't touch warriors," he whispered.

Evliit drew his hand back and did his best to stand at attention. The monk's arms remained folded within the sleeves of his robes.

"I am Jaros," the monk finally said.

"I am Evliit," he replied.

"My lords, the Elders, have sent you to me, I see," Jaros said. "While the support of the Elders is always appreciated, I must warn you, Evliit, you may find yourself a bit bored at this post. It's quiet here. We've not been attacked in many years. I truly believe this monastery holds no strategic interest to any party."

"I accept their wisdom," Evliit answered. "I've offered my sword to the Elders, and they have commanded me to defend it. I give you my word: I will defend this monastery with all that I have."

"Then welcome," Jaros said. His face revealed nothing. "I trust Brother Ebert will give you a grand tour and see you to your quarters. Peace be with you, Evliit."

With a slight bow, the head monk turned to leave.

Is that it? Evliit wondered. Then, remembering his manners, he called out, "And with you, Jaros."

The abbot gave no sign he had heard him.

Evliit did his best to fit into monastery life. He spent most of his time with Ebert, helping the young monk tend the gardens in the courtyard or caring for the messenger birds Ebert had trained to carry news back to the Elders far to the south.

The monks' routine was exhausting—hours of prayer and singing, endless studies and writing, gathering food and supplies. And more prayer. Always more prayer.

The sheer amount of time spent in silence had a profound effect on him. There was so much space to think. Their quiet rituals, their chanting songs about creation and the Creator—all of it pushed Evliit inward. And whenever he turned inward, he found the same memories waiting for him: the mountain, Jenna, Broeden.

He dreamed often of the mountainside. The name Aleris surfaced again and again, but the images were fragmented and strange. The sword had given him the power to defeat the monsters in Rion's arena—he knew that much— but how? And why? He still had no answers.

Ebert, for his part, had a servant's heart and seemed eager to shadow Evliit's every move. Evliit enjoyed his company, even if the young monk was sometimes more talkative than he preferred. Over the next few weeks, the two became fast friends.

ᘔY⌇ᕼᏖ⌐.

"Want to come with me?" Ebert asked. "I'm going to feed the birds."

"Versus waiting here in the courtyard for the sound of an alarm?" Evliit pointed to the monastery bell, as large as a haystack. "I've spent the past hour staring at that thing. I'm not even sure it *can* ring anymore."

"Come on," Ebert said. "You can help me."

"Of course," Evliit said. "Let's go."

It was a beautiful day; sunlight poured through the windows as they ascended the winding stone steps to the eastern tower, where Ebert's birds roosted.

"How do you get them to carry your messages?" Evliit asked. He'd been curious for weeks but hadn't wanted to seem ignorant. Today, curiosity won.

"I give them a lovely home," Ebert said, smiling. "When they mate, I keep the pair together here in the loft and feed them very well. And every time I feed them, I shake this gourd."

"Your little dinner bell?" Evliit asked.

"Exactly." Ebert's head bobbed with enthusiasm. He bent toward the cages, speaking softly to the birds. "Every time I feed them, I shake this gourd and remind them that Brother Ebert is the one they want to stay with — that this is home."

"How long before they're convinced?" Evliit asked.

"About a month," Ebert said. "Then I let out one mate but not the other. I don't feed them before I release them, and though they fly around to get their bearings, when I rattle this gourd, they always come home."

He shook the gourd, and every bird snapped to attention.

"But does he return for the food or his mate?" Evliit asked, crouching to peer into a cage.

Ebert laughed. "Hard to say. All I know is, if I let them fly for an hour each day and feed them well when they return, within two or three days they're trained. Then I keep them inside while I do the same with their mate."

"After that you can let both out to fly together?"

Ebert nodded. "Once they're accustomed to the surroundings and come when I rattle the gourd, I make a small message tube and attach it to their legs. Then I give them to runners who take them farther and farther away. When the runners release them, they fly home."

"I was trying to figure out how you made them fly somewhere," Evliit said. "Turns out you don't. You teach them to fly home."

"You've got it," Ebert said.

Evliit looked over the thirty or forty cages. "So these birds — the ones you don't let out — they're from other places? They fly back to where they came from?"

"That's right."

"Where are they all from?"

"Throughout the known world. We watch for signs of the evil one, and when I release these birds to return home, they'll carry our warning across Rion faster than any horse — certainly faster than an army. The outposts' warnings protect the people, and my birds… they're the key."

Ebert's face glowed with pride.

"You are like Watchers, then?" Evliit asked.

"Oh, no, brother. We are monks. Watchers are something altogether different. They are supernaturally gifted with the Creator's own power."

"Hmm. I think I'd rather be known as a doer," Evliit said with a chuckle.

"You shouldn't say such things," Ebert said. "The Watchers are just beneath the prophets in the Creator's domain. I only hope that through prayer and discernment, I might align my spirit with the Creator's will — then I, too, could channel the power to heal the broken and stand against those who ravage the weak."

"I meant nothing by it," Evliit said, still laughing. "It was a joke."

Ebert didn't appear amused. Evliit's tone shifted. "I'm sorry, Ebert."

"We are more than simple monks," Ebert said. "Jaros believes in action, just as you do. You shouldn't underestimate what the quiet mind can conjure."

"I wouldn't dream of it," Evliit said. "It's always been the quiet ones that worry me."

Finally, Ebert laughed. "I can't argue with that."

He put away the bird feed, grabbed a broom, and began sweeping the loft floor. "Seriously, though," he said, "Abbot Jaros believes the Creator has given us all great powers — that each of us can understand the very rules that govern the universe. And we can use that understanding to affect the outcome of any situation."

Though he spoke of Jaros, his demeanor suggested he was sharing something deeply personal. Evliit gave him his full attention.

"Monks pray for long hours, but they also study — study for years, their entire lives," Ebert continued. "And Abbot Jaros… he knows things you and I will never know."

"I'm sure," Evliit said.

Ebert calmed. "People say the outposts have outlived their purpose — that we can't just watch the horizon anymore. They say the enemy is upon us and we must take the fight to him." He paused his sweeping. "Do you believe that?"

"Yes, I do," Evliit said. "But that doesn't mean the monks' work lacks value. Your watchful eye is vital to saving lives, if not stopping an invasion outright."

He looked out the window at the courtyard below — families living their lives without fear of the monsters beyond the Black Mountains. "Still, who wants to wait for an invasion? Better to confront evil head-on. Let the horrors of war stay there, not here."

"No!" Ebert exclaimed. "We can't go into the Forgotten Lands! We should stay away from the evil one — as far away as we can! Let there be no war at all!"

He resumed sweeping, silent now. When he finished, he returned the broom and started down the stairs.

Evliit followed, respecting his friend's quiet. But as they crossed the outer court, he placed a hand on Ebert's shoulder.

"Understand the very rules that control the universe, huh?" he said with a friendly pat.

"Yes," Ebert said. "The heat of summer is coming. You'll see."

The look on Ebert's face caught Evliit off guard. "Not looking forward to the heat," Evliit said automatically, too busy processing Ebert's expression to offer anything more meaningful.

Without a word, Ebert turned and walked toward his quarters. Evliit did the same.

That night, Evliit prayed to the Creator — but this time, not out of desperation. Curiosity drove him.

"Creator?" he began.

He glanced around the room as if the Bhre-Nora might appear at any moment. His eyes settled on the sword and scabbard propped against his bedside.

"In Rion's arena, you showed me that my calling was true — that you bestowed upon me this holy weapon. And yet you place me here, in the service of monks, isolated in this remote place. What must I do to strike at the heart of Broeden as he has struck at mine?"

He paused, testing the weight of his words.

"I don't understand this path you've placed before me."

Silence followed. He wasn't sure what he expected, but he suddenly felt a little foolish. Compared to the monks, he felt like a novice at prayer. He knelt beside his bed, as he'd seen them do countless times. What the Creator wanted from him was a mystery — but for the first time, he felt the urge to stop worrying about it.

Words he'd heard the monks speak again and again rose unbidden to his lips.

"May your will be done. Bring forth your glory, Creator of all."

And there it was again — that strange sense of peace. He didn't understand it, but it felt as though a weight had lifted from his shoulders.

Murmuring outside his room cut his prayer short. He walked to the doorway and cracked it open. Torchlight flickered up from the courtyard. He stepped onto the balcony, easing to the edge.

Below, monks — some in ornate robes — were singing in the old tongue. Something about the harvest, he thought. A creaking sound came from above; the metal frames holding the stained glass over the courtyard were shifting, opening the space to the night sky.

Jaros stood at the center of the gathering. He raised his hands, and the chant faded.

"We pray for the drought of summer to pass over us," he said. "We pray that Erathe shower her mercy on our crops."

He looked skyward and cried, "*Ca-la!*" throwing something onto the stone floor.

A blue flame burst to life.

The monks spread out as the flame moved before Jaros, swirling like a small whirlwind. "*Yah!*" he cried, and the flame surged waist-high, dancing across the courtyard. The monks began a humming chant, and somewhere under the portico, a stringed instrument joined in — its haunting melody echoing through the stone.

The song grew faster, more intense. The blue blaze rose until it reached the height of the balcony. At its peak, Jaros stepped into the base of the fire — now ten feet across.

The music stopped. The monks fell to their knees.

Evliit heard the whipping of the flame in the sudden silence. Jaros's hair and robes whipped about in the wind — but he did not burn. He tilted his head back, and the flames collapsed inward, converging on him and flowing into his body.

Everything went still.

Then Evliit noticed the moonlight shifting on the balcony floor. Subtle at first — then unmistakable. Clouds above the monastery began to swirl. Thunder rumbled. A gentle rain began to fall, tapping softly on the hosta leaves beside him.

Wind followed, whipping the branches of the courtyard maples.

Jaros lowered his hands and gave thanks, and the rain intensified. The monks resumed their chant as they moved under the colonnade and toward their rooms.

Realizing some might be coming upstairs, Evliit suddenly felt like a voyeur. He turned to slip back to his room — and nearly collided with Ebert.

"Ebert!" he gasped. "I didn't see you."

Ebert's face was radiant. "I told you," he said. "Abbot Jaros is connected to the Creator in ways we may never understand."

Evliit glanced upward. The clouds still turned in a slow spiral. "An incredible thing to witness," he said.

"A lot to take in at once, I imagine."

Evliit found the whole thing surreal — and unsettling. It reminded him too much of the storm in the Black Mountains. Of Harot. Of Jenna. He wanted to say more, but the words wouldn't come.

"Without a doubt," he managed.

Silence settled between them, broken only by the white noise of the rain. Water ran in rivulets down Evliit's face.

"Forgive me," Ebert said. "You're getting soaked! Good night, Evliit!"

"Good night, Ebert."

Evliit walked briskly toward his room, but before stepping inside, he looked back.

Ebert stood at the balcony rail, leaning slightly backward, eyes closed, letting the rain wash over him.

When Evliit closed his door, Ebert was still praying.

༄༅།

Jaros called Evliit before him the following day. Evliit felt a little anxious about the whole affair but did his best to hide it. Ebert wasn't fooled. When they were alone in the tower feeding the messenger birds, he spoke up.

"Worried about seeing His Excellency?" he asked, a hint of a smile tugging at his mouth. Evliit suspected his friend was enjoying the teasing a bit too much. "Warriors do that sort of thing, don't they? Worry, I mean."

"Ha, ha," Evliit said with a scowl. "Yes, I'm a little nervous. You monks are so different from anything I've ever been around."

Ebert looked up from his work. "We're not that different."

Evliit shrugged. "Perhaps. What do you suppose Jaros wants with me?"

Ebert chuckled. "To talk, I imagine. You are our protector — our captain of the guard, after all."

"I am the only guard," Evliit said. "You know, you're very little help sometimes."

"I know."

Evliit glanced out the tower window. Rain still fell steadily. "I've got to go.

It's time."

"We're really not *that* different," Ebert said. "You've nothing to worry about."

Evliit crossed the distance from the tower to the courtyard quickly. As he made his way along the colonnade and down a long hallway, the storm clouds made the world dim, but he could see light ahead.

He continued toward it. "Hello? Is anyone here?"

No answer.

At the end of the hall lay a domed room. A flash of lightning revealed a ring of windows high above and a sunken amphitheater with seating for fifty or sixty. An older monk swept by lantern light, the dust rising in a thin haze. Evliit shielded his eyes from the lantern's glare to find his footing.

"This way," said a voice from the stage below.

Another monk stepped from the shadows. "I am Brother Phillip. His Excellency Jaros will see you now."

He led Evliit up the steps to a doorway in the wing. "This way."

Evliit circled the amphitheater's perimeter to the opposite wall and passed through a double oak door into a study. Jaros sat at his desk beneath a stained-glass window that spanned the width of the room.

Jaros removed his reading glasses and stood. "Come in. Please, Evliit, make yourself at home."

He nodded to Phillip, who stepped forward. Jaros handed him a scroll. "With all haste, Brother Phillip. May the Creator watch over you in your journeys. That will be all."

"Your Excellency," Phillip said, and departed, closing the doors behind him.

"I trust things are well with you, Evliit?" Jaros asked. "Do you lack for anything here?"

"No, Your Excellency. I'm well." Evliit's eyes drifted to a long table lined with beakers, flasks, and interlocking glass tubes.

"Good. Very good." Jaros motioned to a chair. "Please, have a seat."

"Thank you." Evliit sat and waited as Jaros returned to his own chair.

Jaros folded his hands and smiled. "I'm told you wanted to fight on the front lines with the Rion Guard."

"I did. I wanted to keep the fight far from towns like Harot."

"I see." Jaros adjusted a stack of letters. "I'm sure serving at an old monastery was the last thing you expected."

Evliit shifted in his seat. "I've never been anywhere like this. It's so different from Harot."

"I'm thankful for your service," Jaros said. "Whatever you need, you have but to ask."

Evliit's mind raced through possibilities. "You're very kind. I will."

Jaros leaned back. "I'm sure you could raise the hair on my neck with the story of what they put you through. The Rion Guard is not to be trifled with. If the Elders sent you to me touting your skill with a sword, I have no doubt you're an impressive warrior."

"It was… trial by fire," Evliit said, remembering the crash of the rhama's war hammer against Mategaladh's barrier.

"Yes, of course." Jaros sifted through his papers until he found what he sought. He put his glasses back on, lifted a document, scanned it briefly, then set it down and looked at Evliit over the rims.

"The safety of the monastery is paramount to me," Jaros said. "These are my brothers, and we are doing important work here. What you saw last night was nothing compared to what we've tapped into."

"I didn't mean to overstep," Evliit said. "I heard the chanting and—"

"Think no more of it." Jaros flipped the parchment around for Evliit to see. "This message says we are to secure our secrets 'with all haste,' for there is word the enemy moves again on the far side of the mountain."

He exhaled slowly.

"It seems I was wrong about your seeing no action here. We are to expect the enemy to find us — to attack us. Perhaps very soon."

Evliit's jaw slackened. "But the Monastery of Ardidhus is so close to Rion. Surely the enemy wouldn't dare—"

"How quickly things change." Jaros cleared his throat. "I'm sorry to say I wasn't entirely forthcoming about our work here. I wasn't told you had a need to know." He tapped a finger on the desk. "But now, with this latest information…"

"What information?"

Jaros sighed. "Broeden is attacking outposts and abducting monks. The Elders have reconsidered our situation. They're sending reinforcements —

and it is my understanding those reinforcements will report to you."

"To me?" Evliit shifted again. "Well… I'm honored the Elders place such faith in me. I'll serve you to the best of my ability until they arrive."

"I expected as much, warrior. But there is more I must ask of you."

Jaros rose. "Come here."

Evliit followed him to the table of laboratory equipment. Shelves behind it held stacks of dusty books and scrolls — some so yellowed and fragile Evliit couldn't guess their age. Jaros lifted one scroll and blew the dust from its parchment.

"These documents represent the combined learning of some of the finest minds in all of Erathe," he said. "How to control the winds and rain, the elements — some even believe they contain secrets of the spirit world. They will give us power against the enemy that even the Rion Guard cannot imagine. This is our hope against the evil one."

He set the scroll back gently.

"The Elders believe the dark one may have discovered our possession of these tomes. They insist the words within never fall into enemy hands. So I must assign you a new task."

He met Evliit's eyes.

"You are to remove these writings immediately to a hiding place in the mountains. If the monastery is lost, they are to burn before the enemy can claim them."

Evliit picked up one of the books. "All of this?"

"All of it," Jaros said firmly.

Evliit straightened. "As you command, Your Excellency."

"And one other thing."

"Yes, Your Excellency?"

Jaros returned to his desk. He removed his glasses, tapped them against his palm, then folded them carefully and set them down.

"The enemy would fillet the flesh from a man to uncover the whereabouts of these tomes," he said quietly. "That cannot be allowed to happen."

Evliit's shoulders drooped slightly. "I'm not sure I understand."

Jaros fixed him with a misty, unwavering stare. "You must order the men under your new command to do what is necessary to ensure no monk of this monastery is taken alive."

Evliit flinched. "Sir?"

"If it comes to that, they must be martyrs of our cause."

Evliit cleared his throat. "Are you saying you want me to order them to kill you — and the other monks — rather than let the dark one take any of you?"

"Yes," Jaros said. His gaze did not waver. "We cannot risk the dark wizard acquiring this knowledge."

Evliit set the book back on the table. "I was called to protect the innocent, not kill them. I can't—"

"Can't or won't?" Jaros pressed.

The air thickened with tension.

Jaros leaned forward, placing both hands on his desk. "I know how wrong this must sound, but understand: I do not ask this lightly."

Evliit shook his head. "I don't really care how you ask me."

Jaros exhaled sharply. "Broeden will stop at nothing to acquire the knowledge we possess. Do you think he will simply ask them to share their secrets? I assure you, there are worse things than a quick death. You would be sparing us."

Evliit felt an ache in his gut. "What secret could be so important? These are your brothers."

Jaros started to answer, then stopped. With a long breath, he lifted a wax-sealed parchment. "I've written this letter. It documents everything I've told you — what my brothers have asked of you. It also includes a formal request for a change of assignment."

Evliit frowned.

"Take the books," Jaros continued. "Stay with them. Protect them from the prying eyes of the evil one. If it comes to it, you won't have to participate in any of this unpleasant business. Leave the orders for your men with me, and in a few short weeks this letter will put you on the front lines with the guard. My word can make that happen."

"I'm afraid you ask too much," Evliit said.

Jaros's expression darkened. "For all our sakes, I hope you reconsider." He picked up a bottle of wine. "Drink?"

"Please."

Jaros poured a cup and handed it to him. Evliit studied the dark liquid, thoughtful.

"Answer me this," he said at last. "What kind of god murders and pillages?"

"God?" Jaros echoed. "Broeden is no god. He is a man."

"He seems to have been a thorn in the Elders' sides longer than any man should live," Evliit said. "My grandfather spoke of Broeden's tyranny as if it happened when he was a boy."

"And there you have it," Jaros said. "The Elders have asked the same questions. How can a man live so long? Command such dark forces? Defeat our finest warriors and holy men time and time again? These are the mysteries this monastery has been tasked with unraveling."

"And the answers are in those books?" Evliit asked.

Jaros nodded. "As I said — there you have it." He took a long drink and set his cup down. "The fruits of collaboration between the finest minds in Erathe. Incantations. Elementals. Secrets of communing with the spirit world—"

"Secrets?" Evliit raised an eyebrow.

"Yes," Jaros said, unflappable. "Secrets. It has cost us much blood and treasure to uncover ways to connect with the power of the spirit world."

Evliit looked into the swirling red wine. "I'm about as simple a person as you'll ever meet. Son of a peasant farmer. My friends and I spent our youth living free on the streets of Harot, unseen by royals and high priests. And yet the Bhre-Nora visited *me*."

He took a long drink.

"There's no secret to contacting the immortals. If they have business with you, *they'll* do the contacting."

Jaros laughed. "I believe the Elders may have sent you to me as penance for my sins."

"I meant no offense," Evliit said. "Secrets of the spirit world aside, I understand these books are important."

"None taken," Jaros said. He tilted his head. "So — we have an agreement? You'll take them tonight, under cover of darkness, hide them, and if all is lost, destroy them before they fall into the wrong hands?"

"Of course, if that's your wish," Evliit said. "But how am I to find this hiding place?"

"Ebert will take you," Jaros said, clearing his throat. "The three of us will be the only ones who know its location."

There was a faint tremor in his voice — worry, perhaps. Evliit noticed, but before he could ask, a sudden knock sounded at the door.

"Your Excellency, forgive me! I must speak with you at once!"

Jaros strode to the door and opened it. A stout monk stumbled in, sweating and breathless.

"Forgive my interruption, my lord."

"What message do you bring, Ermos?" Jaros asked.

"We've news of an army north of the Crescent Hills," Ermos said. "Flying the black flag of Broeden. Mostly foot soldiers, but riders as well."

Jaros's brows drew together. "Assemble the others in the eastern tower immediately."

Ermos nodded and hurried out.

"The Crescent Hills?" Evliit asked. "That's the northern edge of the Black Mountains. That puts them here in what — five days?"

"On horseback, yes," Jaros said. "Longer for foot soldiers. We can only hope Rion's reinforcements arrive first."

He shook his head, as if clearing it, then met Evliit's gaze.

"It matters not. Grab those chests. We pack now. I'll arrange a wagon and supplies while you gather Ebert. Leave with all haste, and stay hidden until you receive further word from me."

"As you wish," Evliit said.

"Thank you, Evliit," Jaros said. "Now go — fetch Ebert and be on your way."

CHAPTER 7

THE TOMES OF JAROS

By the time Evliit and Ebert reached the first peak of the mountain, it was too dark to see the trail.

They stopped for the night, chocked the wagon wheels, and released Angwen from his burden. The air was sharp with cold, and both men were tense with worry about what lay ahead. Evliit didn't sleep, and the tossing and turning he saw from Ebert made him think his friend didn't either.

At first light, they broke camp and started down the mountain's eastern slope. It bore little resemblance to its sister slope on the western side. Here, trees and grasses were sparse, clinging only where the black shale had not claimed the ground. A frigid wind blew in from the north.

Evliit wasn't sure how Angwen would handle the combination of terrain, weight, and incline, but the horse held his own. Ebert was unusually quiet, but Evliit didn't mind; his own thoughts kept circling back to his conversation with Jaros, and the hope that Rion's soldiers would come quickly.

Toward the end of the day, they reached a plateau nestled between the mountains' two highest peaks. To their left, Evliit could see the northeastward curve of the range sloping down toward the Northern Plains.

Ebert pointed to a lush green patch just off the trail — an oasis of trees and knee-high grass. "We need to go that way."

They guided the wagon into the cover of the trees, and Evliit was surprised to see a cabin tucked into the mountainside. Its wooden door was stained green with algae, and its small square windows were shuttered.

Ebert produced a key, unlocked the heavy door, and pushed it open with a long creak.

Inside were books — many books — a small bed, a woodstove, and a narrow table just large enough for two. Cabinets and shelves lined the walls, filled with strange paraphernalia not unlike what Evliit had seen in Jaros's study.

He and Ebert unloaded the chests from the wagon, but the cramped quarters left no room for the trunks themselves. They removed the books and supplies and, with considerable effort and rearranging, managed to fit everything into the shelves and cabinets. They returned the empty chests to the wagon and pushed it into a thicket, pulling thorny vines over it until it was well hidden.

Evliit fed and watered Angwen, tying him off among the trees beside the cabin. Then he and Ebert settled inside.

Now all they could do was wait.

After four days, there had still been no word from the monastery. Evliit and Ebert had shared their life stories, then stories of friends and acquaintances; after four straight days of talking, the conversation had run its course. They sat at the little table in silence.

Ebert stood. "I think I'll stretch my legs."

"I might lie down for a bit," Evliit replied.

"Right then. I should be back in a couple of hours."

Ebert stepped out into the fading light, and Evliit pushed off his boots and lay across the bedspread. He had grown quite fond of Ebert, but the silence was lovely. He drifted off for a short while on the soft feather bed, only to wake to a flash of lightning and a crack of thunder. Wind whipped outside, and through the small window in the door he saw the willow tree thrashing, scattering its seeds. Rain began to fall — hard and steady.

Evliit watched the storm without worry. Mountain weather was unpredictable, but Ebert knew how to take care of himself. He opened the door and let the fresh scent of rain fill the room.

Boredom crept in. He paced the cabin, and when he reached the shelves, he pulled out one of the books and opened it. The illustration showed a man with his arm outstretched and a grotesque creature rising from the dirt. Evliit recoiled, slammed the book shut, and shoved it back into place.

He walked to the door and looked out for Ebert. The rain still fell, but the wind had turned strangely warm. He sat back at the table, facing the doorway, waiting.

A few minutes later, without thinking, he rose again, returned to the shelf, and opened the same book. The image of the golem was less terrifying this time. He traced the lines with his finger, imagining the hand that had drawn them. The slight tremors in the strokes made him wonder if the artist had been old — or terrified.

"Evliit!"

Ebert's voice cut through his concentration. Evliit snapped the book shut and slid it back onto the shelf just as Ebert burst through the door.

"Evliit! I was calling for you!" Ebert said, a hint of annoyance in his voice. "I thought something had happened to you."

"To me? You're the one wandering around in this storm like a madman," Evliit said. "I was about to come looking for you."

"Yes, well…" Ebert flashed a sly smile. "I found something."

"What kind of something?"

"You've got to come see."

"Right now?" Evliit gestured outside. "In the rain?"

"Yes, right now. You won't melt!"

"Oh, really," Evliit said. "You certainly look like you've dropped a few pounds."

"You're hilarious. Come on!" Ebert said, leading him around the mountainside to a small, nearly invisible path climbing the hill. Ahead, the slopes of the two peaks seemed to converge, and the trail appeared to end.

"Can't go that way, can we?" Evliit asked.

"Watch this," Ebert said.

He continued forward, and as Evliit followed, the path reappeared, cutting around the northern peak. They squeezed through a narrow gap in the rocks, and then the trail widened. The wind calmed.

Hidden in the hollow, surrounded by mountains on all sides, was a beautiful garden — flowers, vegetables, even a small apple tree. The floor was carved into the mountainside, its precise stonework unmistakably Rionese. Six or eight raised rectangular beds dotted the space, and shoulder-high pillars stood throughout, each etched with images and words. Grass and weeds had begun to reclaim the place, but the plants were healthy.

"If you had to, you could survive the winter with this," Ebert said, his voice cracking. "It's like the Creator provided for us to stay here all winter long if need be."

"Take heart, Ebert," Evliit said. "We're not going to be here much longer." He placed a hand on his friend's shoulder. "Jaros will contact us soon."

Ebert wouldn't meet his eyes. "Actually… I was hoping you'd agree to ride back to the monastery tomorrow. I need to check on my birds — make sure they're all right. You've your tasks, and I've mine." He scuffed the ground with his boot.

"I'm sorry, Ebert, but we're not going anywhere until Jaros sends word," Evliit said. "For now, your tasks and mine are the same." He folded his arms. "Jaros said to stay put. Those were his exact words. And that's what we'll do."

Ebert finally looked up. "I know, I know." He looked close to tears. "I'm just afraid no one's taking care of my birds properly."

"They're fine, Ebert. No one's going to let those birds starve." Evliit leaned against a nearby pillar and pointed to the etched words on it, trying to change the subject. "What does this say?"

"Can you not read the words yourself?" Ebert asked.

Evliit shrugged, cheeks warming. He couldn't read the common tongue, much less this ancient script.

"Oh," Ebert said softly. "I'm sorry, Evliit. I didn't know."

The rain suddenly shifted, dropping from a downpour to a few scattered drops.

Ebert held out his hand and laughed. "You see? It's a sign the Creator himself thinks you should read!"

"No worries, Ebert. I don't need to read them."

"No, no — let me help you." He brushed water from his hair and pointed to the image of the Creator on the arch marking the garden entrance. "We'll start at the beginning, with the Creator at the center of it all."

He led Evliit to the arch and pointed to the pillars supporting it. "These images tell of the beginning of men. Do you see?"

Evliit studied the carved panels. Each contained inscriptions so small one had to stand at arm's length to notice them. Someone had carved those tiny letters one at a time. The patience required was staggering.

"Such skill," he said. "You can help me understand them?"

"Of course," Ebert said. He pointed to the etched letters. "This is written in the language of Rion. This symbol is for 'Creator.'"

"Creator," Evliit repeated.

They worked through each panel on the first two pillars. When they finished, Evliit insisted on continuing. They moved from pillar to pillar, Ebert explaining the words and symbols, Evliit asking a thousand questions. They stayed until the light began to fade, then made their way back to the cabin.

Evliit had never cared much about reading. It wasn't a skill the streets of Harot valued. But he could see that refocusing Ebert helped stem his friend's growing cabin fever — and, if he were honest, he took great pleasure in this new skill. So over the next few days, they repeated the ritual: walking to the garden, studying the pillars, reading the stories again and again.

By the third day, Evliit could read them to Ebert with some help.

By the fifth, he could read them flawlessly.

"Someone must have shown you the old language before," Ebert said. "I've never seen anyone pick it up so quickly."

"I swear to you, this is the first I've seen of it," Evliit said.

"It's uncanny," Ebert said. "Give praise to the Creator, the one from whom all blessings flow." He grinned. "And keep reading!"

Evliit laughed. "Yes — and keep reading."

They walked back to the cabin discussing the stories, sharing what each one meant to them. Inside, Ebert took a seat at the table, but Evliit went straight to the pantry; he was hungry. After rummaging through jars, he found some strips of dried beef to his liking. When he turned back, he saw the worry etched on Ebert's face. The silence from the monastery — from Jaros — was wearing on him.

Evliit held out a handful of jerky. "Want something to eat?"

Ebert glanced at the offering. "No, thanks."

"Lack of word is troublesome," Evliit said. They had been avoiding the subject, but it was time.

"Yes, it is," Ebert admitted. "And as much as I want to celebrate your newfound reading skills, my friend, I can't take it anymore. Something's not right. We should have heard something by now. I've got to return to the monastery."

Evliit pointed to the shelves full of books. "And what of the task Jaros assigned us? Do we just leave these things here?"

"Oh, no — we can't leave them unattended," Ebert said.

Evliit saw the apprehension in his friend's eyes, and he understood.

"So you need to go," he said quietly, "and I need to stay."

"I don't see any other way," Ebert said.

Evliit sighed. "Jaros said reinforcements were coming. I can't imagine what kind of trouble I'm in. The Rion Guard arrives, and I'm not at my post." He set the jerky on the table and headed for the door.

"Where are you going?" Ebert asked, jumping up.

"I'm going to check Angwen's tack for you," Evliit said. "If you're going, the sooner the better. Take the horse, Ebert, and get down the mountain."

They stepped outside, and Evliit checked Angwen's saddle and reins.

"Whatever you do," he said, "come back for me — or at least get me word."

"I'll do it," Ebert said quickly. "I promise you, as soon as I get back and figure out what's going on, I'll get right back on that horse."

Evliit looked at the sun. "You'll need light to get down the mountain. Angwen can get you back to the monastery by nightfall, but you'll have to go now."

Ebert nodded and mounted Angwen. "Take care, my friend. I'll return in a few days — sooner if I can."

"See you in a few days," Evliit said.

Ebert turned and urged Angwen into a trot. They disappeared into the trees, and Evliit was alone.

Without Ebert's endless commentary to keep him company, the quiet around the cabin felt far less peaceful. After nearly an hour of listening to birds chirp outside, he began to feel stir-crazy himself. He walked up to the garden and pulled weeds until the tops of his forearms and forehead began to sting. Too much sun. He gathered the weeds and tossed them into the tall grass along the path. Tomorrow, he decided, he would dig up some carrots and potatoes.

Back at the cabin, he watched the horizon until shadows crept up the mountainside and darkness claimed it. He made a simple meal of cheese and flatbread and even found a bit of red wine to go with it. Between bites, he busied himself by tidying the cabin — organizing flasks and vials, sorting powders, and even arranging Jaros's tomes into two neat groups: white-leather bindings on one side of the shelf, red-leather on the other.

The night air was cool, but not cold enough for a fire. Unlike the valley, there wasn't a single mosquito. It was pleasant to leave the door open and listen to the breeze rushing through the trees. When he finished eating, he dug his pipe out of his pack and sat at the little table, thinking he might try reading again.

Alongside the pipe, he found the letter Jaros had written — the one meant to return him to the Elders' good graces and the front lines. The wax seal had broken in transit. He hesitated, then unrolled the scroll and began reading.

Evliit,

By now you should be at the cabin, and I can share more of my plan with you.

Although I truly acted to protect the tomes, I also wanted the sword and its bearer far from the monastery; I hope you can forgive my deception. I feared that you'd somehow lost your way — that you'd forgotten your calling and the meaning of bearing the sword you carry. I could not let you face the enemy in that condition.

To survive the trials to come, you must be clear about why you possess the sword. You must master its use and recall your position within the Watchers.

Within the tomes, you will find the answers you seek, sword bearer: who you are, the powers you can command. May the Creator be with you, and may you soon remember your place in the destiny of Erathe.

— Jaros

There was nothing about a transfer to the front lines.

Evliit shot to his feet, knocking over his chair. He crushed the letter in his fist and hurled it across the room. Turning to the shelf, he saw the neatly organized tomes. Rage surged. He swept his arm behind them and shoved the entire row onto the floor.

"Damn you, Jaros! What have you done!"

For several minutes he paced the cabin, trying to calm himself. In doing so, he stepped on one of the fallen books. Seeing the boot print on its white leather cover, he cursed again.

"Barodhma!"

He snatched the tome up and wiped the dirt away with his sleeve, embarrassed by his outburst. Beneath the smudge, he saw the title:

Mimir na Stydhra.

"Well of Kings," he whispered.

He opened it to check for damage. The beautiful script and decorated borders drew him in. Without thinking, he righted the chair, sat down, and began to read.

The words leapt off the page. Within these ancient lines was the story of the Old World — how the Elders battled the dark wizard Broeden. The scenes the tome conjured in his mind captivated him, but more than that, there was something surreal about it all. He read one line aloud:

"In their darkest hours, a sword bearer will hail from the land of Harot."

He devoured the pages. When he reached the section describing the calling of the Watchers, he felt as though he already knew what came next — as if he remembered it before turning the page. It unsettled him, but he couldn't stop reading.

He lost all track of time until the lamp beside him sputtered. The wick was nearly gone. He rubbed his eyes and glanced out the open door. A faint glow above the treeline told him dawn was moments away.

Evliit stood, stretched, and yawned. The wick gave its last flicker, and the room went dark. He couldn't even see the book on the table.

Then a word formed in his mind — unbidden, instinctive.

"Flodh."

A sphere of energy burst into existence above the table. Tendrils of white crackled and rolled around a glowing core suspended within a cloudy, translucent shell. Its intense light illuminated every corner of the cabin.

Evliit froze, stunned. The orb was both terrifying and beautiful.

Just as the brightness began to pain his eyes, the cloud swelled and collapsed inward, vanishing in an instant. A trail of tiny sparkles lingered like the remnants of fireworks he'd once seen in Harot.

The sudden darkness left him blind. Purplish-white spots burned across his vision. He turned toward the doorway and let the dawn light restore his bearings. As his sight returned, he sat heavily in his chair, overwhelmed by what he had witnessed.

Then, slowly, he rose and began placing the tomes and scrolls back onto the shelf — carefully, reverently.

For the next three days, Evliit tried to piece together the story of Jaros and the Elders from their correspondence. He read from dawn to dusk and often deep into the night.

On the eve of the third day, there was still no word from Ebert, but Evliit barely noticed. The letters consumed him.

There were accounts from distant battlefronts — dark wars fought against creatures Broeden had conjured, and descriptions of how the Elders' warriors were repeatedly defeated by the dark spirits. Evliit wondered what the runners who carried these messages must have felt, fleeing scenes like these. *Could they have imagined their letters would be preserved for centuries?*

Then he found a letter written by an Elder named Faldhra. Its tone was heavy with despair. Faldhra declared the unthinkable: unless the Rion Guard found a way to stop Broeden's creatures, Rion would not survive the coming year. In the absence of the sword bearer, Faldhra proposed taking control away from Broeden's spirits by spellmaking. They would train the most potent Watchers to fight fire with fire — to conjure, cast, and experiment. A young monk named Jaros would oversee these Spellmakers in secret.

"Jaros?" Evliit said aloud. He looked at the ancient parchment again. "How can that be?"

Two more days passed. Evliit organized and read every letter, and a thread emerged. Jaros, though dedicated to his task, feared the Spellmakers' experiments blurred the line between good and evil. He lamented that their work had created a rift within the Watchers.

Jaros had written:

> For all time, the Elders have believed that miracles could be performed by channeling the Creator's power through their bodies like an aqueduct directs water. Now Amphileph and many of his fellow Spellmakers propose that the Creator's power resides within them, granted at birth and sharpened by knowledge of the natural world. The Elders are very unpleased with this turn of events.
>
> Amphileph's beliefs have even separated him from his brother Watchers, saying that the natural world must be discovered not through prayer and meditation but through experimentation and examination. He attempts to fill the void left by the sword bearer, much to the disdain of the remaining Watchers.

The Watchers had always believed the Creator's holiness would overcome Broeden's evil. But Broeden had been killing their people and claiming their lands for years. The commoners had lost hope. The Elders appeared powerless. Their coffers emptied. Their stores vanished.

Then came the breaking point. Amphileph declared that if the Elders' religion could not defeat Broeden, it should end. The Elders sent a furious letter, accusing Jaros of losing control. They stopped just short of calling the Spellmakers heretics.

Jaros's personal journal filled in the final pieces:

> It is by my hand that tragedy befalls them, for though the Spellmakers have grown truly powerful in their magic, there

has been a high price to pay. Darkness encircles all who have engaged these spirits, and I fear it will always be there, watching and waiting to claim them.

"What a mess," Evliit muttered. He stacked the letters, shoved them back onto the shelf, and began packing his things. He could wait no longer. He had to understand how he fit into this tapestry of Jaros's story. He grabbed his pack and headed for the door—

Hoofbeats?

Evliit burst outside as Angwen trotted into the clearing. *Riderless.*

"Ebert?" he shouted.

No answer.

He rushed to the horse. Angwen was bleeding from several cuts. He smelled of smoke.

"Ebert!" Evliit yelled again, scanning the darkness. Only wind and crickets answered.

"Stay, Angwen."

He ran up the path, searching both sides, but the darkness swallowed everything.

"*Flodh!*"

The orb of light appeared instantly, illuminating the mountainside all the way to the peak — but there was no sign of Ebert. He would need Angwen to search further.

A soft pop, and the orb vanished.

Evliit hurried back. Angwen stood trembling in the lantern glow. Several cuts looked deep.

"Steady, boy."

Evliit placed his hand over a wound. "*Hrast na Sura.*"

His hand glowed. A reddish-pink outline formed around his fingers, brightening as energy flowed from his body into the wound. When he lifted his hand, the cut was closed.

"*Flodh!*"

The orb reappeared. In its bright light, the healed wound looked perfect. The words from *Mimir na Stydhra* were powerful indeed.

Evliit gave thanks to the Creator and healed each of Angwen's wounds.

He gathered his things, blew out the lantern, locked the cabin door, mounted up, and spurred Angwen toward the monastery. The orb lit the hillside for a few minutes before fading. Evliit continued in darkness, slower now, trusting Angwen's sure footing.

They reached the plateau at the mountaintop — and Evliit's heart sank.

Far in the distance, fires burned where the monastery should have been.

He wanted to drive Angwen forward, but the night was moonless, the trail invisible. *Should he conjure the light again? If the monastery was under attack, the orb would be a beacon.*

But the trail was deadly in darkness.

"Ebert!" he screamed into the void.

He nearly urged Angwen down the mountain anyway — but then he pulled back. *Remember your promise.* If this was the moment Jaros had warned him about, his place was with the tomes, ready to destroy them if necessary.

He watched the fires rage, the stars flickering in the rising smoke. Then he turned Angwen back toward the cabin.

Evliit spent the night at the table, alert to every sound. The sack of the monastery had changed everything. He knew the tomes were powerful, but he would burn them all to see Ebert walk through the door again.

But Ebert did not return.

When dawn arrived, a weary Evliit checked Angwen's wounds. The skin had knitted perfectly, leaving only faint ridges. Angwen seemed himself again.

Evliit mounted and rode down the mountain as fast as he dared. Angwen nearly slipped more than once, but by midmorning they were flying down the last trail toward the monastery.

As he approached, he saw Mategaladh and Tophian on the lawn — a welcome sight, though his relief vanished when he saw the ruins. A gaping hole yawned where the main gate had been. Beyond it lay devastation. The living quarters had been dismantled stone by stone.

Evliit leapt from his mount. "What happened here? Where are Jaros and Ebert?"

"Jaros has been taken to Rion with serious injuries," Mategaladh said grimly. "He may not live. From what we found, the monks are either missing or dead. We thought you were dead too." He gripped Evliit's arm. "I'm glad we were wrong."

Evliit's stomach twisted. "Ebert? Is he in there?"

"I'm afraid we don't know," Tophian said. "Some of the Guard are still searching. Whatever attacked them tore them apart. It will be difficult to say."

"And Broeden's army? Do they march on Rion?"

"No," Mategaladh said. "It's as if they got what they came for. After destroying the monastery, they turned north." He looked at the smoking ruins. "We came too late."

"Where were you when all this happened?" Tophian demanded.

The question struck Evliit like a blow. "Ebert and I were given a task. By Jaros. I have to speak with him."

"Jaros won't be back anytime soon, if at all," Tophian said. "What's this task he gave you?"

Evliit shook his head. "I'm sorry, but I can't say. He took me into his confidence."

Tophian looked at Mategaladh. "Right. Well, as far as I recall, your task was to defend this monastery." He swept his arm toward the devastation. "Which doesn't appear to be working out so well."

A vein throbbed at Evliit's temple, but he forced himself to stay calm. "I must speak with Jaros at once," he said through clenched teeth. "I've got to go to him — now."

"You keep your distance from the Elders," Tophian said. "Right now they think you're dead, and they'll be none too pleased to learn you didn't die at your post like a good soldier."

He threw his hands up. "I don't think you understand. This was one of the worst attacks on Rionese soil in memory. Ardidhus was a stronghold. Maybe not much for offense, but its defenses were formidable. Those walls were meant to withstand Broeden's worst. For the monastery to fall so easily will send shockwaves through the Elders and the Guard."

He stepped closer. "And for it to fall so easily, and for *you* — the Elders' chosen protector — to appear out of nowhere without a scratch... well, that's going to raise more than a few eyebrows."

Evliit's face tightened in dismay. "I did nothing wrong. I did exactly as Jaros asked of me."

"Your best hope is for Jaros to confirm that," Tophian said. "Otherwise, the next battle you fight may be with the Elders, not Broeden."

Mategaladh scanned the horizon. "So when this happened, you were staying in the mountains?"

"Yes. In a secret place known only to Jaros, Ebert, and me," Evliit said. "At least… I think we were the only ones."

He wanted to tell them everything — the letters, the Spellmakers, the truth about the sword, the tomes, the power he'd invoked. But revealing any of that meant revealing the tomes' location, and he had sworn to protect them.

So he held his tongue. It hurt to do it.

"Then I suggest you go back there until this is sorted out," Mategaladh said.

Evliit thrust out his chin. "I'll not run and hide like a coward."

Mategaladh sighed. "Listen to me, Evliit. This is serious."

Evliit cringed but held his ground. "I can't leave yet. What of Ebert's birds? Were any of them left?"

"Birds?" Tophian exploded. "Have you heard a single word we've said? You need to get out of here!"

"Now," Mategaladh agreed. He grabbed Evliit's arm and pulled him toward Angwen. Evliit resisted, craning his neck toward the tower. The outer wall had collapsed, but in his mind he could still see the birds' perch. He looked again. Nothing but rubble.

"If any of Ebert's birds survived, we'll bring them to you," Mategaladh said, turning Evliit to face him. "How will we find you?"

Evliit hesitated. He was torn in two. He had sworn secrecy — but these were Mategaladh and Tophian. Brothers in all but blood. He needed their help. He needed to tell them everything.

"Follow this trail to the top of the mountain," he said. "Once you cross the peak, there's a wooded area on your left where the slopes meet. You'll find a small cabin hidden in the trees. I'll be waiting there."

"Very well," Mategaladh said. "Now go, before someone sees you."

A deep rumble sounded, and the last standing section of the monastery wall collapsed. Dust billowed outward, engulfing them. Shouts rose from within the ruins.

"You need to go, now!" Tophian yelled. "We'll come to you! Go!"

"I'll see you soon!" Evliit called. He mounted Angwen and galloped up the trail. He stopped once and looked back — just in time to see Mategaladh and Tophian disappear into the wall of dust.

At the mountaintop, he turned Angwen toward the valley. A murky haze hung in the air. He drew a deep breath and exhaled, feeling ashamed, confused, defeated.

What now?

He couldn't think. All he could see was Ebert — tortured, killed, over and over in his mind until his stomach twisted.

He spurred Angwen over the ridge toward the cabin and held on.

When he arrived, he collapsed onto the soft bed. Still, all he could see was Ebert suffering in a hundred imagined ways. He curled onto his side, pulling his knees to his chest, longing for rest but finding none.

CHAPTER 8

HARBINGERS

The next afternoon, Tophian and Mategaladh appeared on the lawn of the little cabin.

"You found me!" Evliit exclaimed. He embraced Mategaladh with a hug and a pat on the back. Tophian dismounted but didn't step forward. Evliit nodded to him.

"We bring news, Evliit," Tophian said.

"We have a few of Ebert's birds," Mategaladh added, pointing to cages strapped across a mule behind his horse. "The rest were long gone."

"That's wonderful," Evliit said. "Thank you." Relief washed over him—until he saw their faces. "I suppose there's more."

"Well—" Mategaladh began.

"Yes, kid, there is," Tophian said. "Jaros is dead. He never made it to Rion."

"No." Evliit felt light-headed. "That's impossible."

"Not only possible," Tophian said, "but fact."

"And I'm sorry, Evliit," Mategaladh added, "but it gets worse."

Tophian nodded. "Before he died, he told the guard that when the attack began, you fought valiantly—killed dozens of Broeden's lesser creatures. He said you died trying to reach the keep before you could release the keep stones."

Evliit stared at him. "But why... He said I *died*?"

"Yes," Tophian said flatly.

"Why would he say that?"

"I have no idea," Mategaladh said. "But as you can imagine, this complicates things."

Evliit's mind raced. "Wait. Wait. Maybe it's because he didn't want the Elders to know—"

"Know what?" Tophian asked.

"Yes, I'm not following," Mategaladh said.

Evliit motioned toward the cabin. "Come inside. I'll explain."

Mategaladh's jaw tightened. "Wait, Evliit. That's not all." He ran a hand through his hair. "Ebert…"

Evliit froze. "Yes?"

"Jaros told the guard that Ebert was in the tower, releasing birds to alert Rion and the other monasteries, when Broeden's forces overran them. Ebert was taken by a huntress leading the attack."

"Taken?" Evliit asked. "So… not dead?"

Tophian shrugged. "That's what's causing the stir. If he'd been killed, no one would've thought twice. But taken alive? People are furious. Men are volunteering to take up arms."

"Unfortunately their anger is great—too great," Mategaladh said. "Many people—present company excluded—believe you and Jaros failed to protect the monks. They curse your name. Even with Jaros's story of your valiant death, their wrath is upon you."

Evliit hung his head. "Poor Ebert."

"That's all you can say?" Tophian snapped. "It'll be 'Poor Evliit' if anyone realizes you're alive. Time to do what you do, kid. Disappear."

Evliit blanched but pressed on. "It was Jaros's fear of something like this that led me up here. Please—come inside. There's much you need to know."

Mategaladh looked to Tophian for approval, then stepped through the doorway. Tophian followed reluctantly, muttering as he went, "The Guard is preparing a counterattack. They'll march right past the monastery. You don't want to meet them. The Elders won't appreciate your resurrection; being alive again might erase what little forgiveness dying bought you."

Evliit went straight to the bookshelf. "Listen—none of that matters. Look at these." He pulled a book free and opened it. "Jaros feared something was coming. He sent me here to protect me, to protect the sword, and to destroy these books if the monastery fell."

Mategaladh and Tophian stopped cold.

"Jaros gave you these?" Mategaladh asked.

"Yes. Along with his journal and letters. They describe a secret plan the Elders devised centuries ago to deal with Broeden. Several tomes record experiments the Spellmakers performed."

"When you left the Third Domain and returned here, the Elders were divided," Mategaladh said. "Their prayer had always been for the Creator to bring forth the sword bearer—to lead the people into the next age."

"You were with us in the Third Domain for almost a year," Tophian added. "Then you vanished without a word."

Evliit blinked. "But I was gone from Harot for only a few days. Most of that was the trip to the mountain!"

"Oh, Evliit," Mategaladh said gently. "Time there and here is not the same."

"Jaros trained Spellmakers for years," Tophian said. "It was heresy. The Elders knew it, so they hid his projects in monasteries along the borderlands."

"I don't think anyone was more surprised than you when conjurers and alchemists appeared at our calling," Mategaladh said.

"Yes, that still baffles me," Tophian admitted. "But I don't deny they were there."

"I also read *The Well of Kings*." Evliit flipped the white tome around. "It was like I already knew the words. I could remember what came next. I can do more than heal—I can conjure light. I feel connected to the sword more than ever."

"Now, Evliit—" Mategaladh began, but he stopped when he saw the red-bound tomes. "Did you read those?" He didn't touch them. "Tophian, look."

Tophian joined him as Mategaladh carefully lifted one of the red tomes. He didn't open it.

"No," Evliit said. "Something about them frightened me. Those are the Spellmakers' writings."

Tophian shook his head. "Our brothers dabble in darkness. They think they can control it, but they can't. Darkness is chaos—formless, void. Believing you can master it is the illusion of fools."

"Jaros said that if the monastery fell, these must be burned," Evliit said.

"If that's true, why didn't he tell the Elders before he died? How could they not know these existed?"

"I'd wager the Elders commanded Jaros to destroy them long ago," Tophian said. "Put it back, Mategaladh. Are we so desperate to defeat Broeden that we call upon the Underworld? Our power comes from the Creator, not spells and witchcraft. It should all be destroyed."

Mategaladh slid the red tome back into place. "Some of these are the writings of Watchers." He motioned to the white tomes. "Holy books. Wisdom from the Creator. They cannot be destroyed."

"If they're mixed with heresy, let them burn with the rest," Tophian said.

"Let them burn?" Evliit said. "These are the only proof I have that I'm not a coward. If we burn them, I have no way to explain what happened—what I was doing out here."

Tophian opened his mouth, but Mategaladh raised a hand. He turned to Evliit. "So what are your intentions?"

"I'll take them to the Elders. I have letters in Jaros's own hand." Evliit grabbed his pack and began stuffing letters inside—then froze. "Wait. I can't go to Rion. We have to go after Ebert!"

He looked between them, desperate. "We can't just let them take him, right?"

Neither man answered. Evliit sank into a chair and buried his face in his hands.

Mategaladh pulled out a chair and sat across from him. "We need to think."

"If it's any consolation, kid, we want to help you," Tophian said. "But you've stepped in a fairly large pile of Barodhma."

"Yeah, I know," Evliit said. "But forget clearing my name—how do we get Ebert back? Do we know for sure they went north?"

"Listen, Evliit," Tophian said. "As much as it pains me, odds are they killed Ebert long before we can catch them. You're wasting your time. I know he's your friend, but face the facts—he's a dead man."

"That doesn't make sense," Evliit said. "Why not kill him at the monastery like the others? Why take him?"

"To toy with him, perhaps," Tophian said. "You can't underestimate Broeden's cruelty."

"Give me a moment," Mategaladh said. He rose, walked to the door, and stared out. "What if something more sinister is at work? What if the Spellmakers were truly onto something? What if they found a way to defeat Broeden? Maybe this wasn't random. Maybe it was a surgical strike to stop them."

Tophian half-laughed. "The monks were here to watch the borders. These monasteries are outposts, not laboratories. This feels more like Jaros's personal dabbling in darkness than any strategy of the Elders. Why would they ever adopt such a plan?"

"Because we were losing; that's why," Evliit said. "Broeden's reign of terror only stopped because the centuries were catching up to him — not because we were getting better at fighting him. The Elders must have known it was only a matter of time before he came farther south. Only a matter of time before they met him on the battlefield again."

"But this time, with their backs to the ocean, there'd be nowhere left to run," Mategaladh said. "They could have seen this as a last resort."

"And this was their secret weapon?" Tophian spat. "To swim in this dark filth? And what of Ebert? Are you telling me Broeden's army marched all this way to snatch the pigeon boy because he was somehow tied to the Spellmakers?"

Evliit shot to his feet, fists clenched. "Ebert is my friend. Don't talk about him like that."

"Settle down," Tophian said. "I'm trying to get you two to hear yourselves."

"Let's say you're right," Evliit said. "How do you explain Jaros keeping silent about all these books on his deathbed?"

"Because out here in the borderlands, maybe monks talk openly about them," Tophian said. "But in Rion? Anyone speaking of such things would be hanging from the nearest tree. I don't think this is conspiracy — I think it's survival. If you take these to the Elders, there'll be a witch hunt. More monks will swing — if the peasants don't fillet them first. Is that what you want?"

"Of course not," Evliit said.

"Then burn *everything* and go back to Harot."

Evliit looked to Mategaladh for support, but Mategaladh looked away.

"Mategaladh, let the man think," Tophian said. "Better to get a start on the trail while there's still light."

Mategaladh hesitated. "What will you do, Evliit?"

"I'm going after him," Evliit said.

"What?" Tophian's eyes widened.

"I told you. Ebert is my friend. I'm not leaving his body out there for the birds. If nothing else, I'll bring him home and bury him properly. And if he's alive, I'll do everything in my power to save him."

"Oh, Evliit," Tophian said, exhaling. "Let's not go over this again."

"I'm not asking you to come," Evliit said. "I can do this alone."

Mategaladh looked between them. "No, you can't."

Tophian crossed his arms, studying Evliit's face. "So you've read *The Well of Kings* and now you're a force to be reckoned with? You're going to take on Broeden's entire army by yourself?"

Heat rose in Evliit's cheeks. "Just leave, Tophian. I don't need your help."

His heart hammered in his chest.

"Okay, you two — enough," Mategaladh said.

"It's fine," Tophian said, still staring at Evliit. "Here's the deal: you listen to us. You do not charge headlong into Broeden's forces the first time we see them. If Mategaladh and I say we're done, then we're done — and you come back to this cabin and wait until we say otherwise. If you can do that, the three of us will make an honest effort to find Ebert and bring him back. What do you say?"

Silence stretched. Evliit became painfully aware of his own breathing, the heat in his face, the pounding in his ears. He closed his eyes and forced himself to think. Tophian often made him angry, but the Watcher was not his enemy.

He swallowed what pride remained.

"Yes."

"Good," Tophian said. "Then I'm in." He nodded to Mategaladh. "You?"

"Yes," Mategaladh said.

"Then get your things together, boy. We ride now," Tophian said.

"But what about Jaros's books?" Evliit asked.

"They stay here," Tophian said. "We'll have to trust they'll be safe for a while."

Evliit bit back his protest and nodded. He didn't like leaving the tomes unguarded — but if he had to choose between them and Ebert, he would choose Ebert every time.

ᘔᎩᕼ�6ᕐᘔ᛫

They were still riding when dawn came.

The morning sunlight stabbed at Evliit's eyes, each ray a needle of pain, but he clung to the saddle horn and forced himself upright. He felt as though he could slide off either side of the horse and fall asleep where he landed. His eyelids were unbearably heavy.

Tophian glanced back and laughed. "Pretty much sapped the hero out of you, huh?"

"Pretty much," Evliit muttered.

"I'm about done myself," Mategaladh said.

"The crescent is just ahead," Tophian told them.

"Crescent?" Evliit blinked. He realized he didn't even know where they were going — only that they were headed north.

"The Crescent of Ardidhus," Mategaladh explained. "A plateau between the northern peaks of the Black Mountains. From there we can see for miles. If Broeden's forces haven't crossed the Northern Plains yet, we'll spot them."

As he finished speaking, the trail curved, and the foothills of the Black Mountains opened before them. Tophian dismounted and motioned for the others to join him.

"The peak looks a long way up," Evliit said.

Tophian pointed to a crease in the rock a third of the way up the mountainside. "We won't be exposed long. We just need to reach that cut. Once we drop into it, we disappear — and it's clear sailing to the peak."

A sudden thunder of hoofbeats filled the air.

"Back!" Tophian hissed.

They pulled their horses off the trail and into the trees just as a company of Rion Guard thundered into the field ahead. The captain raised his hand, and the cavalry halted.

Two riders approached from the north. The captain and his lieutenant met them, then turned to address the company.

"Our scouts say the enemy lies just beyond the Black Mountains!" the captain shouted. "The Creator is with us!"

"Hoof! Hoof! Hoof!" roared the guard, pounding their spears against their shields.

"These monsters prey upon the meek! But today they won't stand against a group of monks! Today they meet the guard!"

"Up close and personal!" the lieutenant bellowed.

"Swift and merciless!" the company answered.

"Rest your horses!" the lieutenant commanded. "We move out shortly! We'll deal justice to them on the Northern Plains!"

Mategaladh's horse whinnied, pulling at its reins. Evliit held his breath, but the guardsmen didn't seem to hear.

Mategaladh soothed the horse. "Shhhh." Then he leaned toward the others. "This is too close. How do we get around them?"

"I have an idea," Tophian said. "Wait here."

He handed his reins to Mategaladh and strode to the forest's edge. He lowered his head and raised his palms toward the sky.

Evliit frowned. "What's he doing?"

"Wait," Mategaladh whispered. "Just wait."

A murmur rose among the soldiers. Evliit craned his neck, trying to see past the trees. Something dark moved on the horizon — a blot growing larger.

The guardsmen pointed, shouting. They scrambled to mount their horses, pulling scarves over their noses and mouths.

Evliit looked back at Tophian. His lips were moving.

What are you doing, Tophian?

The dark shape grew clearer — a massive whirlwind of dust, fifty yards wide at its base, roaring in from the north. Its howl grew louder by the second.

Horses reared. Men shouted. The captain tried to rally them, but his voice was lost in the rising gale.

Sand-filled wind struck the trees with a sizzling hiss. The whirlwind hit.

Evliit threw up his arm to shield his face. Dirt blasted into his eyes and mouth. He coughed, choking, eyes watering. Branches snapped like bones in the storm.

A sudden tug yanked him sideways. He stumbled — and the tempest vanished.

He spat dirt and blinked. He, Mategaladh, Tophian, and their horses stood inside a shimmering sphere. Dust spiraled around them, but none entered. A tree crashed nearby, but the sound was muffled, distant.

"Stay close," Tophian said. His face was taut with concentration.

"Do as he says," Mategaladh urged.

Tophian lowered his arms and began walking toward the hills. The sphere moved with him. Evliit and Mategaladh led their horses, staying close. Sunlight flickered through the swirling dust outside, making the world shimmer.

They passed within yards of the guardsmen, who were still in chaos, but the three men went unnoticed.

Once they reached the passage and the shelter of the mountain, Tophian exhaled sharply. The sphere dissolved. Evliit braced for another blast of dirt — but the whirlwind was gone, as suddenly as it had come.

"Can you see them?" Mategaladh asked.

Evliit climbed a short steppe and peered over the rock wall. "They're regrouping west of us."

"Good. Let's keep moving," Tophian said. He clicked his tongue, and his horse stepped forward.

They stayed on foot until the passage walls rose high enough to hide them even on horseback. Then they mounted and trotted up the mountain toward the Crescent of Ardidhus.

"That was a lot of soldiers," Evliit said at last. "I mean… *a lot.*"

"And out here this quickly," Mategaladh said. "Interesting. Jaros's activities clearly had someone's attention."

"Or he wasn't as good at keeping secrets as we thought," Tophian said.

"No," Evliit said. "The Guard was already en route before the attack. A dispatch came to Jaros before Ebert and I left with the tomes. We hoped they'd reach the monastery first."

"Then they mean to make war on Broeden," Mategaladh said. "We need to move quickly. If Ebert is alive, he'll be caught in the crossfire."

"Let's be about it," Tophian said, spurring his horse.

Half an hour later they reached the crescent. The wind howled across the exposed ridge. Tophian dismounted.

"Leave the horses. We go on foot to the northern peak." He pointed to a crown-like outcropping above them. "We can see everything from there."

Even in late summer, the wind was bitter. Evliit's eyes watered, but he climbed steadily. Soon he stood atop the peak, gazing down at the vast Northern Plains. Far across the valley rose the sheer Faceless Mountains — the northern border of Etharath.

They all saw the flickering black banners at once.

"There!" Evliit said.

Mategaladh clapped his shoulder. "Yes, we see them."

"They'll have to go northeast," Tophian said. "There's no crossing directly north."

"Look there!" Mategaladh pointed.

The Rion Guard appeared below, charging toward Broeden's forces, red banners snapping in the wind. A deep, booming horn sounded, and the black banners shifted to meet them.

Behind the front line, a cluster of dark-skinned creatures surrounded a wagon. Two chained beasts strained to pull it from a bog. A small creature leapt and whipped them viciously.

"That wagon!" Mategaladh said. "Do you think—"

"A wagon for prisoners!" Evliit cried. "Ebert could be in there! We have to get down there."

"Follow me!" Tophian shouted, already scrambling down the slope.

Evliit and Mategaladh raced after him. They leapt onto their horses.

Evliit turned toward the trail — but Tophian galloped to the far end of the crescent.

"Get over here!" he yelled. "I'm taking us through the mountain!"

"Do as he says, Evliit!" Mategaladh called.

They rode up beside Tophian, one on each side. He had dropped his reins and lifted both hands toward the sky.

"Hold on!" he shouted.

The ground vanished beneath them.

Evliit felt the earth swallow him whole. He buried his face in Angwen's mane as the world dissolved into darkness. The smell of damp soil filled his nostrils. Pressure closed around him like a fist. It felt as though he were being buried alive.

Angwen screamed and bucked, but Evliit clung to the saddle horn with everything he had.

He couldn't breathe.

How much longer can this last?

Just when he was certain he would suffocate, the pressure released. A rush of cold air swept over him. He gasped, blinking grit from his eyes.

Through the swirling dust, he saw Tophian's silhouette ahead.

"Hurry!" Tophian cried, spurring his horse into a full gallop down the newly formed tunnel.

"Quickly, Evliit!" Mategaladh shouted, close behind.

Evliit kicked Angwen forward. The tunnel collapsed behind them as they rode, the rumbling earth chasing their heels.

They burst out onto the plains at the foot of the mountain. Evliit wiped dirt from his eyes and rode hard.

The two armies had already clashed. The field was a nightmare of screams, steel, and blood. Horses reared. Men fell. The grotesque foot soldiers — the small, dark-skinned creatures — darted beneath the guardsmen's blades with impossible speed. The larger brutes towered over mounted riders, smashing men from their saddles.

A third of the Rion Guard already lay dead.

"Come!" Mategaladh cried.

They spurred their horses toward the fray, dust streaming from their hair and clothes.

As they closed in, Evliit saw Tophian free one hand from his reins and raise it high. His fingers curled as though gripping something invisible. Suddenly his arm jerked backward, as if pulled by an unseen rope. He grimaced and thrust his hand forward.

The earth answered.

A massive stone tore free from the ground, spraying dirt and smaller rocks. It tumbled end over end behind Tophian. At the last instant, he veered aside, and the boulder thundered past him — straight into the ranks of the little creatures, crushing them in a rolling wave.

Mategaladh leapt from his horse into the opening the stone created. Evliit followed.

For a heartbeat, he saw the creatures clearly — the things that had slaughtered Rion's finest. They stood like men but were twisted mockeries: too many teeth for their squat heads, black eyes that revealed no direction of focus, swarms of flies buzzing around them, and a stench so foul it made Evliit gag even from yards away.

Evliit drew his sword.

Time slowed.

Mategaladh's face froze mid-shout. A second stone Tophian had hurled rotated lazily through the air. A creature driving a guardsman's helmet into his own chest cavity hung suspended, droplets of blood floating like rubies.

Evliit felt alive. Power surged from the sword into his veins. Somewhere — distant yet intimate — he heard chanting. Soft voices. Ether spirits.

"Camonra na Flodh."

The hilt pulsed with warmth, matching the rhythm of the chant. A faint flame flickered along the blade, growing brighter.

"Camonra na Flodh."

Time snapped back.

The roar of battle crashed over him. The stone smashed into the enemy line. The creatures surged toward him and Mategaladh.

Heat radiated from Evliit's sword. Flames climbed the blade, licking up his forearm. They burned hot — but did not burn him.

A half dozen creatures leapt at him.

Evliit flipped the sword and drove the tip into the earth.

A wall of fire erupted outward in a sweeping arc. It washed harmlessly over Mategaladh and the guards — but ignited the creatures' fur. They fell from the air shrieking, rolling and thrashing as flames consumed them. The larger brutes bellowed, beating at their burning armor.

Broeden's warriors faltered. Then they broke.

The guard stood stunned, frozen in disbelief.

"Attack!" Evliit roared.

Angwen galloped toward him. In one fluid motion, Evliit ripped the sword from the ground, grabbed the saddle horn, and vaulted into the saddle. Mategaladh and Tophian were right behind him.

The fifteen surviving guardsmen snapped from their stupor and fell in behind them.

They charged toward the knot of thirty or forty creatures encircling a wagon at the rear of the field.

Someone moved inside it.

Evliit squinted — leaned forward —

Ebert.

"I see him!" Tophian shouted.

"Ebert!" Evliit cried.

"Evliit!" Ebert pressed his face against the bars. A creature struck the cage with its blade, forcing him back, but he seemed unharmed.

"We're coming!" Evliit yelled.

A bright blue object dropped from the sky.

It struck the earth in front of him with a force that shattered the ground. For an instant, Evliit saw a crouched figure bathed in blue plasma at the center of the blast.

Then weightlessness.

He was thrown from the saddle. The world spun. The ground slammed into him. Angwen rolled over him, crushing him beneath a wave of agony.

Evliit lay on his back, stunned, unable to move. The sky blurred above him. He tried to call out to the Creator, but he coughed up something wet — blood, or bile, or both.

He cleared his throat and gasped for breath.

Give me strength.

Instantly, energy surged through Evliit's body. The stabbing pain in his ribs dulled, and he lifted his head. The blast had thrown him nearly twenty yards. Angwen lay on his side at Evliit's feet, and dread seized him — but then the horse kicked, rolled to his knees, and pushed himself upright.

Broeden's creatures had not been so fortunate. Those closest to the impact lay scattered, dead or dying.

Evliit rolled to his side. A sharp pain still stabbed beneath his left ribs.

Give me strength, he repeated.

Mategaladh and Tophian were sprawled among several Rion guardsmen who had been farther from the blast. They were already stirring, moving toward the crater. On the far side of the depression, the prisoner wagon sat half-collapsed in the mud. One whole side had been blown away. The door was gone.

Ebert was inside — dazed, bleeding from the head, but alive.

"Ebert!" Evliit called.

He reached for his sword — but his hand met only dirt. Panic flared. He scanned the ground, frantic.

A slender young woman rose from the center of the crater.

The Huntress.

She ignored the approaching guards, calmly adjusting her gauntlets. Her cape drifted around her like black mist suspended in water. Her face was hidden behind her upturned collar, but Evliit saw long black hair and skin pale as death. Steam rose from her body like winter fog. Her grey sleeves billowed elegantly around the black bodice and knee-high boots she wore.

She fixed her gaze on Evliit and began walking toward him.

A guardsman rushed to intercept her. She extended her hand lazily in his direction. He raised his blade to strike — then arched backward in agony. Every vein in his face and neck bulged purple. A wisp of ether escaped his mouth and flew into her palm. He collapsed, lifeless.

Without a glance at him, she turned toward the wagon.

With a flick of her arm, the debris blocking the wagon flew aside.

"Come," she commanded — her voice resonant, powerful.

Ebert was ripped from the wreckage and thrown at her feet.

"Tophian! Mategaladh! Get up!" Evliit shouted, still searching for his sword.

Three Rion guards rushed to help him — but the Huntress repeated her sorcery, killing them instantly.

Evliit spotted his sword. He staggered toward it, but his balance failed and he fell to his hands and knees. He crawled, dragging himself through the dirt, and seized the hilt just as the Huntress reached him.

She raised her hand at the same moment he lifted the blade.

Evliit braced for death.

Instead, energy burst from the sword and poured into her palm. She cried out in pain.

Evliit couldn't let go. The sword clung to him like a living thing. His strength drained away, flowing into her. His vision dimmed. His skin tightened over his bones. His lips pulled back from his teeth. His arms thinned, every vein stark beneath the skin.

Then a stone slammed into the Huntress's hood, hurling her backward.

Evliit collapsed.

He lay on his back, staring at the sky. He was so thirsty. It reminded him of walking the monastery walls in the heat of summer.

"Get away from him!" Tophian roared.

Evliit forced himself to roll over. Darkness crept at the edges of his vision. He fought to stay conscious.

Tophian stood with Mategaladh beside him, calling another stone from the earth — nearly as large as he was. He floated it above his head, preparing to hurl it.

But the Huntress, already recovered, slapped her palms together.

The stone exploded.

Tophian fell. Blood spurted from a gash in his scalp.

"Tophian!" Mategaladh cried.

The Huntress advanced — but roots burst from the ground, wrapping around her leg.

"No, you don't!" Mategaladh shouted.

More roots erupted, binding her arms, her torso, her neck. She hunched under their pull.

Her head snapped up. Her eyes glowed bright, burning red. The roots blackened. The corruption spread down into the earth.

Mategaladh screamed. The veins in his arms turned black. He fell to his knees, clutching his chest. With trembling hands, he drew a short blade and slashed both forearms. Black blood poured out, smoking as it hit the ground.

The Huntress tore free of the dying vines. She seized Ebert around the waist. She looked back once — then shot straight upward into the sky.

In a blink, she vanished into the clouds.

"Ebert!" Evliit cried.

Only the wind answered.

Evliit looked around. The Huntress had annihilated the Rion Guard. No survivors.

He stumbled to Tophian's side. The wound in his scalp was a gaping hole.

"Tophian!" Mategaladh called weakly. He tried to rise but collapsed again.

Evliit forced himself upright. Mategaladh looked up at him, pale as death.

"There are herbs… in my saddlebags," he said. "Come!"

His horse trotted to him.

Evliit leaned against the animal for support and fumbled with the saddlebag straps.

"It's a purplish root," Mategaladh whispered.

Evliit found one and held it up.

Mategaladh shook his head. "It's not enough." He struggled to his feet.

The cuts on his arms now bled red — rivers of scarlet dripping to the dirt.

"Let me help you." Evliit guided him to a piece of the wagon's roof. "We won't need the root. I can fix this."

"Evliit… you can't even stand. " Mategaladh protested. "If you try to channel like this, your body will give out."

Evliit shook his head. "The Creator isn't done with me yet."

He placed his hand over the wound. The sword in his other hand glowed. Mategaladh grimaced as the wounds closed. When Evliit finished, he gasped and nearly toppled.

"Sit. I have to help Tophian."

He stumbled to Tophian's side and dropped heavily beside him. Tophian was unconscious, grey, barely breathing.

"He's lost a lot of blood," Evliit said. He placed his hand over the wound. Light flared between his fingers. When he lifted his hand, the skull was whole — but Tophian's breaths were shallow.

Evliit looked at the devastation and bowed his head. He rubbed his eyes.

"Take him home, Mategaladh. Ebert is gone. There's nothing more to be done here."

Mategaladh stared into the distance. "How do we even combat a sorceress like that?" he whispered. He rose unsteadily and knelt beside Tophian, placing a hand on his chest. "Tophian?"

"Mategaladh?" Evliit said gently.

No response.

"Mategaladh!" Evliit barked.

Mategaladh jolted. "Yes!"

Evliit softened his voice. "Let me help you get him ready to travel."

"Yes… of course," Mategaladh murmured, still dazed.

Evliit fashioned a travois from the wagon's broken beams, lashing them with rope. Together they lifted Tophian onto it and secured the poles over his horse's saddle.

Mategaladh mounted his own horse. Evliit handed him the reins to Tophian's.

"May the Creator watch over you," Evliit said. His leg buckled, but he caught himself. "I'm going back to the cabin. I must tend to Jaros's tomes. I'll await word from you there."

Mategaladh nodded, though his eyes were distant. He spurred his horse gently and rode away.

"You heard me, right?" Evliit called after him. "I'm going back to the cabin."

Mategaladh didn't answer. He seemed to be praying — or simply mumbling to himself.

Does it really matter? We've failed. On all accounts, we've failed.

Evliit looked up at the passing clouds. The image of Ebert and the Huntress shooting into the sky was burned into his mind, and he had to look away. All this destruction — all this death — only reminded him of Harot and Jenna. A hollow ache spread through his chest. For a moment, he felt the pull of surrender, the quiet temptation to lie down beside the fallen and let his own life drift upward with theirs.

"Tophian should have been dead, but you channeled the Creator's healing upon him," a voice said behind him.

Evliit turned.

Mategaladh had stopped his horse and was staring back at him. "You saved him. Saved both of us." His voice wavered, and his eyes shone with the threat of tears. "You are the sword bearer, Evliit. No one else could have survived her attack. Don't you see?"

"We escaped that sorceress with our lives, Mategaladh," Evliit said quietly. "Few can claim the same. And it wasn't just me. It was you and Tophian as much as anything."

"Maybe," Mategaladh murmured, though his tone was flat, distant. He looked down at Tophian on the travois. "I'll nurse him back to health. When he's better... we'll speak of this again."

He nudged his horse forward, and Tophian's horse followed. Evliit watched them until they disappeared into the haze of the plains.

Then he called Angwen, pulled himself into the saddle, and turned toward the western side of the Black Mountains.

Evliit returned to the cabin by way of the northern shore of Aertos, giving the monastery a wide berth and avoiding any sign of life. The Huntress had done something to him; he could feel it. His strength bled away faster than it should have. More than once he had to slip into the cool shadows beneath the trees lining the northern bank, resting until he could force himself onward.

There, alone in the musky mulch of the forest floor, Evliit found himself questioning everything. *How was it that Broeden always found a way to prevail? If the Creator was infinite and omnipotent, why did darkness continue to triumph at the expense of so many innocents?* The questions twisted inside him, gut-wrenching and maddening.

What are you waiting for?

He stared up at the sky, but no answer came.

He had just begun moving again after another long rest when a thunderous crack split the air. He turned toward the sound and saw the last of the monastery towers collapsing. The rumble rolled across the lake, echoing for what felt like minutes.

When Evliit reached the eastern shore, he kept low, watching for movement — but even the ferry operator was gone. No one left to ferry.

The climb up the mountain to the cabin was hard and lonely. Every step felt heavier than the last.

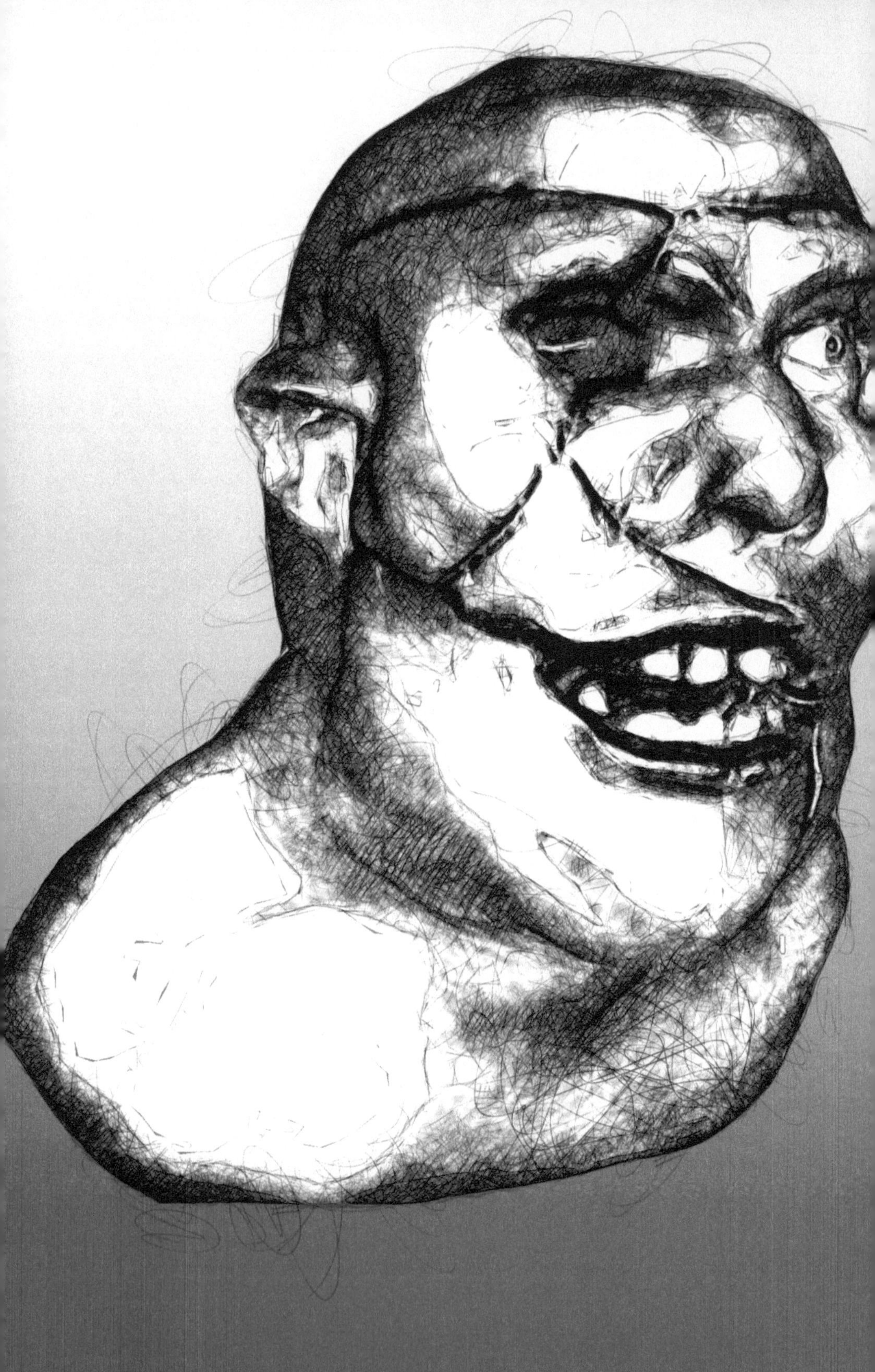

CHAPTER 9

THE SUFFERING OF OTHERS

Rendaya landed just outside the western entrance of Broeden's castle, releasing Ebert from under her arm a heartbeat before her boots touched the ground. He hit the earth hard enough to knock the wind from him — not enough to injure, just enough to keep him compliant.

The western sally port burst open, and Broeden's minions came scrambling out.

Rendaya straightened. "Give the master this message," she said to the first creature that reached her. "I have seen the thing he desires, and I have captured one we may bargain with. Now run."

The creature's eyes narrowed. It glanced at Ebert, and its face stretched into a drooling grin. It nodded violently and scampered off.

Rendaya turned to Ebert. "Get up."

He lay gasping, struggling to draw breath. He rolled to his side.

"Rise," she said. "Or I'll drag you."

"I'm… coming," Ebert managed between ragged breaths. He pushed himself to one knee, wobbling.

Rendaya seized his chin and hauled him upright. "Keep up. I'm not staying down there any longer than I must. The dungeons always put me in a foul mood."

She marched him through the sally port and down six flights of stairs into the castle's depths.

She hated this place — the reek of mold, damp stone, and old smoke. When it mingled with the stench from the cells, it clung to her skin and hair for days. It was beneath her, all of it.

At the chosen cell, she grabbed Ebert by the shoulder and threw him inside. She was impatient to report to Broeden — and she was certain he would want every detail about the monk's friend, the sword bearer.

She slammed the cell door.

Ebert's eyes slowly adjusted to the darkness. Distant crying, moaning, and screams echoed up the stairwell like the voices of the damned. A voice behind him made him jump.

"It never stops."

Ebert spun around. "Who is that?"

Something shifted across the cell, but he couldn't make out the figure. He stepped closer.

A man in peasant's clothing sat slumped against the wall, legs sprawled before him. Rats crawled over his right foot in a writhing pile.

"In the name of the Creator!" Ebert cried. "Get away!" He kicked a handful of them across the floor. "Get away!"

The remaining rats scattered. Most of the flesh on the man's ankle was gone, gnawed to the bone. When Ebert bent closer, the stench of rot hit him like a blow.

"I'll help you, brother," Ebert said — but the man had already slipped into unconsciousness.

Ebert dropped to his knees and prayed. "Help us, Creator of all."

His hands began to glow. A warm golden light filled the cell. Ebert placed his palms on the man's ankle and held them there. The light flowed from his hands into the man's body, spreading outward until it enveloped him entirely.

The man awoke with a gasp. Seeing Ebert so close, he cried out and pressed himself against the wall, eyes wide with fear.

"It's all right," Ebert said gently.

He removed his hands. The wound was closed. The bleeding had stopped.

"My foot!" the man exclaimed. He bent his knee, turning his leg to see the healed ankle. "What'd you do?"

"The Creator healed you," Ebert said. "We give thanks for the Creator's power."

"Thanks be to the Creator!" the man repeated. "You're a healer!" With effort, he pushed himself upright. Only then did he notice Ebert's robe. "A healer and a monk!"

He hobbled to the cell door. "I can't tell you how thankful I am to be off that floor. I've been sitting there for so long — not something you want to do when you're bleeding." He inspected his ankle again. "Amazing. Thank you… I'm sorry, what's your name?"

"I'm Ebert."

"Loren," he said, offering a hand.

"Where is this place, Loren?" Ebert asked. "A Huntress and these creatures attacked our monastery. I think they killed everyone but me. My friends tried to rescue me, but she fought them fiercely. I don't even know if they're alive. She carried me into the sky — I must have passed out. I woke only as we approached this castle."

Loren's expression softened. He placed a hand on Ebert's shoulder. "I'm sorry, brother. We're captives of Broeden himself. This is the dungeon of the dark one."

Ebert drew a sharp breath. "I feared as much."

A rusty gate screeched open down the hall. A towering Camon lumbered toward them. Ebert gasped. The creature wore a blood-stained leather apron, freshly spattered with something foul. He limped, his body a patchwork of stitched-together parts.

Loren backed away from the door.

The Camon entered, locking the door behind him. As he turned, the left side of his face swung loose. He growled and shoved the skin back into place, removing piercings from his brow and cheek to secure the flap. He stretched his mouth wide, testing the rings, then drew a gruesome blade from his belt.

"Time to take a limb, the master says," the Camon rasped, pointing at Loren. "You. Come with me."

Loren began to cry. "Help me," he begged Ebert. "Don't let them take me!"

Without thinking, Ebert stepped forward — but the Camon raised the blade to his face.

"Stand there," the creature growled. "I'd hate to open you up."

His tone made it clear he'd enjoy it.

The torturer's left eye — shrunken and dead — stared straight ahead while the right eye jerked around, searching for Loren. "C'mere, you!"

"No!" Loren cried, sliding into the far corner, sobbing.

"I got all the time in the world," the Camon said. "Come now, and I'll make it quick."

"Let no harm come to him," Ebert whispered. "*Sepe.*"

Black vines burst from the moldy stone around Loren. The Camon froze, confused. Ebert stepped back as the vines sprouted long, sharp spines and branched outward, forming a protective barrier.

"Witchcraft!" the Camon snarled — and grinned. "I welcome it."

He grabbed a vine.

Five spines punched through his hand.

He howled and jerked back, but the thorns split and curled like hooks, anchoring themselves in his flesh. He slashed himself free with his knife — but the vine whipped around and struck him in the cheek.

He screamed. The spines had pierced his cheek and hooked his tongue. He tore the vine free, ripping flesh with it. Blood poured down his face.

He freed his other hand with another brutal cut, then turned toward Ebert, fury blazing.

"Master wants a limb," he snarled through his mangled mouth. "One of yours will do."

He shoved the knife into his belt, crossed the cell, and seized Ebert by the arm. Blood dripped down Ebert's sleeve.

Dragging him, the Camon fumbled for the key ring — dropped it — roared, and punched the lock. The bolt snapped. He kicked the door open so hard it sheared off the upper hinge.

"You're gonna wish I'd taken him," the Camon grunted, hauling Ebert down the hall.

ZⱯⱤᏱᚢ.

Rendaya sat before the vanity in her chamber, staring into the looking glass as though trying to recognize the person reflected there. Her seventeenth year on Erathe had been complicated, full of questions she had never dared ask. For as long as she could remember, her purpose had been simple: please Broeden. Serve him. Hunt for him. Kill for him.

But something in her was changing.

Thoughts she had never allowed herself to dwell on now pressed at the edges of her mind.

The scouting trip had been productive. Broeden would be pleased once she learned more from the monk. The man with the glowing sword — he had resisted her powers. No one had ever done that. She was certain the sword he carried was the one Broeden desired so desperately. And this monk, this *Ebert*, would tell her everything she needed to know.

She looked again into the mirror.

Her reflection stared back blankly, as if the girl in the glass were someone else entirely.

There was still blood in her hair and a streak of it on her neck — the blood of the man at the outpost, the one she had killed before the attack on the monastery.

His death haunted her in a way nothing ever had.

Why?

She dipped a cloth into the bowl of water on her vanity, pulled her black hair aside, and wiped the dried blood from her neck. As she did, the memory returned with painful clarity.

Her scouts had cornered the man in a bell tower north of the monastery. She had wanted to strike unseen, but the watchman had spotted them and was about to ring the alarm. The Camonra were battering the tower door when the man appeared at the top, pulling back the bell's hammer.

"Stop!" Rendaya had shouted.

Two Camon had dragged a woman and two children from the house below the tower and thrown them at Rendaya's feet.

"If that bell rings, they die," she said.

The man's face twisted in horror — a look she had seen a thousand times.

"No!" he cried. "No, wait!"

"Ring it!" his wife screamed. "They'll kill us anyway!"

A Camon moved to silence her, but Rendaya waved him off. The children sobbed uncontrollably.

"You have my word," she called up to the man. "Come down to me, and they will be left alone."

His expression shifted — horror to defeat. She knew that look as well.

He lowered the hammer, raised his hands, and shouted, "I'm coming down!"

The moment the bolts slid back, a Camon yanked the door open and dragged him out, throwing him at Rendaya's feet beside his family.

"I love you," he whispered to them. Then he looked up at Rendaya. "Please… let them go."

All at once, Rendaya couldn't breathe.

A memory — buried deep — surged up: her father and mother kneeling in front of their little house, her mother's voice begging her to look away.

The Camon's voice snapped her back. "Your orders, Huntress?"

She pointed to the open doorway of the house. "Put them inside."

The Camonra dragged the woman and children away. The woman never took her eyes off her husband, as if trying to memorize him.

"I have your word they will be safe?" the man asked.

"Yes," Rendaya said.

He knelt before her, staring into her eyes with defiance.

She drove her dagger between his collarbone and neck with perfect precision. He did not scream. He did not speak. He simply closed his eyes and fell.

The memory faded. The red-stained towel on her vanity took its place.

Rendaya picked up her brush and ran it through her hair, thinking for the hundredth time about the man's final act. It made no sense. *Why surrender a perfect defensive position to save three others? What was this love that could make a man trade his life for theirs?*

Ebert would know.

He was young — about her age. Surely he understood this strange thing that drove people to sacrifice themselves.

She set her jaw. The monk would tell her what Broeden wanted to know… but he would tell her more as well. About the world beyond these walls. About something other than blood and terror.

Rendaya rose from her vanity and headed for the dungeons.

When Rendaya reached the cell, the door stood open. She glanced inside and saw the cocoon of thorned vines in the corner, the older peasant still cowering behind them. Ebert was gone.

She spun, scanning the hall.

"What are you up to, monk?" she muttered.

She rounded the corner — and froze.

Ebert knelt on the floor, one arm stretched across a chopping block. Blood streaked his face and hair. The jailer loomed over him, a cleaver nearly as long as Ebert's arm raised high. The Camon torturer squinted down the blade with his one good eye, as if deciding exactly where to sever the limb.

"No!" Rendaya screamed.

The blade fell anyway — but her cry startled the jailer. He jerked back at the last instant, burying the cleaver into the block at an angle. The back edge still sliced into Ebert's arm, deep enough to draw a gush of blood.

Ebert cried out, crimson running down the side of the block.

"Get back!" Rendaya commanded.

The jailer's eyes narrowed with fury, but he obeyed, releasing the cleaver and stepping away. "Yes, Huntress. At once."

"What are you doing, you fool?" she demanded.

"The master wanted limbs," the jailer said. "I was collecting them for him."

Rendaya ripped the cleaver free and spun.

With a single stroke, she severed the jailer's left arm at the elbow.

The Camon howled, clutching the spurting stump as blackish blood poured through his fingers.

Rendaya tossed the cleaver aside and pointed to the twitching limb on the floor. "Take that one."

"I did nothing wrong!" he wailed. But he snatched up his severed arm, staggered to a brazier of glowing coals, and shoved the stump into them. The smell of burning flesh filled the hall. He collapsed to his knees, screaming.

Rendaya had no sympathy to spare. "Leave me."

Whimpering, the jailer dragged himself out of sight.

Rendaya turned to the monk. He had freed his arm from the block and bowed his head, one hand pressed over the wound. When he lifted it, she saw the skin had closed — the cut healed by his incantation.

She grabbed his arm and examined it. "Amazing," she murmured. "We have much to discuss, monk."

She seized him and threw him onto the rack.

"I'll tell you what you want to know," Ebert said. "You don't have to hurt me."

"Yes, you will," Rendaya said. "One way or another."

"Please… no," Ebert begged. He tried to twist away, but she caught his leg in one hand and squeezed until he screamed. She looped a rope around his ankle and pulled it tight. When he lunged forward again, she backhanded him, knocking him senseless. She tied the other leg — but when she reached for the ratchet, the handle was missing.

"Bring me the ratchet handle!" she shouted.

The jailer growled something down the hall, but she ignored him. She focused on binding Ebert's left hand.

Footsteps approached behind her. She turned to take the handle — and saw a flash of metal instead.

A sharp sting tore across her neck. Warm blood sprayed across the jailer's face.

My blood, she realized.

"You shouldn't have hurt me!" the jailer shrieked. He raised the cleaver for another strike. "I'll cut off your—"

Rendaya tried to speak, but blood filled her throat.

The jailer's body exploded.

Gore splattered the far wall.

Rendaya pressed her palm to her neck, trying to stem the flow, but the spurting blood was already slowing on its own. She sank to the ground, her head resting in the warm pool spreading beneath her. The torchlight dimmed.

Her childhood rushed back — running through the fields behind her father's house, laughing at a butterfly. The blue sky. The flowers. The joy.

If this was death, she welcomed that memory as her last.

Then pressure touched her neck.

The monk was kneeling over her. His hands pressed against her wound. His voice murmured a prayer she could barely hear. Warmth spread through her body, thawing the cold places.

She gasped for air.

He lifted his head and looked into her eyes.

She saw determination. And kindness.

She tried to smile — but his face faded into darkness.

SPELLMAKER

Since Evliit's confrontation with the Huntress, summer and fall had slipped away, and winter crept into the Black Mountains. Its northern winds curled around the windows and doors of Jaros's little cabin, chilling it with icy breath.

Fatigue plagued Evliit through the early winter. He ventured little beyond the cabin door. There was plenty to eat in the stores Jaros had left, but his appetite had faded. He was certain he'd lost twenty pounds, maybe more.

Now, in late winter, he stood at the cabin's small window, watching snowflakes as large as coins drift past. A thick white blanket covered the mountainside.

As he stared dully into the storm, a magnificent blue jay burst from a pine tree and landed on the stone path. It darted back and forth, flashing royal blue feathers and leaving tiny three-toed prints in the snow. In its beak was a scrap of parchment, which it dropped before vanishing into the sky.

Evliit slipped on his shoes, wrapped a sheepskin around himself, and stepped outside.

The frigid air bit into him. Teeth chattering, he bent and carefully unfolded the parchment.

The lettering was tiny, but he made it out:

No sign of Broeden. Tophian still mending. Numbness in left arm.

Will come to you in spring. Leave message for jay.—M.

Evliit hurried inside, found a quill, trimmed its point with a paring knife, and wrote in letters as small and precise as Mategaladh's:

No word here. Praying for Tophian's healing. Better now. Looking forward to spring. —E.

He folded the note and returned outside, clearing a patch of snow on the stone path before placing it down.

As he turned to leave, the blue jay appeared again. Evliit froze so as not to startle it. The bird danced around the message, snapped it up, cocked its head as if to say *I've got it*, then shot northward over the mountains.

A chill wind swept across the ridge. Evliit retreated into the cabin, bolted the door, and returned to the tomes of the Watchers.

Winter solitude had been both a curse and a gift — time alone with the knowledge of ages, an alchemy lab, and an unrelenting desire to avenge Ebert's abduction. Jaros's volumes would reveal the secrets behind Broeden's power. They had to.

He had replayed the battle with the Huntress countless times. Her ability to drain life without touching him had been devastating. Without Mategaladh, Tophian, and the sword, he would have died.

Broeden's minions were no less deadly — especially the larger ones.

The sword remained his greatest weapon. Beyond its ability to cut through anything, it amplified his thoughts and words. It channeled the Creator's power. When he held it, energy flowed into him, reviving his body. That same power allowed him to heal.

But he was increasingly convinced the sword alone would not be enough — not even one forged by the Bhre Nora.

He set aside the white tomes and stared at the red-trimmed cover of a Spellmaker volume. It looked harmless enough — just a book. Tophian's warnings echoed in his mind.

But Tophian isn't here. And Ebert needs my help.

He took a deep breath and opened it.

A cold chill ran down his spine.

These books were nothing like the Watchers' philosophical prose. Each page stated an objective — sometimes with ingredients and instructions, sometimes with only a phrase, a spell spoken into existence. Pronunciation seemed critical. Mispronouncing a word could mean the difference between commanding a conjured creature… or being devoured by it.

He turned a page and saw a drawing of a person impaled on a stake.

Jenna's face flashed before him — the desperation in her eyes. Then Ebert's face, full of fear as the Huntress carried him into the sky.

Shame and anger twisted in his gut.

He squeezed his eyes shut.

Words slipped out.

"Barodh Ira Mor!"

Evliit opened his eyes.

A dark object hovered beside the stove — a void, a hole in the air. Sunlight dimmed as if drawn into it.

"Why do you call upon us, sword bearer?"

Many voices spoke at once, each wracked with agony.

Evliit stood, backing away — but the darkness slid between him and the door.

"I didn't call upon you!" he shouted.

The floor beneath the void cracked.

"You spoke the words!" the voices howled.

"Depart!" Evliit cried. "Depart at once!"

Cackling erupted. *"He doesn't know us! He doesn't know us!"*

The darkness surged toward him.

Evliit snatched up his sword, unsheathed it, and held it upright. A brilliant golden light burst along its length. The beams bent into the darkness, and the void convulsed. A faint glow appeared at its center, no larger than a copper coin.

The voices shrieked in pain. *"You do not command us!"*

The cabin shook. The darkness stretched from floor to ceiling. The sword's light intensified, filling the room with blinding white.

Clawed hands reached from the void, grasping for him — but bands of light streamed from the sword, burning them back.

Evliit's hair whipped around his face. The void sucked the air from the room. His lungs strained. His feet slid across the floor, dragging him closer, closer, until he stood just beyond the reach of the claws.

Within the darkness, illuminated by the sword's glow, he saw them — an undulating mass of faces, their soulless eyes desperate to claim him.

"Depart!" Evliit screamed.

The darkness collapsed inward and vanished.

The sword dimmed. Evliit staggered, catching himself on the table. Sweat poured down his face. His breath came in ragged gasps.

A clay pot fell from a shelf and shattered on the floor with a great crash, but he was oblivious.

Evliit placed his palm on the sword's hilt and let its energy flow into him. He closed his eyes, steadied his breathing, and gave thanks to the Creator.

Tophian's words echoed in his mind:

To dabble in darkness is dangerous at best.

It was going to be a long winter.

The weather in the following two months was the coldest Evliit could ever remember. He counted the days, waiting for winter to break and the snows to melt. In the dead of that season, in the silence of the cabin, he read Jaros's tomes from cover to cover — and the things he experienced defied explanation.

Then one morning, Evliit awoke to a familiar voice.

"Evliit?"

"Evliit, it's us."

He lifted his head with a grimace. He'd slept with his arm as a pillow, and his neck was stiff. He rolled his head, trying to focus. "Mategaladh?"

Tophian came into view behind him. "What happened here?"

The cabin looked like a battlefield. Broken furniture littered the room. Burn marks streaked from the floor trim up the walls and across the ceiling. Shattered flasks and twisted tubing lay everywhere. A thin layer of ash coated the floor.

"I've destroyed them," Evliit said, pointing to the woodstove.

Inside, soft pillows of ash filled the chamber — some still holding the shape of the shrunken tomes.

Mategaladh stared. "The Elders made contact?"

"No." Evliit braced himself against the wall and stood. "Tophian was right. Those books could destroy us all."

"So you destroyed them?" Mategaladh asked.

"Yes, Mategaladh. All of them."

"Well, son," Tophian said, "I didn't think you had the brass."

Mategaladh did not share his satisfaction. "Evliit! What have you done?"

"Tophian was right," Evliit said, unmoved. "When the darkness found them here, I had no choice."

"The knowledge in those books cannot be replaced!" Mategaladh cried. "It was a fool's errand Jaros gave you! And now you've taken it upon yourself to—"

Tophian grabbed his arm. "Stop, Mategaladh! Look!"

Mategaladh turned — and confusion filled his eyes. "Evliit?"

"Oh no," Evliit whispered.

A fire burned inside him. He held up his hands, and they glowed with the same light shining from his face.

"Evliit… what have you done?" Mategaladh said softly.

Evliit looked into the broken mirror shards on the floor. His eyes glowed like yellow-red spheres of fire. He shut them in disbelief, but when he opened them again, the air itself seemed to reignite them.

He could see dark spirits moving in and out of the cabin walls.

"Do you see them?" Evliit shouted.

Mategaladh and Tophian looked around, bewildered. "See what?" Tophian asked.

"You should leave!" Evliit boomed. The force of his voice startled them both. "I'm not sure how long I can keep things in check. Leave me!"

Tophian backed away. "Come, Mategaladh!"

"Oh, Evliit…" Mategaladh whispered, heartbroken.

"Come on!" Tophian pulled him through the door.

Evliit followed them outside as they mounted their horses. "Hurry!"

Clouds gathered overhead. The darkness appeared again — now as large as the cabin.

"Go! Go now!"

Mategaladh and Tophian spurred their horses. The darkness surged toward them.

"*Cera Orbita!*" Evliit cried.

A spherical wave of energy burst outward. Their horses cleared its expanding edge at nearly a hundred paces. The darkness slammed into the barrier and rebounded, brimstone and fire bursting from within it. It struck again, and Evliit felt the concussive force in his gut.

"You'll go nowhere!" he shouted.

The darkness hurled itself at the barrier repeatedly, howling in fury. Evliit held fast. A sharp pain stabbed above his left eye, and his nose began to bleed. His vision blurred. He dropped to one knee.

Mategaladh and Tophian turned their horses back.

"Evliit!" Mategaladh shouted. They leapt from their saddles and tried to reach him — but the barrier held them back.

Mategaladh ran along its edge. The darkness slammed into the opposite side, making him jump back.

Evliit waved him off. "Leave!"

The darkness moved toward Evliit's voice.

He drew his sword. Flames climbed the blade, rising three feet above its tip. He charged into the darkness, fire streaming from his eyes, mouth, and sword.

"I am the sword bearer!" he roared.

The ground vanished beneath him as he plunged into the blackness.

He drifted downward. The sword's flames roared brighter, illuminating a mass of hideous creatures below — a sea of fangs and claws stretching as far as he could see. They hissed and leapt at him like wild dogs fighting over a butcher's bone.

Above him, the ring of daylight shrank, leaving behind a cavern of jagged black slag. Thousands more creatures poured from every crevice.

Evliit whispered a desperate prayer. "Creator, protect me."

All seemed lost.

But when he drifted within thirty feet of the cavern floor, the creatures nearest him burst into flames. Their ashes rose past him like black snow.

The sea of monsters recoiled. The howling died. They hesitated, confused.

When he touched the cavern floor, they decided as one.

A deafening roar shook the chamber.

They charged.

Thousands upon thousands.

Creatures burst into flames as they neared him, but still they came. The wall of bodies pressed closer.

Evliit stood firm on black brimstone, engulfed in the sword's fire. The demons screamed in agony, but they kept coming.

He brought his feet together, held the sword upright, and closed his eyes.

Then pain — sharp, searing — tore through his right thigh.

One had reached him.

Claws raked his body from all sides. They tugged him, tore at him, bit at him. Energy poured from the sword, sealing wounds as fast as they opened — but still they pressed in, grabbing his arms, trying to wrench his hands from the hilt.

Suddenly he was sitting with the Creator in the garden.

Quiet.

Peaceful.

The sword lay on the table.

He remembered taking it.

He remembered everything.

A scream rose from deep within him — primal, absolute, born of calling and conviction.

He roared.

A blinding flash of light.

Then he fell forward onto his face.

Silence.

Evliit felt something wet on the back of his neck. He pushed himself up.

He was lying just outside the cabin.

It was raining — quiet, peaceful — as if nothing had happened. But the stench of brimstone clung to him, and his hands and clothes were black with soot.

It was early evening.

Tophian and Mategaladh were gone.

He grunted as he stood, then again as he bent to pick up his sword. He walked inside, bolted the door, rolled up a scrap of tablecloth into a makeshift pillow, and lay down beside the shattered remains of the bed.

He tried to sleep, but the darkness haunted him.

"You will never take me," he whispered.

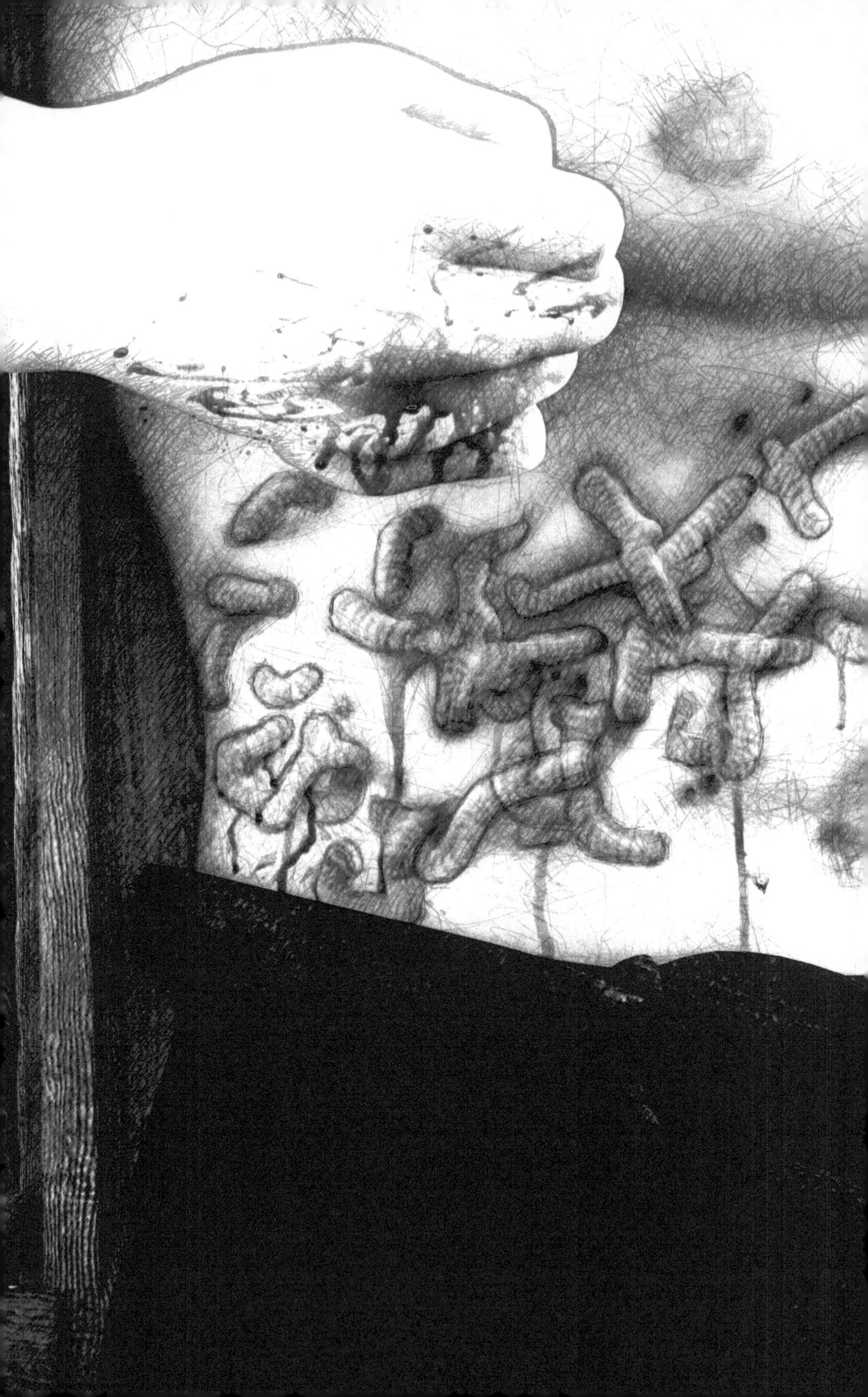

CHAPTER 11

THE WEAVING WORM

A few hours before sunrise, Evliit awoke to someone shouting at his cabin door. For a moment he jolted upright, thinking he was under attack — but the fear passed quickly. He had heard only one voice. Demons from the Underworld never came alone.

It had been a little over three weeks since Evliit, with heroic effort, had sealed the gateway he'd opened. Since then, he had manned his lonely post without fail. He repaired the cabin, tended the grounds, and watched over the portal — a duty he imagined might last the rest of his life.

He remained completely isolated. Not even Mategaladh or Tophian could pass through the barrier he had erected, though they had come once to bring news from Rion. After the fall of the monastery and the Huntress's slaughter of the Guard, Rion's leaders considered the mountain too far from their protection. The superstitious whispered that the land was cursed — that when the monastery fell, all manner of evil began to roam the place.

"You'll not likely have a living soul come this way anytime soon," Tophian had told him.

But the voice outside his door now sounded very much alive.

Evliit kept his eyes closed, listening. Silence. Maybe he had dreamed it. He hadn't heard a voice outside his cabin since the first time he'd crossed into the Underworld.

He was about to lie back down when the shouting came again.

"Ev-li-it!"

Something in the air had changed. Ever since the portal appeared, he had felt a constant drag on his spirit — and suddenly, it was gone.

Evliit's eyes snapped open. He swung his feet to the floor, exhaling a cloud of frosty breath. His little wood-burning stove was losing its battle with winter.

He stood behind the heavy-timbered door, shook the sleep from his head, and slowly opened the window shutter. He wrapped his blanket around himself as the cold seeped through the wood. Torchlight flickered through the gaps, casting long yellow-red stripes across the cabin walls.

Peering through one, he saw a middle-aged man in soldier's garb standing on the lawn. The stranger stepped back onto the path, raising his torch. His eyes were glassy and bloodshot.

Evliit withdrew into the shadows.

"Show yourself!" the man shouted — then jerked his hand to his side in pain.

He's injured.

Evliit opened the door and leaned out. "Are you hurt?"

The soldier looked confused by the question. He staggered, dropped his torch, and fell to his knees.

Evliit stepped outside.

The man's face was panicked. "Are you the one they call Evliit?"

"Let me help you," Evliit said, dropping the blanket and moving toward him.

"Are you the one called Evliit?" the soldier repeated. His skin was pale even in the torchlight, sweat beading on his brow.

Evliit met his gaze. "Yes. I'm Evliit."

"Thank the Creator," the soldier breathed. Evliit reached around his waist to lift him — but the man cried out and recoiled.

"This is why I've come," he gasped, lifting his chainmail and shirt.

Fresh and dried blood covered his side. Something like wet leather strings protruded from his skin — except the strings were moving, weaving in and out of his flesh.

Evliit snapped to attention. "A weaving worm."

He had never seen one, but he had read enough to know the danger.

He hooked an arm under the soldier's armpit and half dragged, half carried him inside as the man moaned in agony.

"Why does it burn so?" the soldier cried. "It did not burn so before!"

"It feels threatened in this place," Evliit said, shutting the door and window. "Quickly — your shirt."

The soldier hesitated, then stripped off his shirt, sword, and chainmail, letting them fall in a heap.

"The head of the serpent is here today," he said, pinching a pointed tip protruding from his abdomen. He drew his short blade, pulled the worm outward several inches, and sliced it off. The severed piece recoiled, and the rest of the worm vanished beneath his skin. The man screamed and made to throw the piece into the stove.

"Stop!" Evliit shouted.

The soldier froze.

"I need that," Evliit said more gently, taking it from him. He handed him a clean rag. "Tend to your wound."

The soldier obeyed, trembling.

"First of all, that's the tail, not the head," Evliit said. "And cutting it only slows the worm. It will regrow."

The soldier's voice cracked. "Can you help me?"

"Only the Creator can help you now," Evliit said. "But I will use the skills He's given me."

He laid the worm's tail on the butcher block, split it lengthwise, and mixed it with two vials from the cabinet. The mixture formed a thick black cake. He tapped it into his hand and showed it to the soldier.

"This will be uncomfortable. Are you ready?"

The soldier's eyes were wide, but he nodded.

Evliit pressed a piece of the black cake onto one of the bleeding holes.

The soldier screamed. The weaving worm began to unravel, whipping beneath his skin at terrifying speed. Foamy blood oozed from every opening.

He kicked and clawed at the red ribbon of worm unspooling from his flesh. A fist-sized bulge rose near his right kidney. He pressed against it — and his skin tore open. Hooked teeth pushed outward, forcing his fingers aside. When the creature finished evacuating itself, several feet of worm lay in a bloody heap on the floor.

The soldier lost consciousness halfway through.

Evliit made a makeshift cot on the floor with blankets and rags, then lowered the unconscious man onto it. He stuffed a rag into the gaping tear in the soldier's lower back to slow the bleeding.

As he worked, the first pale light of dawn crept through the shutter cracks.

Evliit looked up. *Light.* He needed more of it.

He crossed the room quickly and threw open the shutters. Sunlight spilled across the cabin floor, chasing the shadows from the corners. The cold blast of air stirred the soldier, but Evliit was already kneeling beside him again, hands pressed firmly over the wound.

A soft blue light spread beneath Evliit's palms, sealing the torn flesh beneath a transparent, shimmering membrane. The soldier gasped awake mid-healing, eyes wide with confusion.

"What—what is happening?"

"Easy," Evliit said, gently pushing him back down. "While you slept, I called upon the Creator to close your wounds."

The last of the healing light faded. Only then did Evliit pull the soldier's shirt back down over the injury.

The man blinked up at him, dazed. "Praedhos," he said weakly. "Praedhos of the Rion Guard—ah!" He clutched his side as the membrane tightened.

"That was a nasty bit of business," Evliit said. "I wasn't sure you were going to make it."

Praedhos lifted the edge of his shirt and stared in horror at the shimmering blue membrane. "I can see my insides!"

"Only for a time," Evliit said. "This wound is different. It will take longer to mend."

Praedhos let his shirt fall back over the injury.

Satisfied Praedhos would not bleed out, Evliit scooped the worm from the floor, stuffed it into a jar of preservative, and sealed it with a plate-sized cork. The creature sank slowly, ribbons of red drifting in the clear fluid.

He was a little in awe of the soldier. Given its size, the worm should have killed the man by now. He would have had to cut the tail off it every single day to keep it from consuming him — and the pain he must have endured doing so repeatedly… well, he was incredibly tough; that was certain.

Evliit tilted his head. "Where did you cross paths with such evil? Who infected you?"

"About eight days northeast by horse," Praedhos said. "Broeden's land."

The words seemed to wound him. Tears welled in his eyes.

Evliit snapped to attention. "You faced Broeden? The dark one himself?"

Praedhos nodded grimly. "The sorcerer lives. He blasphemes the very name of the Creator. He spreads darkness over all the land. He—"

Evliit raised a hand, stopping the rising torrent. "From where do you hail?"

"Rion," Praedhos answered.

"Rion," Evliit echoed. His pulse quickened. News from Rion meant news of the Huntress — and if he met her again, things would be very different. His winter alone had not been wasted. *And Praedhos's knowledge of Durageim… that could change everything.*

Evliit pointed to the emblem on Praedhos's chest. "You're in the Guard. I honor your service."

Praedhos straightened, pride flickering through the pain. "It's my honor to serve."

Evliit fetched his teapot from the cast-iron stove and set it on the table. "We need a little heat. I'll get a fire going and make you some tea; it will help you heal."

He rummaged through his jars of herbs, lifting a glass lid and inhaling the aroma.

Praedhos licked his lips. "Tea sounds very good right now."

"Excellent," Evliit said. He found a fire stick, tossed a few pieces of wood into the stove, and struck the stick against the iron. "This wood's so dry it's no problem. Quick and easy to light."

They waited in silence until the familiar crackle of flame filled the room.

Evliit poked the wood. "I remember Rion being near the ocean. The cliffs looked as though they went on forever."

"Yes," Praedhos said, eyes brightening. "When you stand back and look out over the ocean, it's like an illusion. Blue Water goes on forever. Word is the Elders had masons cut steps into the cliffs last year — all the way down to the sea."

Evliit closed the stove door and gathered the teapot and herbs. "That'll be a sight to see. Rion must be growing in leaps and bounds."

"All the tribes of the Forgotten Lands are represented in Rion now,"

Praedhos said. "It's taken more than a century for my people to abandon the northern lands. About a generation."

"In search of a place far from the sorcerer," Evliit said.

Praedhos nodded tightly. "I grew up hearing stories of Broeden's minions stealing our people in the night, dragging them to the dark places beneath his castle. Our fathers were powerless to stop him. This time we thought we'd strike at the heart — at Broeden himself." He shook his head. "We failed."

"What made the Elders act now?" Evliit asked.

"After seven years of silence, we believed the ancient one had finally passed. But then word came from the old country that Broeden lived — and was more desperate than ever to find some 'key' to his immortality. Thirteen moons past, in the dead of northeastern winter, news reached us that Broeden was marching an army south. With it came reports of monks abducted and monasteries destroyed in the borderlands."

"Rion claims all lands west of the Black Mountains?" Evliit asked.

"And north to the Faceless Mountains, and south to the sea," Praedhos said with a sigh. "We take on too much, if you ask me — but guardsmen have no say in matters of state." He grimaced as he shifted on the cot. "When Broeden's armies drew near, our people were terrified. The Elders sent us on a sacred mission to the old country to find Broeden's lair — to remove the head of the snake."

"But if Broeden had an army," Evliit said, "what hope did your Elders have with so few warriors?"

"Graeson, our captain, dared to propose what no one else would — a covert plan to assassinate the sorcerer in his own home. He led us around Broeden's army, far north into the icy tundra, then back south to the rear of the dark castle."

The teapot whistled. Evliit poured two steaming cups and listened as Praedhos continued.

"We were two hundred strong when we began," Praedhos said. "Only six of us made it out alive."

"Six," Evliit whispered. "So few..."

Praedhos's face darkened. "Six. But a sickness befell us." He pointed to the jar where the worm floated. "Some were less lucky than I. The worms appeared in their faces, or in several places at once. I had only the one, here."

He motioned to his side. "We made it back to our country, but when the priests of the Temple of Rion could not cure us, we were declared unclean. Even Elder Jonas could not save us. The Elders commanded that we leave Rion immediately, under penalty of death."

He swallowed hard.

"The Rionese shunned us like lepers. Every healer, every peddler — nothing helped. We died one by one as the worms consumed us."

He lay back, staring at the ceiling.

"After eight months, I was utterly alone." His voice cracked. "I decided to take my own life rather than endure the pain any longer."

He used his sleeve to wipe his eyes. "That's why I came to the Black Mountains. I thought only to reach their peak and gaze one last time upon Rion to the south before I died. But yesterday I grew weary and could go no farther. I sat beside the path and thought I might die there."

His voice trembled.

"But a kind soul found me. She took pity on me."

"A woman?" Evliit asked. "Where did she come from?"

Praedhos shrugged. "She walked out of the mist surrounding the road as if sent by the Creator himself. She knelt beside me, and when she touched my hand, she was cold as ice — but the pain of the weaving worm eased. For the first time in months, I felt hope."

Evliit's breath caught.

"'You must find Evliit,' she told me. 'He lives close by and can heal evil afflictions such as this.'"

"But where is she?" Evliit asked. *Who is this woman who knows my name… and what I can do?* "Didn't she come with you?"

"For a bit, yes," Praedhos said. "She led me to the path into your woods, then stopped. She said she could come no farther. She looked… sad. I told her she'd already done more than anyone could ask."

He swallowed.

"'Tell Evliit that Jenna sent you,' she said. 'And tell him to fret not for her; she is at peace.' Then she smiled and walked back into the mist. She disappeared."

"Jenna." The world seemed to go still around him.

"Yes, Jenna," Praedhos said. He studied Evliit's face. "You know of her, I assume?"

A wave of emotion washed over Evliit — grief, wonder, disbelief, and something like joy. He drew a deep breath and steadied himself.

"You are fortunate she passed your way," he said quietly. "She saved your life."

"I know it," Praedhos said. "She led me directly to you." He hesitated. "Is she—?"

"She is a friend," Evliit said. He rose and fetched clean dressing from the cabinet. "Now let me redress your wound. You should rest. One does not recover from an ordeal such as this easily."

"Thank you," Praedhos said, grasping Evliit's hand. "Truly."

"Thank the Creator for your healing," Evliit replied. "In His infinite power and wisdom, He has blessed us both with this gift of His grace. Now rest, and let His healing finish its work."

"When next you see your friend," Praedhos murmured, "give her my thanks as well."

"I will," Evliit said softly. "I will indeed."

He thought of Jenna — and for the first time since her death, he saw her not in agony, not crucified, not broken… but alive. Smiling. Radiant.

Praedhos would never know how his search for healing had begun the closing of Evliit's own wounds.

CHAPTER 12

A New Calling

On the morning of the third day after Praedhos's arrival, Evliit opened the cage and watched Ebert's messenger pigeons scatter into the grey morning sky. He worried for them; the winds along the Black Mountains could be vicious. Yet the birds danced on the shifting currents with effortless grace.

Their wings beat madly at first, tossed high and low as if they had no control — and then, as always, order emerged from chaos. A direction. A purpose. Evliit smiled as they twisted and sped toward their destinations.

"You've sent out the pigeons. What's the occasion?" Praedhos asked. He had come up the hill without Evliit noticing.

"Well, good morning!" Evliit said. "How are you feeling?"

"Much better now, thanks to you," Praedhos replied.

"I pray your healing continues," Evliit said. "As for the occasion — there are things my friends must know. The energy in the Black Mountains has changed. The darkness I guarded here no longer occupies this place. And though I thought I might never leave these mountains again, I've realized my time here is ending."

"Your time here is ending?" Praedhos asked. "Then you're leaving?"

"Yes," Evliit said simply.

"But where are you going?"

Evliit paused. "When you attacked Broeden's castle, did you see a female warrior — a witch who drew the life force from her victims?"

Praedhos frowned. "No, I'm sorry. I never saw any women there. Why do you ask?"

"I lost a friend to this Huntress not six months ago. I mean to find him and bring him back. Your appearance here — the weaving worm — these are signs. Signs that change everything. Now I must send word to Mategaladh, Tophian, and the others. The Watchers must gather against Broeden and his Huntress."

"Watchers?" Praedhos repeated. "The chanting of monks is not what I pictured when I picked up my sword to make war on Broeden."

"Broeden does not die easily, as you've discovered." Evliit closed the pigeon cage. "And be wary of assumptions. Not all Watchers are healers and chanting monks."

"If they're capable of infecting a man with a weaving worm, then I already count them as deadly," Praedhos said. "My eyes have been opened."

Evliit remembered Elder Faldhra's letters. "Dark magic to fight dark magic," he murmured.

"You call upon dark wizards?" Praedhos asked. "But darkness is evil — pure and simple."

"Is not evil a matter of the heart?" Evliit asked. "Some of the holiest Watchers were chosen as Spellmakers." He looked toward the early morning sky. "My friend Tophian would say that those who surround themselves with darkness are eventually consumed by it."

A faint smile touched his lips.

"And Mategaladh would respond that even the smallest light can be seen in the darkest night."

Evliit placed a hand on Praedhos's shoulder. "I know not whether such darkness can be controlled. My problem with the Spellmakers is simpler: how to know where their loyalties truly lie."

Beautiful shades of purple and red streaked the thin clouds on the horizon.

"I myself have been swallowed by darkness," Evliit said quietly. "Only by the Creator's grace was I not destroyed. I cannot help but think the Spellmakers were doomed from the start. Such battles wither even the most heroic hearts."

"I don't follow," Praedhos admitted.

Evliit smiled. "No matter. It seems that after months of isolation, the curse of Jaros's tomes has lifted from my shoulders. Something new is unfolding. I know in my soul that the Huntress and I are destined to meet again."

Praedhos shielded his eyes and scanned the horizon. The birds were long gone. "What makes you think the Watchers will come?"

"There are no assurances," Evliit said with a shrug. "Mategaladh and Tophian will be glad to know our time apart has ended. They'll come. But the others… my only hope is that Mategaladh's and Tophian's influence will be enough."

Evliit gathered the last scraps of parchment from the warped grey table where he had scrawled his messages.

"The Watchers have always been a force for good. Their disciplines often require solitary lives, but they will not fail mankind in its greatest hour of need — regardless of what they think of me."

"What is it they hold against you?" Praedhos asked.

"I gave up a chance to lead them for the woman I loved. When they needed me, I wasn't there." Evliit stared at the drifting clouds. "And I had charge over two things: a monastery and a pile of old books." He exhaled. "Neither still exists."

"Oh," Praedhos said softly, lowering his head.

"Come," Evliit said. "Let's go back down. I'll show you my garden."

"Your garden?"

"Yes. Are you up to it?"

Praedhos glanced at his side. "Yes. It's still painful, but I can't tell you how good it feels to be rid of that thing." His voice thickened. He looked up at Evliit with misty eyes. "I don't know these men you speak of, but I can tell you this: you saved me. No matter what's come before or what they think you've done, I owe you my life. I will spend the rest of my days repaying that debt."

He extended his right hand.

The emotion in Praedhos's face caught Evliit off guard. "Oh, Praedhos," he said gently. He grasped the man's hand with a firm, steady grip. "You owe me no debt. Give your praise to the Creator."

Evliit gestured down the path. "The garden, shall we?"

"Of course," Praedhos said.

They started down from the small hill where the pigeons' cages sat. Evliit noticed Praedhos grimacing once or twice when the shin-deep snow forced him to shift his weight suddenly, but the man never complained.

Evliit felt a renewed sense of peace as they stepped into the garden. The longer days at winter's end had left only a dusting of snow upon the pillars and planters. Grinning, he swept a hand around him.

"Welcome to the Garden of Huergol."

"You did this?" Praedhos asked.

"No — this garden is ancient. I merely cleared away the years of neglect. This is what one does when they've too much time on their hands," Evliit said with a smile. "At first I tended it in honor of my friend Ebert. I didn't know how much joy I'd find in caring for it." He pointed to one of the pillars, where artisans had etched images of the Watchers of old and the Bhre-Nora. "I wish we could have seen it in its heyday."

Praedhos surveyed the twisting paths and stone planters. "It really is beautiful."

Evliit sat on the grey stone edge of a planter and took in the garden's quiet majesty. "Yes. Especially now that spring's coming."

Praedhos sat opposite him. "And peaceful. It's very peaceful here."

They sat in silence for a short while, letting the stillness settle around them.

"You know," Evliit said at last, "the Watcher Huergol lived in a time of turmoil. He once wrote, 'I begin to fear we might lose our belief in the one Creator and the land of the spirits, that the followers of the Creator would never see a new generation of believers.'" He plucked a leaf from a crimson barberry bush and twirled it between his fingers. "When I read that, I knew exactly what he meant. The Creator seemed distant — unresponsive. His brotherhood was crumbling beneath doubt, beneath the fear that they had dedicated their lives to nothing more than the four winds and an empty sky."

Praedhos shifted, clearly uneasy with such talk, but Evliit continued.

"Just days ago, I felt as Huergol did. For the first time in years, my prayers went unanswered. I questioned everything. I wondered if the answers I'd received in the past were nothing more than tricks of the mind — coincidences." He looked up at the grey sky. "But now… suddenly things look very different."

Evliit rose abruptly and brushed the snow from his trousers. "We should be getting back. You need your rest."

"Of course," Praedhos said.

They walked most of the way back to the cabin before Praedhos spoke again. "You are a man of great faith, Evliit. I grew up in Rion. I listened carefully to the Elders' words… but the things that happened on my journeys — I cannot begin to tell you how they've changed me."

They reached the cabin door. Evliit opened it and gestured for Praedhos to enter, but the soldier remained outside, brow furrowed in thought.

"I, too, thought as Huergol did," Praedhos said quietly. "When the people I served cast me out because of my affliction. I prayed to the Creator, but no answer came. I was filled with such anger."

Evliit nodded. "When things seemed darkest, I came to the garden to pray — but I broke down. I shouted my anger to the heavens. A numbness overtook me, and I sat there for some time, listening to the wind in the honeysuckle. I was broken, ready to give up the fight." He smiled softly. "That night, you appeared on my doorstep."

He gestured again toward the cabin. "Now come in and get some rest."

Two days later, Mategaladh and Tophian's little blue bird returned with a message. On the fourth day after Praedhos's arrival, Evliit awoke at dawn, giddy with anticipation. Praedhos rose not long after.

"I'm going to ride to the top of the mountain to properly greet my friends," Evliit said. He pulled on his boots, stepped outside to saddle Angwen, then poked his head back through the cabin door. "Please, help yourself to food. I'll be back before nightfall — maybe sooner."

"Safe journey," Praedhos said, already rummaging in the pantry.

Evliit smiled and closed the door, mounting Angwen without delay.

When he reached the place where the barrier had once stood, he stopped instinctively. He dismounted and put out his hands, feeling for the familiar repulsion of the energy field — still half expecting it to be there. But there was nothing. After so many months of being unable to pass, it felt surreal that he could simply walk forward now.

With a relieved sigh, he remounted and rode to the mountaintop to watch for Mategaladh and Tophian.

By midmorning, he spotted movement in the distance. Within minutes he recognized his friends — but several other riders, dressed in black, followed behind them.

One of the black-clad riders peeled away from the group and increased his speed, catching up to Mategaladh and Tophian. As they drew closer, Evliit saw gold trim on the rider's black metal pauldrons and delicate red stitching along his robes. The stranger drew even with Evliit's friends at the foot of the final ascent.

Mategaladh had seen Evliit by now. He pointed up the slope, and the three riders exchanged words. The black rider looked up at Evliit, then pulled his horse aside as if to wait.

As Mategaladh and Tophian climbed the mountain, tents began rising below them — many flying black banners that looked disturbingly similar to those flown by Broeden's armies. Evliit frowned.

But his misgivings vanished when Mategaladh galloped up with a broad smile. Both men dismounted and embraced.

"Evliit!" Mategaladh said. "I can't tell you how good it is to see you!"

Tophian dismounted as well and embraced him, though with less enthusiasm.

"My friend," Evliit said.

Tophian grunted. "Glad to see you outside your bubble."

A flap of a banner caught Evliit's eye, reminding him of his concern. "It's good to see you both, but I must ask — what's happening? Who are these men?"

"These are our brothers," Mategaladh said, clapping him on the back.

"Spellmakers?" Evliit asked. "Why do they fly Broeden's flag?"

"Oh no, Evliit — that's not Broeden's flag!" Mategaladh exclaimed. "These are the followers of Amphileph."

"I wouldn't lead with that when you greet them," Tophian muttered.

Evliit shot him a look. "You haven't changed a bit."

"My skills are exceeded only by my manners," Tophian said. Then, unexpectedly, he smiled — a real smile, the first Evliit had ever seen from him. "I didn't have a chance to properly thank you for saving my life when last we met." The smile faded, replaced by earnestness. "Thank you, Evliit. Truly."

"Well, I stand corrected," Evliit said. "The world may actually have come to an end."

The three of them laughed.

"You would have done it for me," Evliit said.

Their laughter died quickly.

"That brings up an excellent point," Tophian said. "Because you see, Evliit, I *couldn't* do that for you. Neither can I open a portal to the Underworld or construct a barrier through which other Watchers cannot pass — especially one as resourceful as Mategaladh."

"You've made quite the stir," Mategaladh said. "The destruction of Jaros's tomes, the opening of the Underworld, the creation of this barrier — when you sent word that the barrier was gone, our brothers were beside themselves. They all want to know your intentions — especially the Spellmakers."

"The problem," Tophian added, "is that we're not entirely sure *why*. We can't tell if they want to hail you as their leader… or kill you."

Evliit looked down at the assembly of black tents. He counted thirty-two riders. "Are you *trying* to make me regret closing the portal?"

"He who can lock someone out can potentially lock someone in," Tophian said. "That worries them."

"Then they haven't come to join me in my attack against Broeden?" Evliit asked.

"I'm sorry… no," Mategaladh said. "This is about the destruction of Jaros's tomes. Some of the men below are none too happy with you."

"I suppose this is what Clogren calls 'giving us a moment,'" Tophian said, flicking his head toward the tents.

The black rider had left the camp and was making his way up the mountainside toward them.

Mategaladh placed a hand on Evliit's arm. "Evliit, Tophian and I are with you."

Evliit leaned toward him. "Things are not as they once were. These past months have changed me. You need not worry about my fearing the Spellmakers."

Mategaladh and Tophian exchanged a look — not of doubt, but of recalibration. Evliit was not the man they had left behind.

Clogren closed the last three hundred yards between them. He halted his horse a few yards away.

"I am Clogren, a conjurer and follower of Amphileph," he said. His face was unreadable. He did not extend a hand.

"I'm Evliit."

"We have come to discuss Jaros's tomes," Clogren said. "Would you meet with us in our camp?"

"I welcome the discussion," Evliit replied. "But I would invite you and your brothers to my garden. It is peaceful, secluded. We may speak openly there."

"Then it will be so," Clogren said. "Tonight?"

"Forgive me, Clogren," Evliit said, "but I did not expect so many. I would gladly host you, but my stores are too meager for a group of your size."

"Then I insist you join us in our camp," Clogren said. "My brothers are eager to meet you."

"I cannot," Evliit answered. "I am caring for an injured man — Praedhos, a soldier of the guard — and I will not leave him alone for so many hours. I must return to tend to him this afternoon."

"Then let us meet in the early morrow," Mategaladh said. "We can share morning prayers in the gardens. Tophian and I will show them the way."

"Excellent," Evliit said. "The garden is beautiful in the morning light."

Clogren nodded curtly. "Until tomorrow, then." He turned and spurred his horse back toward the tents.

Mategaladh waited until Clogren was well out of earshot before turning to Evliit. "So what's the plan here?" He cocked his head. "I assume you have one."

"It's time to avenge the wrongs of Broeden," Evliit said. "The Watchers must revolt against him and end his terror for good."

"Maybe you misunderstood," Tophian said. "The Elders threw the Spellmakers to the wolves. They owe the Watchers nothing. They've come to pass judgment on you for destroying Jaros's tomes — not to join your personal vendetta."

"If they're here, together, I don't care why," Evliit said. He swung himself onto Angwen. "I'll see you tomorrow. Enjoy your dinner, my friends."

Evliit rose before daybreak. He dressed quickly and took a few fire sticks from the hearth to light the urns he'd placed along the trail, illuminating the way for their guests.

Praedhos rolled over in his cot. "Going down now?" he rasped. "When should I bring the wine?"

"When their attendants come with food," Evliit said. "We'll have morning prayers first. It'll be a little while."

"Very well," Praedhos murmured, rolling back over.

Evliit walked the trail, lighting each urn as he passed. The temperature had risen overnight; spring was fighting to reclaim the Black Mountains from winter's last grip.

When he reached the garden, he knelt and prayed for wisdom in dealing with the Watchers. Peace settled over him. A hint of jasmine drifted from the brass burners along the path. He gave thanks to the Creator for the trials of the Underworld — for they had remade him, forged something stronger in him than he had ever imagined.

He rose, squared his shoulders, and walked to the garden gate to wait.

Before long, torchlight crowned the mountainside. A line of men came over the summit, making their way toward the garden. Evliit stood tall at the arched entrance.

Mategaladh and Tophian arrived first, followed by a large group of men in light-colored robes. Behind them came a smaller group dressed in black, led by a dark-haired figure. Clogren walked at his side, somber as ever.

I remember you. You are Amphileph.

For a moment, Evliit was back in Aleris's vision — the blackened earth, the robed figures, the burning eyes. They were the eyes of this man, Amphileph, the Spellmakers' most potent conjurer.

Tophian's voice pulled him back. "Our host," he said, stepping forward. "Evliit — a man willing to do what is right, regardless of personal sacrifice."

Mategaladh's voice was smaller than usual. "Amphileph... will you lead us in morning prayers?"

"Ardidhus loves his prayers," Amphileph said. "Let him lead."

One of the black-clad Spellmakers stepped forward. "Yes, of course," Ardidhus said. "In honor of his passing, I will lead the Liturgy of Jaros."

He took his place at the head of the group. The others faced him and recited the liturgy in unison. Evliit knew none of it, so he bowed his head and listened.

The liturgy continued until shortly after sunrise, when the clatter of bottles made everyone turn toward the garden entrance. Praedhos stood just outside the gate, holding a tray of red wine and dried venison.

He gave an embarrassed cough. "I'm sorry to interrupt."

Ardidhus finished the last words of the prayer. The group murmured among themselves. Evliit waved Praedhos inside and pointed to a planter.

"Set it there, Praedhos. Thank you."

Praedhos flushed. "I'm sorry."

"Not to worry," Evliit said with a reassuring smile. "We were nearly done. Besides, they have more pressing matters on their minds."

"What do you mean?" Praedhos whispered.

"Take a look around."

Praedhos did — and leaned in. "I've seen friendlier faces across a battlefield."

"Some are friends," Evliit said. "But the Spellmakers look none too happy."

After the meal, Evliit set down his pipe and cup beside a planter of gardenias. Winter had stolen their blossoms, but their dark green leaves still held a faint, sweet fragrance. He inhaled it, smiled, and glanced at the clear sky.

"Lead us now," he whispered to the heavens.

Then he turned and walked to the center of the garden.

"I have something else to show you — something extraordinary I discovered during my time alone here. Will you indulge me?"

"Very well," Ardidhus said.

"We delay this further?" Clogren asked.

"Just a moment more, Clogren," Evliit said. "Please — follow me."

He led them out of the garden and a short way up the mountainside. The

Black Mountains were majestic in the midmorning light, their inky peaks steaming where snow had fallen overnight. But even as Evliit admired them, a sharp pain stabbed through his body. He stumbled.

Mategaladh hurried to his side. "Are you all right?"

"Yes," Evliit said. "It isn't far now."

But the pain spread. The dark spirits had returned, clawing at him from within. The voices were louder than ever — visceral, panicked, *terrified.*

Evliit stumbled again and gripped Mategaladh's arm.

"I'm concerned," Mategaladh whispered.

"Almost there," Evliit said through clenched teeth.

The path ended at a plateau. Stonemasons had carved a wide walkway into the mountain's glossy stone. Evliit led them beneath a stone archway into a courtyard centered around a round marble prayer table eight paces across. A second arch rose above it, its pinnacle thirty feet high.

"This is where prophets of old bore witness to their brethren," Evliit said. "A holy place — and fitting that I should do likewise. Gather round, all of you."

He didn't want to rush them, but the pain was becoming unbearable.

He climbed the steps and stood at the center of the table. The Spellmakers looked skeptical, but they filed into the courtyard, each finding a place with a clear view.

Ardidhus spoke quietly with Mategaladh and Tophian, then motioned toward Evliit. "It is time for Evliit to give his witness regarding Jaros's tomes."

"Yes, very well," Evliit said. "I—"

A searing pain tore through his chest. He doubled over. The screams of the Underworld roared in his ears. His whole body felt aflame. He saw Praedhos and Mategaladh speaking, but their voices were drowned out.

Get control. Get control.

With immense effort, he straightened.

Mategaladh stepped to the edge of the table. "Evliit — something's wrong."

"The curse of the tomes," Evliit gasped. He looked out over the assembly. "My brothers… a moment, please. Let us begin with Praedhos. Let him tell you of his encounter with Broeden."

"We did not come all this way to listen to your servant!" Clogren shouted.

Praedhos bristled. "I am a guardsman of Rion!"

"Praedhos, please!" Evliit cried. Sweat poured down his face. "Brothers — listen to this man's story. I will prove to you that there are far greater threats to the people of Erathe than I will ever be — far greater losses than that of Jaros's tomes!"

"He speaks the truth!" Tophian shouted. "I told him to burn the tomes the moment I laid eyes on them!"

A rumble of dissonance swept through the Spellmakers.

"Let the soldier bear witness!" one of the Watchers called.

"Hear, hear!" another said.

Ardidhus stepped onto the table. "Quiet! Quiet down! If we are to judge well, then we have time to hear all. Say your piece, soldier."

Praedhos looked at Evliit, eyes wide. "Where do I begin?"

"Tell them the task the Elders gave you," Evliit said. "Tell them what happened at Broeden's castle."

He locked eyes with Praedhos — and when he saw fear give way to resolve, he stepped down from the table.

Praedhos walked up the steps to the center of the table. He told them how the Elders had sent his company to kill Broeden in secret, how he had seen the old wizard with his own eyes. He recounted the horrors in the pits behind Broeden's castle, his infection with the weaving worm, and the efforts Evliit took to save him.

Then Praedhos defiantly lifted his shirt. Several Watchers and Spellmakers stepped closer to inspect his side.

"The wound is almost completely healed!" one Watcher marveled.

Still, a snake-shaped strip of purple scar tissue ran from just below Praedhos's ribs to his hip, and dozens of pockmarks riddled his skin — the trail of the weaving worm's tail.

The crowd erupted in noise.

Praedhos pointed to Evliit and shouted over them. "This man saved my life! No matter what you think of him for what happened to those books, he saved my life. He could have let me die. He owed me nothing — but he healed me instead!"

"You did well, Praedhos," Evliit said. "You have my thanks."

Praedhos looked indignant. "But what of Broeden? Will they help us or not?"

"Come down, Praedhos," Evliit said, offering a hand.

Praedhos flushed. "Of course."

"What about the creature's source?" Tophian asked. "Who else but Broeden can conjure such magic?"

Evliit pointed to the Spellmakers. "They can."

Silence fell like a hammer.

"What did you say?" Ardidhus demanded. "Does he dare lump us in with Broeden?"

Tophian winced. "That wasn't exactly where I was going with that, kid."

"The Darkness knew of the tomes' existence," Evliit said. "It was only a matter of time before they acquired them. There was too much potential for destruction. Tophian saw it at once — I did not."

"Is this what we traveled here to hear?" Amphileph spat. "Judgment from one whom we have come to judge? This man is not part of our brotherhood! Did he not have every assurance — even the blessing of the Creator Himself? And yet he denied the Creator's wishes! Did he not abandon us when Broeden ravaged our lands?"

He pointed at Evliit. "Where were you when the Elders sacrificed blood and treasure to stop Broeden?"

He turned to the others. "And now he has destroyed one of the greatest treasures of our age — texts whose mere reading could impart incredible abilities. Knowledge some of our own died to obtain! And what of the barrier? The opening of the Underworld? He is no leader of ours! How can someone so reckless deserve the title of Sword Bearer?"

Clogren began circling Evliit, studying him. "And what other abilities will he manifest? We'll never know — he destroyed the tomes that revealed them!" He turned to Mategaladh. "You feared he had been consumed by darkness when last you saw him, did you not?"

Mategaladh looked at Evliit. "Yes, but—"

"What better distraction from the real issue than to stir up talk of Broeden!" Clogren shouted.

The Spellmakers murmured their agreement.

"Calm yourself, Clogren," Tophian said. "It's beneath you to insult your host."

"Speak not to me, Tophian!" Clogren snapped. "I'll not bear your lectures!"

"Enough!" Ardidhus barked. "Bickering gets us nowhere. Amphileph — what do you propose?"

"Surely some penalty must be administered for such a crime!" Amphileph said. "There is no question of his guilt. He does not deny destroying the tomes!"

Evliit looked over the assembly. Some of the older monks looked away. The Spellmakers glared at him. A distant chant rose — words he could not make out. The pain inside him surged.

He turned to Praedhos. "You are not in my debt, my friend. I release you from whatever service you believe you owe me. Leave now."

Praedhos looked stricken. "How can you say that? You shame me by turning me away."

"Praedhos, I beg you."

There isn't much time now.

"You saved my life," Praedhos said. "How does a man repay such a debt? Am I not worthy to serve you?"

"Only the Creator is worthy of your service," Evliit said. He clutched his stomach. "I must ask something of these men now — and I must do it alone." He lowered his voice. "Leave before things spiral out of control."

The fire ignited in his belly. The voices screamed in unison:

"No! No! Praedhosss! S-stay with ussss!"

Praedhos recoiled.

Evliit forced his eyes shut and wrestled back control. "There's no more time, Praedhos."

"Back, everyone!" Tophian shouted. "Mategaladh — it's happening again!"

The Watchers retreated. The Spellmakers conjured shields of shimmering force.

Praedhos stepped back but hesitated. "I will not leave! Tell me what I can do!"

Evliit grabbed his arm. "It's too late!" He pushed Praedhos away and staggered back up the steps onto the prayer table.

"Another sign!" Amphileph cried. "He cannot hold the darkness at bay!"

"We must destroy him now!" Clogren shouted.

Mategaladh and Tophian moved forward. "No!"

Evliit lifted his trembling hands to the heavens. "I have read Jaros's tomes — and now I come to you a man in ruin!" He looked down at the Watchers. "Darkness waited untold years to be released from those tomes! It is inside me now! Pray for me, I beg you!"

Several Watchers raised their hands to the heavens.

Evliit shouted upward: "Let them witness Your power, O Great One! Let them know You alone are the Creator, ruler of the Third Domain, spirit world of our ancestors! Take me now — or leave no doubt that I *am* the sword bearer!"

His body convulsed. His mouth opened, and screaming voices poured out.

"Destroy us!"

Black vapors streamed from his mouth. The spirits swarmed above him, then drifted toward the Spellmakers.

"Now!" Amphileph shouted. "*Escorpa! Ha-rha!*"

"*Escorpa! Ha-rha!*" the Spellmakers cried.

The spirits shrieked. Several burst into showers of sparkling light. The rest hurled themselves at the Spellmakers' shields. Some scattered red embers across the surface; others passed through.

Nine Spellmakers screamed as invisible claws tore into them. Their bodies fell. The spirits surged toward the Watchers, killing seven of the oldest first.

Evliit threw back his cloak, revealing the hilt of his sword. The spirits halted their attack and streaked toward him. He leaned back his head and opened his mouth. The vapor streamed back inside.

He closed his mouth and held his breath. It felt as though the spirits were shredding him from within.

He looked out over the devastation. Shock was etched on every face.

He placed his bare hand on the hilt. Warm, prickling energy danced across his skin.

"This sword was given to me by the Creator Himself!"

He drew it. A bolt of energy erupted from the blade and struck him in the chest. With all his strength, he held on.

"Creator!" he cried. "We are ready to watch over these lands as You have commanded! Let each one know his calling!"

Everything froze. The Watchers and Spellmakers stood motionless.

Evliit felt his heart skip — once, twice — then stop. He fell to his knees. He wanted to cry out, but the dark voices screamed in agony. He fell forward, catching himself with one hand, clutching the sword with the other.

He heaved up a black liquid. It sizzled on the sacred table like water on hot steel. His strength failed. He collapsed.

Evliit rolled onto his back, resting his head on the cold stone. His clothing felt weightless, floating around him.

For the first time in months, there was silence.

Nothing but peaceful silence.

He opened his eyes again, and his body began to float upward, turning slowly in the air above the prayer table. He relaxed his grip on his sword's handle and watched it drift from his hand. It rotated in the air until the tip pointed downward, then slowed to a stop, hovering just below the arch at the center of the prayer table. The sword began to glow with an intense white light, and as Evliit turned in the air, he saw the survivors' eyes reflecting the radiance like mirrors.

Search our hearts, oh Creator of all things!

Time itself seemed to slow. Evliit watched sequential arcs of lightning leap from the sword. One by one, each arc struck a Watcher or Spellmaker in the chest. Their faces softened, and each slowly closed his eyes as though falling into a peaceful sleep.

Evliit drifted downward. His feet touched the stone beside the prayer table. His heart lurched—once, twice—and then thundered back to life. He gasped a deep breath.

Lightning from the sword carved glowing grooves into the tabletop, dividing its surface into segments like slices of a great wheel. When the bursts finally ceased, symbols and writing adorned each section.

Time resumed.

Before their limp bodies could collapse, an unseen force lifted each man touched by the sword's power and placed him gently on his knees around the table, facing its center. To Evliit's relief, their eyes opened. They looked upward.

"Watch over my people!" boomed a voice from the heavens. "Submit yourselves to Evliit, for I have named him master over all who gather here!"

All turned toward him.

Evliit knelt before the segment etched with the sword. Slowly the others regained their senses. One spoke—and then all joined in:

"Sword bearer."

They bowed their heads.

Amphileph and the Spellmakers avoided his gaze, but Evliit sensed no threat from them now.

Including Evliit, there were twenty men in all. Citanth and Ardidhus had come from the Lakes of Aertos in the west. From Calarph in the north knelt Tophian, Mategaladh, and Hiadhlian. Clogren, Odhramorus, Hrast, and Sardhor represented the Northern Plains, while Amphileph alone stood for the Black Mountains. Riandhian, Arondar, and Lodhnra hailed from the lands bordering the eastern deserts. Madhis and Emordhos had journeyed from the southern cliffs near the sea, and Rorindan, Olidan, and Faldhian from the deep forests of the West.

And when Evliit saw who occupied the final place at the table, he doubted his eyes.

Praedhos.

The sword descended to the table's center, its tip hovering just above the marble. Evliit stood and reached toward it. The blade drifted into his hand as though eager to return. He grasped the hilt and sheathed it.

"It is time," he declared, turning toward the garden.

Ardidhus called after him. "What do you command, sword bearer?"

Evliit stopped and faced them.

"Let us bury our dead," he said, "and prepare for war."

At Evliit's request, most of his brethren returned to their lands to gather what forces they could from the loose alliances of tribes and villages scattered across the known world. He, Tophian, and Mategaladh prepared to ride southwest over the Black Mountains to seek aid from the Elders of Rion.

As they topped the mountain peak, they stopped and looked down upon the ruins of the monastery. All three dismounted. Evliit bowed his head and prayed for Ebert's safe return. Then they remounted and began the slow descent, speaking as they went.

"Amphileph was none too happy," Tophian said.

"Nor Praedhos," Mategaladh added. "He wanted to bear witness to the Elders of his healing."

"An attack on Broeden's stronghold will require the strength of an army unlike any ever seen," Evliit replied. "The scattered militias of the tribes will never unite unless the full force of the Rion Guard stands with them."

"But the two of them together — you think that's wise?" Tophian asked.

"I need Amphileph in the south to gather men and wood for building catapults. There's no assaulting Broeden's fortress without them. He can return to his Spellmakers once he secures the resources. Praedhos will oversee the construction."

"How did you convince Praedhos to leave your side?" Tophian asked.

"By emphasizing both the challenge and the necessity of the task," Evliit said.

"Overseeing the building of the catapults and getting them to the Northern Plains before the second full moon is a tall order indeed," Mategaladh said.

"Time is against us," Evliit replied. "We must launch this campaign before summer has come and gone. A prolonged siege of Broeden's castle would force us to endure the winter of the Northern Plains."

"Which will thin our ranks and give Broeden's creatures the advantage," Mategaladh said. "They seem immune to the cold."

"It's all for nothing if you can't convince the Elders," Tophian added.

"Then I'll convince them," Evliit said.

Over the next four days, they made their way south into Rion. When the dirt road gave way to cobblestone, signaling their entry into the city's outskirts, Mategaladh leaned back in his saddle and sighed.

"So we return to Rion," he said. "Bearing grave news, no less."

"Let's keep out of the arena this time," Tophian suggested. "Could we try that."

Evliit smiled. "Yes, I vote for that."

They rode through throngs of citizens and past a magnificent fountain on the northern side of the city. At its center stood a marble figure on a pedestal — Elder Jonas. Marble guardsmen encircled him, heads bowed in reverence, shields resting at their feet.

"He doesn't think much of himself, does he?" Tophian muttered.

"Oh no, no, no," Mategaladh warned. "None of that. The Rionese love Jonas. Watch your tongue."

"I'd rather him say it now and get it all out," Evliit said.

The three men laughed and eased their horses down the Northern Road toward the Temple of the Elders.

As they approached, Evliit noticed something different from their last visit. He was no longer an anonymous traveler. People stared. Some followed. Their expressions were not exactly warm.

No sooner had they dismounted at the temple steps than someone shouted, "Is this not Evliit, the one who supposedly died to protect the Monastery of Ardidhus? Seize him!"

The temple guard surged forward.

Evliit raised his hand. "Things have changed, brothers. I come of my own volition to speak with Elder Jonas. I'll not be manhandled."

The Rion Guard drew their swords. Townspeople scattered.

Evliit drew his sword. Eerie blue flames rose from it.

The guards froze.

"Gives you some pause, does it not?" Evliit said. He wasn't smiling.

"I'm not sure this is how we want to go about this," Mategaladh murmured, moving closer.

"We're here to talk with Elder Jonas," Evliit said. "There'll be no trouble unless you make it."

"I thought the kid said he was worried about me making trouble," Tophian grumbled.

"You'll not get the chance," Mategaladh replied.

"What's the plan now?" Tophian asked.

"We go to see Jonas," Evliit said, and he began to ascend the steps. Mategaladh and Tophian followed, watching the guard carefully.

"Evliit of Arentis," a voice called from above. "I thought never to see your face again. What business have you here?"

Elder Jonas stood at the top of the stairs.

"We come with news of your kinsmen," Evliit said.

"Please, put away your sword," Jonas said. He waved his hand, and the guards sheathed their weapons. "There's no need for that."

Evliit looked around, then sheathed his sword as well.

Jonas nodded. "Have the stable boys tend to their horses!" he shouted. Draping the excess of his pallium over his arm, he said, "Follow me."

He led them through the temple into a white-columned atrium where Elders, attendants, and guardsmen lined the periphery. Sunlight made the white stone glow. Jonas ascended a dais and sat upon a throne facing them. An attendant brought him a golden chalice; he drank, dismissed the boy, and turned to Evliit.

"What say you?"

"Elder Jonas," Evliit said. "We've come to give an account of Rion's forces sent to the Northern Plains after the attack on the Monastery of Ardidhus."

A hush fell over the atrium.

"Speak," Jonas said.

Evliit squared his shoulders. "My friends and I witnessed the annihilation of an army of guardsmen at the hands of the dark one's Huntress, just north of the Black Mountains. We came to their aid and confronted her, but she prevailed and took away my friend — a monk known as Ebert."

"How dare you call yourself a friend to the monks of Rion!" someone shouted.

"Silence!" Jonas commanded.

Evliit continued. "The Huntress is a clear and present danger to Rion and all its outposts. The dark one builds his armies once more, and she will lead them to the very steps of your temples."

Jonas leaned forward. "You, wizard — you believe this too?"

Mategaladh bowed his head. "Make no mistake, my lord. These are his intentions."

"The Watchers and their sword bearer will take the war to him," Evliit said. "We call upon the guard to join us."

A rumble swept the room, but Jonas raised a hand and silence returned.

"Annihilation, you say," Jonas murmured. "I would hear more. What happened to the guardsmen we sent?"

"The dark one fielded familiars and giant men — seven, perhaps eight feet tall," Evliit said. "The guard held their own, and we joined them. Victory seemed near, but then the Huntress attacked."

He lowered his gaze. "She drew the life force from their bodies, one by one. She nearly killed us as well. When she found us more difficult prey than expected, she fled into the night sky, carrying Ebert with her."

A man beside Jonas spoke. "Is it not strange that this man escaped when our holy warriors did not?"

Jonas nodded. "What my counsel asks troubles me as well. How is this so?"

"Only by the grace of this sword, bestowed on me by the Bhre-Nora," Evliit said.

He drew the sword slowly. Guards moved, but Jonas halted them with a gesture.

Evliit raised the blade high.

"Creator!" he cried. "Give them a sign of my obedience to Your will!"

A blinding light burst forth. The temple shook. Guards rushed to shield Jonas — then froze as three winged beings descended through the open roof. The Bhre-Nora. Aleris among them.

They knelt at Evliit's feet.

Aleris rose and faced Jonas.

"Elder Jonas," he said. "You have long been righteous. We appear so that all may know: this is the sword bearer. He is the Creator's chosen one."

Jonas stared, speechless.

Aleris turned back to Evliit. "You, and your children, and your children's children after them, will carry this charge: defend the weak, battle evil, and guide mankind toward union with the Creator."

"Let it be so," Evliit said.

"Let it be so," Aleris echoed. He bowed once more, and the Bhre-Nora ascended into the heavens.

Evliit sheathed his sword.

Jonas looked around the room, awe frozen on his face. At last he spoke:

"All hail Evliit, the bearer of the sword!"

The crowd answered as one:

"All hail Evliit, the bearer of the sword!"

Jonas approached and knelt at Evliit's feet. The entire hall followed.

"What do you require of us?" Jonas asked.

Evliit lifted him gently. "Stand — all of you. I am a servant of the Creator, the same as you." He turned to the assembly. "The time has come. The dark one's age may be ending, but the Huntress's power grows. He will extend his reach through her, even beyond his own death. We stand together — or we die alone."

"The guard will join you!" Jonas declared. "We will avenge our brothers and end the dark one's reign! What say you, brothers?"

The Rion Guard slammed their spears on the floor in three thunderous bursts.

"War!" they shouted.

"We shall flood the battlefield with our guardsmen!" Jonas cried. "We shall rain arrows and blades upon these creatures! Generals, ready your legions! Let us destroy the great evil of our time!"

The hall erupted in a fevered roar.

"Send word to all tribes and villages!" Jonas commanded. "The Watchers and the Rion Guard call upon every man willing to wield a sword! We march northeast to Broeden's lands — and we will rain all hell upon him!"

CHAPTER 13

THE NORTHERN PLAINS

Rendaya awoke on her side in her bed. The floor swam slowly into focus. Winter must have passed, for the light spilling in from her balcony shimmered like threads of gold across the stone. The curtains rustled gently in the warm breeze drifting through the open shutters.

A man's face leaned over her. He studied her eyes, one at a time.

"Thanks be to the Creator," he murmured. "You've rejoined the living. Do you know where you are?"

Rendaya tried to rise, but her limbs felt hollow and weak. She closed her eyes—and instantly she was back in the dungeon, floating above her own body. The monk knelt over her, hands pressed to her neck, blood everywhere.

Her eyes flew open. She reached for her throat. No blood. The skin was whole, smooth, only a faint ridge marking where the wound had been.

"Just take your time," the monk said gently. "Do you remember what happened?"

"Stand back from the Huntress, slave!" someone barked.

Rendaya turned her head. A Camon guard stood just inside her bedroom door, hand on his sword.

"No," she rasped. "No, wait."

The guard stared, astonished that she was speaking.

"Stand down," she commanded, though her voice was barely more than a whisper.

He hesitated, then obeyed, returning to rigid attention.

Rendaya looked back at the monk. His eyes held only kindness and concern.

"Yes," she said. "I remember. The torturer attacked me." She closed her eyes again, seeing the monk's face leaning over her. "You helped me." She felt strange—lighter, as though some weight she had carried for years had slipped from her shoulders.

"Yes," the monk said. "That's right. I'm glad it's returning to you. I was beginning to wonder…"

Rendaya narrowed her eyes. "Wonder what?"

He sighed. "Much time has passed. You awoke the day after your attack, but you never spoke. You just sat here, staring into nothing. Your master was… quite worried."

She wanted to tell him how different she felt now, but the guard's presence pressed at the edge of her awareness. She needed him gone.

She cleared her throat and hardened her voice. "Tell the master I've returned. Leave us."

"At once." The guard shot Ebert a warning look, then exited.

Rendaya waited until the door closed. "I don't even remember your name."

"My name is Ebert," he said, smiling softly.

"Well, Ebert… I don't understand. Why would you help me? I was going to torture you."

"I was there," he said simply. "You were hurt. The Creator gave me the gift of healing, and He places me where He wills so I can use it. I don't believe in coincidences."

Rendaya looked down at her arms—thin, almost fragile. "How long have I been lying here?"

"For just over two months," Ebert said. "Your master swore to put my head on a pole if you didn't recover." He gave a nervous chuckle. "You can imagine how relieved I am to see you awake. My odds were getting worse by the day."

"Two months…" She couldn't grasp it.

"When the Camonra found us in the dungeon, I'd closed your wound, but you'd lost so much blood I wasn't sure you'd live. When your master learned I could heal, he ordered me to care for you. I've tended you as best I could… but this past week, I was struggling to get you to eat."

Rendaya lifted her hands again, studying them. "Fetch me my looking glass."

"Of course." Ebert retrieved it from her vanity and sat beside her, offering it.

She raised the mirror. The face staring back was gaunt, hollow-cheeked. She pushed back her hair. The scar traced a long, thin line across her neck. Her breath caught. The enormity of it all crashed over her—and she burst into tears.

"Oh my," Ebert said, looking down and wringing his hands. "Perhaps you'd like some food or drink, mistress?"

Her tears stopped as abruptly as they'd begun. Heat flushed her cheeks. She was embarrassed he'd seen her weakness—yet strangely, she felt no anger.

"You may call me Rendaya," she said quietly. "You saved my life."

Ebert looked up, then lowered his gaze again. "Rendaya, then. Would you care for something to eat or drink?"

"Yes. I'm famished." A small, bubbling laugh escaped her before she could stop it. She clapped a hand over her mouth. She couldn't remember ever laughing like that. *What is happening to me?*

Ebert smiled. "Very well. I'll return in a moment."

But as he turned toward the door, it opened again. The Camon reentered and dropped to one knee. Ebert immediately followed suit, lowering his gaze. He had clearly learned the routine.

Rendaya heard the rapid clicking of Broeden's insects in the hallway — the unmistakable herald of her master's approach. Moments later, Broeden entered on his throne.

"You've done well to revive her, monk," Broeden said. "It's good to see you've not outlived your usefulness."

"Thank you, master," Ebert murmured, eyes fixed on the floor.

"My Huntress," Broeden said, turning his attention to her. "I am pleased you have rejoined the living. Do you want for anything?"

"My slave was going to fetch me food and drink," Rendaya said.

"Then be about it, slave," Broeden said with a dismissive wave.

Ebert rose and left, the Camon following him out. Broeden's insects scuttled forward, lifting and carrying his throne closer to Rendaya's bedside.

"The healing powers of this monk are unlike any I've seen," Broeden said. "When you have regained your strength, you will take his life force — and use his powers on me."

The words struck Rendaya like a blow to the gut, though her conditioning held her steady. "Yes, master, of course. But… why not have him use his healing powers on you now?"

"No lover of the Creator will ever pray over me!" Broeden roared. He mastered himself a moment later. "I cannot trust these monks," he said more quietly. "You, my beauty, will be the one to heal my brokenness. In you I place my complete faith. Now eat, drink, and recover so you may return to your service."

"Yes, master," Rendaya said.

"Away!" Broeden commanded, and the millipedes clustered beneath his throne, lifting him and carrying him from the room.

Ebert returned shortly after with a tray of bread, dried fish, cheese, and a carafe of wine. Rendaya narrowed her eyes at the Camon, and he closed the door behind Ebert, leaving them alone again.

Ebert set the tray across her legs and helped her sit up. His hand was cold and clammy.

"The master frightens you," Rendaya said.

"Yes," Ebert admitted. "Yes, he does. I've feared for my life more than once here."

"Fear serves slaves well in this place," she said. "You did well to keep your gaze from my master's face. And don't let the Camonra catch you looking at them either. They are his creation, and they can be difficult to control." She touched the scar on her neck. "I suppose you've gathered that already."

Ebert looked down at the floor.

"You may speak freely to me," she said.

"I don't even like being near them," Ebert said. "When the master entered, during the silence, I heard the Camon inhale and exhale. It sounded like a bull breathing. And even staring at the floor, I saw his fist out of the corner of my eye — fingers as thick as carrots, knuckles pressed to the stone. I never want to be in the clutches of a creature like that again."

Rendaya laughed softly. "The master did not create them for their company. It is wise to fear them. Most have served him for many years, and they are loyal. Incidents like what happened to me in the dungeons simply do not occur. The torturer's treachery was the first of its kind."

She stopped. Ebert was watching her with rapt attention, hanging on every word. A strange warmth bloomed in her chest. She smiled — a small, involuntary thing — and touched his arm. Before he could pull away, she felt his life force. It was strong. Clean.

"Had you not been there," she said quietly, "it seems he would have taken my life."

"As I said, the Creator places me where I'm needed. Without His power, I could have done nothing."

That caught her interest. Her only knowledge of this monk's faith came from the scraps she'd absorbed from the monk Broeden had forced her to consume. "Why would your Creator place you in a situation where you would be called upon to save your torturer?"

"I suppose," Ebert said gently, "you've something more important to do than die in Broeden's dungeon."

The words stunned her. She had never once imagined a life beyond the castle walls. The idea left her speechless.

The silence between them grew cold. Ebert shifted, embarrassed. "I'm sure you're hungry. You should eat."

"Yes. I'm starving." She tore a piece of bread in half.

Ebert bowed slightly and moved toward the door.

"No — don't leave," Rendaya said.

He paused, then returned to the chair beside her. He sat quietly, attentive but unobtrusive, while she ate.

Over the next week, Ebert helped Rendaya move about the castle. At first she ventured only as far as the hallway outside her room. Standing made the scar on her neck feel too tight, as though the skin might tear if she straightened fully. But by week's end, she felt ready to appear in Broeden's court again.

Descending the stairs was still difficult, but Ebert offered his arm to steady her. She realized, with a strange flutter in her chest, that it was the first time a man her own age had ever done so. *It truly is a week of firsts.*

When she arrived at Broeden's court, he was already waiting — and he had cleared the chamber of all attendants except the two Camon guards at the door. That was never a good sign.

"Tell your slave to wait outside," Broeden said. "I would speak with you alone."

"Yes, master," Rendaya replied. Without looking at Ebert, she said, "Wait for me outside." She forced the contempt she knew Broeden expected.

Ebert obeyed at once.

Broeden pointed to the Camonra. "Leave us!" he commanded. The guards bowed and exited, closing the doors behind them.

Broeden wasted no time. "What have you learned of the monk's powers?" he asked, hunger in his eyes.

"He says his powers come from his Creator," Rendaya said. "A god that cannot be seen."

"I know of their mysticism!" Broeden snapped. "How is it that you have spent days with him, walking the castle, and this is all you know? What do you do with all that time?"

He slowly raised his hand and curled it into a fist.

Rendaya's throat constricted instantly. She clawed at her neck as her feet lifted from the floor. She drifted helplessly across the chamber until she hung before him.

"When I tell you to learn the monk's secrets, I mean quickly!" Broeden hissed. "Does it look to you as though I have time for you to dally with him, making conversation?" He coughed violently, spitting phlegm onto the floor. Even this exertion cost him.

A burning pain flared along the scar at her neck.

"I may not possess his powers of healing," Broeden snarled, "but I still excel at powers of destruction!"

Rendaya felt something wet on her hand. She pulled her fingers away — they were drenched in blood.

"I can open that wound without rising from this chair," Broeden said. "Do not imagine my confinement limits my wrath." He lifted his chin.

"Guard!"

The doors swung open. A Camon stepped in. "Yes, lord!"

"Bring in the monk!" Broeden commanded. He shot Rendaya a look of disgust. "You've left me no choice but to let this degenerate pray over me!"

The Camon seized Ebert and dragged him inside. Ebert looked up at Rendaya in terror before remembering himself and fixing his gaze on the floor.

"My Huntress has failed me!" Broeden said. "You care for her, monk — so hear me well: use your powers. Heal my body, or she dies!"

Rendaya stared at him, stunned. Surely he bluffed. She had dedicated her entire life to pleasing him.

"Please, master!" Ebert said. "Rendaya has done nothing to deserve your anger!"

"Do you hear the slave?" Broeden roared. "He calls you by your name as if he holds rank in my court!"

Broeden released his grip on her, and she collapsed to the floor.

"Guard! Rip out his tongue!"

The Camon strode to a cauldron and withdrew a pair of pinchers. Their three-pronged tips glowed red-hot.

Rendaya leapt to her feet, pressing a hand to her bleeding neck. "He must speak incantations!" she lied. "Remove his tongue and we lose the chance to use his healing powers!"

"He has possessed you, my Huntress!" Broeden cried. "His words have you enthralled! Rip out his tongue before he ensnares us all!"

The Camon advanced on Ebert — but another Camon burst into the chamber.

"My lord, forgive me!" he said, dropping to one knee. "Our scouts have sighted an army approaching from the southwest!"

A battle horn sounded outside. Broeden's insects swarmed beneath his throne and carried him toward the southern balcony.

"Take the monk to a cell, Rendaya," Broeden commanded. "I will deal with both of you later!"

The Camon dropped Ebert and returned the pinchers to the cauldron. Rendaya rushed to Ebert's side.

"Get up! Come with me!"

"You're bleeding!" he said.

"I'm fine," she answered. They hurried from the court as Camon soldiers thundered past toward the southern battlements.

Just before they reached the dungeon entrance, Rendaya veered sharply left, pulling Ebert down a hallway he had never seen. She shoved open a door — and they were suddenly outside the castle.

The moment they cleared the threshold, Rendaya seized him tightly and launched into the air, flying west into the night.

Rendaya didn't stop flying until she saw her destination: the great southern forest of Etharath. It was her secret refuge — the place she had always fled to when life under Broeden became unbearable.

Her blouse was soaked with blood. The reopened cut on her neck had bled slowly but steadily throughout the entire flight, and a fog crept into her mind as she descended into a clearing deep within the forest.

She landed hard. They tumbled across the grass until they came to rest beneath towering live oaks, their branches arching sixty feet overhead.

Rendaya staggered upright. "He would kill me? He would kill me?" she screamed into the trees.

Ebert rolled to his side, gasping for breath. "Rendaya... please. Let me look at your neck."

She swallowed her fury and nodded. "Very well."

Ebert pushed himself to his feet and placed his hand gently over her wound.

"You're shaking," he said.

"I have killed for him," she said, voice cracking. "And he would kill me?" The tears came then — hot, unstoppable, running down her cheeks in waves.

Ebert lifted his free hand toward the sky, closed his eyes, and prayed. Warmth radiated from his palm. The pain vanished instantly. When he opened his eyes, he looked directly into hers — and she saw genuine concern there. Perhaps he was the only person in her life who had ever truly cared for her.

"There," he said softly. "The bleeding has stopped."

He withdrew his hand. Rendaya wiped her tears with her sleeve.

"Are you—"

"I'm fine," she insisted. "Follow me."

She turned toward the trees on the western edge of the clearing.

"Where are we going?" Ebert asked.

"There is a place I sometimes go," she said. "A place to be alone."

She scanned the skies, then stepped into the shadowed woodlands.

Ebert fell silent. She led him through her small garden of wildflowers, down a narrow path, and to the door of an abandoned cottage. This was her sanctuary — the one part of herself she had never shared with anyone. Yet she felt connected to Ebert. Safe with him.

"It's quite the mess," she said. "I've never had guests here before."

The old door sagged on its hinges. She pushed it open, and its bottom edge scraped an arc through the dust on the wooden floor. With a flick of her wrist, the candles around the room flared to life, their soft glow filling the cottage with shifting shadows.

"It's very nice," Ebert said. "A fireplace and everything."

She felt a sudden urge to hide the doll sitting on the bed, but she knew that would only draw attention. Much to her dismay, it was the first thing Ebert noticed. He walked over and picked up the dirty calico rag doll.

"This is yours?" he asked.

"Don't touch it!" she snapped, striding over and snatching it from his hands.

Ebert stepped back. "I'm sorry, Huntress. I meant no harm."

"Don't call me that!" Rendaya cried. "Not you."

"I'm sorry, Rendaya," Ebert said — and he didn't sound frightened. Only hurt.

Rendaya drew a breath and spoke as she had never spoken to anyone — from her heart. "No. I'm sorry." She couldn't remember ever saying those words before.

Ebert looked stunned.

She placed the doll back on her pillow. A tear fell beside it. She wiped her face quickly and adjusted the doll so it sat upright.

"This little doll is the only thing I have from my childhood," she said. "I tell myself my father made it for me, but I don't know. All I know is that I had it with me when I was given to Broeden."

Ebert's large brown eyes softened. "I'm sure it must be incredibly special to you." He looked around the room. "Rendaya… what are we doing here?"

"I will not serve a master who would destroy me on a whim," she said fiercely. "I've destroyed all who dared challenge him."

"Don't be discouraged, Rendaya. The best is yet to come." He stepped closer and laid a hand on her arm. "You have a greater purpose than destruction. I know it."

"You still talk like a monk," she said, pulling her arm away. "Don't mistake my choice to save you for weakness."

"I didn't," he said gently. "I saw it as compassion."

"Compassion?" She gave a bitter laugh. She sat on the bed and buried her face in her hands. "I've lived my whole life surrounded by servants who feared me, bringing me whatever I wanted — surrounded, but utterly alone. I didn't bring you here out of compassion. I brought you here out of a desperate desire to be with someone. I don't want to be alone anymore."

Ebert sat beside her. "I owe you my life," he said. "And I promise you — I won't leave you."

ZⱩ⌁6⌐⌐.

From his southern balcony, Broeden watched the gathering forces in the distance. The line of warriors stretched a thousand yards across the Northern Plains. Tents rose behind their formation, snapping in the stiff wind. Flags of the Rion Guard — and many others he did not recognize — flew taut and defiant.

"Rendaya!" Broeden roared. When she did not appear, he turned to his guard. "Find the Huntress!"

"At once, master." The Camon bowed and hurried from the room.

Broeden's fury mounted as he watched the enemy encampment grow. They had brought catapults, ballistae, cavalry, and thousands of foot soldiers.

"Fools!" he shrieked. "You dare challenge me? You have summoned your own doom!" He struggled to stand, gripping the throne's armrests and the balcony rail. "Your coming here only spares me the trouble of hunting you down! Come! Come and taste death!"

The shouting triggered a violent coughing fit. Bursts of white flashed behind his eyelids. His head and chest throbbed.

The Camon returned, head bowed. "Master, the Huntress is nowhere to be found."

"Then find the monk!" Broeden screamed.

"Yes, master!" The guard repeated the order down the hall.

Broeden sank back into his throne. His insects turned it and lurched forward, carrying him through the corridors to Rendaya's room. Two guards followed close behind.

When he entered, he found the chamber exactly as she always left it — her belongings scattered in the familiar disarray she had never outgrown.

The Camon he had sent to search returned empty-handed. "The Huntress and the monk are gone, master!"

"What did you say?"

The Camon dropped to one knee. "Master, forgive me. We have searched everywhere. The Huntress and the monk are nowhere to be found."

"Leave me!" Broeden roared.

The Camonra bowed and withdrew, closing the door behind them.

Broeden moved to Rendaya's vanity and picked up her hairbrush. It still smelled of her. He lifted it to his face and inhaled.

The monk bewitched her. He turned her against me.

"Rendaya?" he whispered to the empty room. "Why have you left me?"

His thoughts drifted back to the day a Camon had thrown her at his feet — small, trembling, terrified. She had cringed at the sight of him. Frail. Helpless. But he had seen greatness in her. Something in him had shifted that day. He had returned to the village that had surrendered her so easily… and slaughtered them all.

In the years that followed, he had shaped her into a prodigy. And in return, she had given him the closest thing he had ever known to fatherhood — even if not by blood.

And now the monk had taken her.

Broeden's fury erupted. He hurled the brush at the mirror, shattering the glass. The broken handle clattered to the floor. The sight of the ruined mirror

— something Rendaya cherished — struck him with a sudden, unexpected pang of remorse.

His fractured reflection stared back at him, accusing.

One of his insects scuttled up the throne leg, retrieved the broken brush handle, and offered it to him. Broeden took it, turning it slowly in his hand. Rage burned through him.

"Guards!" he bellowed.

He would show his attackers no mercy.

Evliit had gathered the leaders of the Watchers and the Rion Guard in his tent at the rear of the encampment. A young man entered carrying a leather document tube and bowed.

"As you requested, Lord Evliit," the boy said. He opened the tube and handed Evliit a rolled parchment.

Evliit unrolled it, studying the freshly inked map of the outer wall and grounds surrounding Broeden's castle.

"Thank you," Evliit said. "You're dismissed."

The cartographer's assistant bowed and departed. Evliit spread the map across the wooden table in the center of the tent. As he did, the entrance flap lifted and Praedhos stepped inside.

"Praedhos!" Evliit said warmly.

"My lord," Praedhos replied. "Your catapults stand ready."

"Well done, Praedhos. Come — hear our battle plans."

Praedhos bowed, placed his fist over his heart, and joined the others around the table.

"Our scouts report Broeden's forces pouring from the castle onto the field," said Perel, commander of the Rion Guard. He moved six carved figures to the front of the drawbridge illustration. "Six regiments of Camonra guard the main entrance, with packs of war dogs before them." He placed three carved hounds ahead of the line. "Each flank is protected by small demons and possessors. Their rear flanks are guarded by Camonra mounted on their two-legged beasts."

"Azrodh, commander," one of the captains said.

"Yes — Azrodh," Perel confirmed, sliding the carved lizards and riders into position. "Our scouts estimate their numbers at fifteen to twenty thousand."

Evliit leaned over the map, the scale of the enemy force weighing heavily on him.

"What are your orders?" Perel asked.

Evliit looked at the carved figures representing the Rion Guard, the Watchers, and the militia. He thought of the faces of the townspeople who had marched with them — the human cost behind every wooden piece.

"To be honest, commander," Evliit said, "I wish to rely on your years of battlefield experience. What do you recommend?"

Perel looked pleasantly surprised.

"With such a large force, we must break their lines," he said. "We cannot allow their pawns to overwhelm our greatest warriors." He moved the shielded warriors to the center of the map. "We should place the Watchers and the militia before the phalanx. They will engage the war dogs, minions, and possessors while our cavalry attempts to flank."

He shifted the cavalry pieces outward.

"The archers and catapults will remain at the rear and launch the first volley. Their rain of stone and arrow is essential to moving the phalanx into position. Once Broeden's front lines fall, we advance to capture the drawbridge."

He pushed the figures forward to the moat.

"Praedhos," Evliit said, "will you command the catapults and archers? Their importance cannot be overstated."

"I would fight by your side, my lord!" Praedhos blurted — then quickly regained his composure. "Of course, my lord. As you wish."

Perel nodded. "Very well. Our laddermen will wait with the catapults until the way is clear. If the bridge remains raised, they will drop the first ladders across the moat here." He pointed to the trench around the rampart. "If the bridge is lowered, we enter there. Otherwise, we take the walls with ladders and swordsmen."

Evliit swallowed hard. The cost in lives pressed on him like a physical weight.

"Yes," he said quietly. "Let it be so, commander."

Perel signaled his captains. They bowed and exited, leaving Evliit with Tophian, Praedhos, and Mategaladh.

"You realize what'll happen to the militia when they engage the possessors?" Mategaladh said.

"It'll be a slaughter," Tophian added.

"Then the Watchers will stand with them," Evliit said.

"And it'll still be a slaughter," Tophian replied.

Evliit's thoughts flashed to Jenna — to Harot — to the horrors Broeden had unleashed. Rage surged through him.

Mategaladh picked up one of the carved townspeople. "I can see the anger inside you," he said. "Its darkness consumes the light of your spirit. Do not let it cloud your judgment."

"Pray that the Creator steadies my hand," Evliit said.

Broeden pushed himself up from his chair and glared out over the battlefield.

"Bring me my armor!" he commanded.

His servants rushed to obey. When they finished fastening the last gleaming plate, Broeden lifted a hand. A great horn sounded across the courtyard. At once, his brigades shifted into formation.

"Their spy has bewitched my Huntress and stolen her away!" Broeden roared, spittle flying. "Their religion will fail today! They will cry out to their god in vain, and I will tear out their hearts and mount their heads on poles!"

His voice rose to a fever pitch.

"We will carry their rotting skulls back to Rion and burn that city to the ground. Let the battle begin!"

He signaled with two short blasts of the battle horn.

Below, Broeden's war dogs, minions, and possessors answered with a chilling, unified cry.

The brand of Harot burned over Evliit's heart. Today he would avenge Jenna — and all the lives Broeden had destroyed.

Dust rose from the field as Broeden's warriors surged forward. Several militia turned to look at Evliit, terror plain on their faces. He raised his voice over the growing roar.

"Good men of Etharath! This is our day!" he shouted. "How long have we lived in fear of this madman? Will we not shake off his bonds forever?"

Gradually, their eyes left the advancing horde and fixed on him.

"Have they not murdered the last of our children? Burned the last of our villages?"

A roar erupted from the phalanx of trained guardsmen behind the militia. The sound startled the front ranks — then emboldened them. Fear drained from their faces, replaced by grim resolve or wild fury. Their transformation made Evliit's heart swell.

Perel rode to his side. "They plan to strike us hard!"

"Stones and arrows!" Evliit commanded. "Drop those you can!"

Perel raised his hand. "Archers!"

A thousand bowstrings drew back. He waved forward — and the air cracked with the release.

Arrows arced high, then fell like rain. Broeden's creatures faltered under the storm. Dozens of the short, hideous demons fell, along with several war dogs. But before Evliit could celebrate, he saw it: a dark vapor drifting within their ranks.

"Mategaladh!" Evliit cried, pointing. "Is that what I think it is?"

Mategaladh's eyes widened. "Possessors!" He turned his horse toward the foot soldiers. "Beware the dark vapor! If it enters you, you'll turn against us — and we'll have no choice but to kill the host to kill the parasite!"

"Catapults!" Perel barked.

The tensioned wood behind them whined and cracked. Evliit looked toward the oncoming fray as the catapults' great arms snapped free. Stones the size of horses hurtled through the air.

The front line of dogs and minions scattered — except those too confused to choose a direction, or too enraged to care. Some froze, eyes wide, realizing too late they could not escape.

The boulders struck with bone-crunching force. One here. Six there. Four more. The impacts sprayed gore across the advancing Camonra. The first volley had fallen well — but Evliit knew it would be precious minutes before the catapults could fire again.

Broeden's front line was ragged, but unbroken.

The war dogs surged forward, weaving across the field in a snarling wave. The militia braced.

"Shields!" Perel shouted.

The phalanx dropped into a squat, shields locking together like dragon scales.

"Spears!"

Spearpoints thrust through the curved cutouts in their shields, transforming the formation into a bristling wall.

Perel drew his sword. "Forward!"

The phalanx rumbled ahead, still crouched in its defensive posture.

"Keep the militia ahead of us!" he called to Evliit.

"Attack!" Evliit cried, and the militia charged.

Tophian rode up beside him and Mategaladh. "I told you!" he roared. "Lambs to the slaughter! Teeth before them and spears behind!"

Evliit nodded toward the oncoming beasts. "We go ahead of them. Are you with me?"

"Keep up with me if you can!" Tophian shouted.

"I'll do my part!" Mategaladh answered.

Perel overheard. "What are you doing? No, my lord! Keep back!"

"Drive the phalanx forward!" Evliit yelled — and spurred Angwen into a full gallop.

The three men surged ahead. When they pulled in front of the militia, Evliit let out a thunderous battle cry. He saw the Spellmakers advancing on the far right. To his left, the other Watchers entered the fray.

Evliit drew his sword — and blue flame engulfed the blade. A roar rose behind him. The militia had seen the legendary weapon and were screaming their allegiance.

The war dogs were nearly upon them.

Evliit leapt from his horse. "Return, Angwen!" He slapped the mare's flank, sending her racing away just as the first war dog struck.

It lunged for him — but Evliit spun and cleaved its jaws apart, splitting the beast to its shoulders. It skidded to a stop before the militia as Tophian and Mategaladh dismounted beside him.

Another dog charged. Tophian raised his hand — and the ground surged upward, smashing into the beast's mouth and knocking it unconscious. It tumbled toward them. Tophian motioned again, and the turf ramped upward, launching the body over their heads and into the militia. The men parted, then fell upon it with blades and clubs.

A horn sounded. The center three columns of Camonra shifted inward and broke into a dead run. The war dogs slowed, forming a pack around Evliit.

"Form up behind Evliit!" Mategaladh shouted.

The militia scrambled into position. Mategaladh closed his eyes — and a ring of thorns erupted from the earth around them.

Screams rose behind them. Three militia hadn't made it inside. A war dog circled the thorns and seized one man by the leg, tearing it off at the knee. The other two hacked at it wildly, but the beast dropped the leg and ripped into the fallen man's torso. Another dog dragged one of the remaining two away, past the advancing phalanx and into a swarm of minions that ended his screams.

The last man panicked, threw down his weapon, and tried to climb the thorns — impaling himself on the four-inch spines.

Another war dog lunged for him — but Tophian seized a catapult stone mid-flight and redirected it downward. It crushed the beast's skull into the earth.

"Well done, Tophian!" Evliit shouted.

He reached through the thorns and grasped the impaled man's wrist. The man calmed instantly.

"Go back! Tell the catapults to rain down their stones!"

The militiaman cried out as he tore himself free of the thorns. Evliit's sword glowed brighter, and the man's wounds closed. He turned and ran toward the catapults.

Mategaladh pointed to a black mist drifting above the minions. "The possessors come!"

Tophian redirected another stone — crushing minions, but the possessor drifted on, unharmed.

The largest war dog howled. The black mist shot down its throat. The beast convulsed — then began to change.

It doubled in size. Its neck and limbs stretched. Skin tore open, revealing swelling muscle. Teeth erupted along its jawline. Its incisors lengthened to a foot.

When the transformation finished, the rakmuut stood six feet at the shoulder. It snarled and hurled itself into the thicket, shredding vines as though they were grass. The other war dogs crowded behind it, waiting for an opening.

Mategaladh summoned more vines, but the pack tore them away as fast as he could raise them. The rakmuut's face was slashed and bleeding, but it never slowed.

Tophian redirected two more stones, crushing only a pair of dogs. The rest scattered, then returned, barking madly, saliva flying.

The militia huddled in the center of the thicket, facing outward. Terror was etched on every face.

As Evliit led the militia slightly left, he saw the Rionese phalanx trudging forward toward the center of the field. At Perel's command, they lifted their shields from the dirt and lurched ahead with a collective grunt, thrusting spears at anything that dared approach.

Beyond the phalanx, Amphileph and his Spellmakers raised golems from the earth. The enormous creatures stood three deep, shoulder to shoulder, swinging tree-trunk arms into a host of Camonra on Azrodh mounts. The Camonra attempted to flank the Rionese, likely to disrupt the archers still raining arrows upon their forward lines. They hacked at the golems with everything they had, but their efforts were futile. Evliit winced as one golem smashed a Camon and his Azrodh into pulp with a single blow.

"Evliit!" Tophian shouted. "The possessors!"

Evliit turned just in time to see the black mist slip effortlessly through Mategaladh's thicket. It darted into the cluster of men within. One militiaman screamed as his body convulsed. His skin split along his torso and limbs. His screams twisted into a roar as he transformed — more monster than man — and he swung his sword wildly at those nearest him. Trapped within the thicket, they had nowhere to flee. He killed three before Evliit brought his flaming blade down, cleaving him from shoulder to hip.

"The rakmuut!" Mategaladh cried.

The beast's snout burst through the thicket and seized a militiaman who had backed against the vines. With a single twist, it tore off his arm and hurled him into the snarling pack behind it. They eviscerated him before he could scream.

"We must retreat!" Mategaladh shouted.

He looked toward the rear of the thicket — the vines there withered and blackened. Evliit thrust out his palm, and the area erupted in flames.

"Run!" Evliit cried.

He slashed through the burning vines, and the militiamen scrambled through the opening. Their flight sent up a cloud of white ash and glowing embers. The rakmuut burst through the front of the thicket just as the last men escaped.

Another catapult stone flew overhead. Evliit raised his hand. Red cracks spidered across the rock, and it burst into molten fragments. Tophian pulled the molten mass downward onto the charging rakmuut. The beast shrieked, rearing and thrashing. It fled back through the hole in the thicket, but the molten stone overtook it, engulfing the vines in a roaring blaze. The other war dogs retreated from the heat.

As Evliit backed away with Mategaladh and Tophian, he saw black mist pour from the rakmuut's gaping maw and disintegrate in the flames.

"We've lost the militia!" Tophian yelled.

Evliit surveyed the chaos. "Let them go! The right front is moving forward!"

Broeden's war horn sounded — a thunderous boom that shook dust from the earth. The squeal of rusty gears followed as the drawbridge lowered behind the central Camonra. When it slammed into place, the ground trembled and a gust of wind swept across the battlefield.

"Broeden's center column retreats!" Mategaladh shouted.

"Follow the phalanx!" Tophian cried.

They sprinted to catch up with Perel and the Rion Guard — but the phalanx had broken from its defensive posture. Perel was charging the opening.

Evliit stopped abruptly. Mategaladh and Tophian halted beside him.

"Something is wrong!" Evliit shouted. "Their strongest warriors retreat? And where is the Huntress?"

He saw the minions pulling back as well, running inward toward the drawbridge.

"The war dogs!" Tophian yelled.

Lines of the beasts were scampering toward the phalanx.

Mategaladh cupped his hands around his mouth. "Perel!" he screamed — but the distance and the din swallowed his voice.

"We must warn him!" he cried, sprinting toward the rear of the phalanx. Evliit and Tophian followed — but before they could reach the Rion Guard, the war dogs crashed into the formation in a thunderous explosion of fur, teeth, spears, and shields.

Perel had seen them just in time. The phalanx dropped shields to the ground and dug in. The dogs impaled themselves in a chorus of cracking wood and shrieks. Some died on the shields; others recoiled, their bloodlust broken by pain. The survivors broke off and looped around toward the rear of the Rionese army.

The phalanx lifted shields and advanced toward the drawbridge again.

"The archers and catapults!" Tophian cried. "The war dogs will ravage them!"

"Go to them!" Evliit shouted. "I will get to Perel!"

"No, Evliit!" Mategaladh yelled. "We must stay together!"

Evliit hesitated. Arrows flew as the war dogs reached the archers — but the beasts darted through the volleys, seizing bowmen and dragging them off by arms or legs.

"Look!" Tophian pointed.

Praedhos burst from behind the catapults, drawing two swords. Two war dogs lunged. Praedhos dodged, slicing the hind leg from one and the ear from the other. The three-legged beast hobbled away, dragging its severed limb. The second shook its head violently, spraying blood. It crouched to attack again — but arrows struck it down.

Praedhos's efforts cleared a small space. Hiadhlian and Sardhor raised a barrier of energy around themselves and several militia. Madhis and Emordhos tended the mangled fallen.

"We must get to Perel!" Tophian said. "He's walking into a trap!"

Evliit nodded, torn but resolute. Together they ran toward the phalanx, now nearly at the drawbridge.

To their right, Broeden's creations were finally tearing the golems apart, heedless of their own losses.

"*Oriuntur!*" Amphileph cried. He and Ardidhus raised more golems from the blood-soaked earth as quickly as the Camonra could destroy them. The right flank was a brutal stalemate.

At last they reached the rear of the phalanx. Evliit shouted for passage. The soldiers parted, and he pushed toward the center where Perel barked orders.

"Perel!" Evliit yelled.

Perel turned. "We take the bridge!"

"Wait!" Evliit protested. "Something's wrong!"

"Your companions have stopped the possessors, lord! It's now or never!"

Evliit glanced left. Clogren, Odhramorus, and Hrast were chanting, gathering the black mist into a swirling vortex. Fire fell from the sky into the whirlwind, consuming the possessors in a column of flame.

A third blast of Broeden's horn echoed across the field.

"Hold!" Perel commanded.

They watched as hundreds of underlings joined the Camonra at the far side of the drawbridge. The smaller creatures screamed curses upon Rion, then knelt. The Camonra executed them with swift thrusts.

Black mist poured from their bodies, flowing over the sides of the drawbridge and into the corpses filling the moat. Tentacles burst from the dead, weaving together a grotesque mass of rotting flesh that rose from the trench in a quivering mound. Dark green fluid oozed from every orifice. Arms from the screaming bodies clawed at the drawbridge, pulling the abomination upward toward Evliit's horrified army.

Praedhos stepped aside from the snapping jaws of the last war dog, spinning with his blade and slicing cleanly behind its left ear. The beast recoiled, and the archers he'd defended returned the favor, sinking three arrows into its flank.

Praedhos turned to shout his thanks — but the archers were staring past him, faces twisted in horror.

He followed their gaze.

A mass of corpses was rising from the moat.

"Oh no," he whispered.

A fist the size of a Camon warrior erupted from the writhing mound and punched through the phalanx, shattering spears and scattering men like leaves. Praedhos thought he saw Evliit and Mategaladh flung from the impact, but he couldn't be sure. He did see Tophian lying on his side among the remaining Rionese.

Then the creature tore free of its cocoon of bodies — skinless, towering thirty feet high — and roared.

The Camonra scattered, but not fast enough. A single crushing foot came down on the drawbridge, pulverizing warriors beneath it. One side of the bridge splintered under the weight. As the creature lurched to regain balance, it swept its massive arm, backhanding four fleeing Camonra into the castle wall.

It clutched a stone column, hauled itself from the trench, and began grabbing anything within reach — friend or foe — ripping bodies in half with its ragged fangs. Blood and limbs rained down on the terrified soldiers below. Its bellow shook Praedhos to his core.

The monster leaped onto the golems. Though some tore chunks of gore from it, the creature ripped them apart, scattering their earthen bodies. The Spellmakers collapsed one by one — their lives tied to their creations. They fought valiantly, but even they could not stop it.

Praedhos stood firm with the archers, but panic clawed at him. He still couldn't see Evliit or Mategaladh. The remaining Rionese were scrambling over the dead in retreat.

On the left flank, the Watchers formed a protective sphere between the retreating soldiers and the monster. The creature hammered the shield, sparks flying with each impact. The plasma flickered. It grasped the orb, but found it immovable. The Watchers' chant rose in volume.

Praedhos could wait no longer. He sprinted toward them. The creature's claws were beginning to pierce the shield.

The Watchers' chant surged. Lightning burst from the orb into the creature's arm. It roared and recoiled. Praedhos was nearly to Tophian when the creature screamed in fury and smashed the sphere with its fist.

The orb exploded.

The Watchers were hurled through the air. The shockwave knocked soldiers off their feet and stopped Praedhos in his tracks. The creature's eyes followed the arc of the Watchers' bodies — and it moved toward them.

From the pile of dead and dying, Tophian staggered upright.

"He's going to kill them!" Praedhos shouted.

Tophian turned, saw the helpless Watchers, steadied himself, and raised a stone the size of a cart. He hurled it with all his strength. It struck the creature's shoulder, toppling it — but it rose again, turning toward Tophian and the dazed remnants of Perel's phalanx.

"Archers!" Praedhos called.

The remaining Rionese archers rushed forward. A volley of arrows struck the beast. It shrieked, then raked its hand across its face, snapping arrow shafts in its flesh. It dropped to all fours and sprang.

It landed among the archers, sweeping both hands and catching three men in each.

"Loose your arrows!" Praedhos cried. "Loose your arrows, all of you!"

Arrows flew from every direction. Some archers held their ground; others advanced, firing without pause even as the creature snapped them up whole. It smashed others beneath its jaws, crushing bows and bodies alike.

The creature lunged again. Praedhos felt its hot breath as it stopped before him. He dropped one sword, gripped the other with both hands, and slashed across its face. The blade opened a deep line of muscle. Blood sprayed like rain.

The creature howled, pressing its wound against its shoulder. Then it turned, searching for the source of its pain. Its eyes locked on Praedhos — sword raised, dripping with its blood.

It charged.

"Run!" Praedhos shouted to the archer beside him. The man fled.

The creature swung. Praedhos ducked. Its claws buried themselves in the earth. Praedhos struck again, slicing open the inside of its upper arm.

The creature screamed, pulled back, and tried to hammer him — but the injured limb faltered. It lowered the arm, fell silent, and staggered backward toward the trench.

Praedhos pursued — but the creature lunged with its good arm, grazing him and knocking him down. It slipped on the trench's edge as it dove, jaws snapping just short of Praedhos's feet. It planted its good arm, reared back to strike again—

A stone the size of a table smashed into its eye socket.

Tophian appeared beside Praedhos. "Get up!"

Grunting, he lifted another catapult stone and hurled it into the creature's chest, driving it backward into the moat.

Its clawed foot tore into the bodies below. Veins shot from the corpses into its legs. The bleeding stopped. The dead began to hiss and screech. The creature's veins bulged, feeding on them. Its wounds stitched shut. It began to grow even larger.

The fallen Spellmakers stirred. Amphileph rose first. He thrust out his hands toward the moat.

"I call upon the spirits of the dead!" he cried. "May the murdered rise and seek your revenge!"

Screams erupted from the trench. The creature looked down — and tried to pull free — but the dead surged upward, sending vein after vein into its flesh, dragging it down.

Praedhos ran. The creature's head was now below the drawbridge. He saw his chance. He sprinted up the three-foot-wide railing of the drawbridge tower and leaped.

The creature roared and swung, breaking free of the veins holding its head. Its maw opened wide, ready to swallow him whole.

Praedhos could not change his trajectory. He stared into the bloody gullet that meant his death.

Then Amphileph shouted.

More veins burst from the moat, seizing the creature's lower jaw and yanking its head downward.

Praedhos had just enough time to grip his sword with both hands before he struck the top of the creature's skull. He drove the blade down with all his strength until the guard slammed against bone.

The creature stopped instantly.

It collapsed.

Praedhos clung to the hilt, but as the monster toppled sideways, he lost his grip and fell toward the pit.

"No! No! No! No!" he screamed — one long cry ending only when he struck the ground.

He couldn't breathe. Pain exploded through him. He looked down.

A broken spear shaft jutted from his chest.

"*Praaedhossss…*" the bodies around him hissed in unison, their arms reaching.

"No… nooooo…" He mouthed the words silently, frantically. He grabbed the spear shaft, trying to climb up and off it — but the hands of the dead pulled him down. His vision dimmed.

Amphileph and several Spellmakers appeared above him at the trench's edge.

"Depart from us!" Amphileph commanded.

The hands released him.

"Why do you shun us?" the inhuman voices cried together.

"Leave us!" Amphileph cried.

He and the other Spellmakers raised their hands. The pit darkened — black first, then gray, then white — until the bodies crumbled into drifting ash that the wind carried away.

What remained banished Praedhos's fear and pain.

All around him stood his comrades — his fellow soldiers. Graeson was there, and Kelae. Their bodies shone with warm light, but he knew them instantly. Every face. Every friend.

"I've missed you," Praedhos whispered.

His body relaxed. He felt his spirit step free of it. He saw his friends clearly then, radiant and whole, and they embraced him with welcoming arms.

"We have done as you required," Graeson said, looking up toward the Spellmakers at the rim of the pit. "Let us now take our friend and go in peace."

"So be it," Amphileph answered.

Praedhos felt his spirit lift. He rose with Graeson and the others, ascending into the evening sky.

ZⳊᚾᏮ⌐ͻ·

Evliit awoke buried beneath bodies and shattered weapons, soaked in a mixture of human and creature blood. Fighting the urge to retch, he forced his head and left arm through the tangle. Warm blood dripped into his left eye. He shoved aside the tip of a sword near his cheek and freed his right arm.

"Evliit!" Tophian's voice rang out. "Mategaladh!"

The sounds of battle echoed nearby, but the monstrous creature lay sprawled halfway out of the pit, a sword hilt protruding from the top of its skull. Evliit blinked hard, trying to orient himself.

"Tophian!" he shouted, waving.

Tophian clambered over the bodies and hauled Evliit free. Then he immediately began tearing through the pile, frantic.

"We've got to find Mategaladh!"

A muffled voice rose from below. "Help me!"

"It's Mategaladh!" Evliit cried.

They dug furiously until they uncovered a moving hand. "Hold on, Mategaladh! We've got you!" Tophian said.

Together they pulled him from the heap and helped him stand.

Mategaladh wiped blood and filth from his face. "What happened? Where are the others?"

"The creature's fist leveled the phalanx," Tophian said. "But it's dead now. Our warriors are inside the castle. We've got to find Ebert before they do — they're mad with battle."

"But we've no idea where he's being kept," Evliit said. He tore a strip from his sleeve and pressed it to his bleeding head. Dropping to his belly, he reached through the corpses and retrieved his sword. "Still no Huntress?"

"Nowhere in sight," Tophian said. "Mategaladh, can you fight?"

"Yes," Mategaladh said. "Go! I'm right behind you."

Evliit hesitated. "Are you sure?"

"Yes! Go!"

Evliit and Tophian moved ahead, Mategaladh limping after them. They crossed the dead and the splintered drawbridge to the outer wall. They watched the parapets for movement, but none came. The sally port stood open, and the main gate hung mangled. Camon bodies lay strewn inside, as though they'd tried to close the gate when the Rion Guard broke through.

They stopped just inside the courtyard and stared up at the castle's looming façade — six stories of jagged stone rising like a cliff. The walkway to the entrance sloped steeply toward two massive steel doors, thrown wide. The sounds of war thundered from within.

Evliit looked up at the arched windows. "Ebert!" he called.

"What are you doing?" Tophian snapped. "Do we look like we need to invite a beating right now?"

Mategaladh caught up, leaning heavily on his staff. "He's right. Think for a moment. Ebert's likely in the dungeon or the servants' quarters — if he's alive."

Evliit scanned the castle for alternate entry points. "The Watchers and Spellmakers must regroup and search together. If we meet the Huntress, we'll need our numbers. Where are Amphileph and the others?"

"Inside," Tophian said. "You must take back command and focus their wrath on Broeden. He hasn't lived a thousand years by being a fool. Don't underestimate him. Waste nothing fighting Camonra — Broeden cares nothing for them. They serve out of fear, not loyalty. Use that."

"Tophian's right," Mategaladh said. "Regain control of your army. Defeat Broeden, and the castle will fall. If Ebert lives, we'll find him." He pointed to a large balcony above. "I'd start there."

As he pointed, he stumbled. His cloak shifted — revealing a piece of wood jutting from a bloody hole beneath his ribs.

"Mategaladh!" Evliit cried. "Tophian, help me!"

They eased him down. "Let me help you," Evliit said.

"No time," Mategaladh gasped. He yanked the wood free. Blood gushed. His shaking hands rummaged through a pouch. He produced a vial and poured it into the wound. The skin glowed red-hot, burning like an ember. Mategaladh arched his back, teeth clenched. "Now — get to your army!"

"Stay with him," Evliit told Tophian.

"Regain control of your army," Tophian growled. "I'll stay."

Explosions boomed from within the castle. Evliit turned and sprinted up the sloping walkway.

Inside, the dead were mostly Camonra. Seeing no movement, he leapt over bodies toward the sounds of battle.

He found wounded Rion Guard and militia behind the front. Several turned on him.

"It's me!" he shouted. "Where's Perel?"

"He didn't make it, sir," a militiaman said. His armor was gone from one shoulder, and blood-soaked bandages wrapped his chest. "A Camon killed him when we took the gates. Amphileph leads now."

"And where is he?"

"He and the Watchers are fighting the dark one even now," the soldier said. "We're to wait here."

"Show me."

The soldier pointed to massive doors at the hall's end, flanked by stone dragons. Soldiers braced them from behind. The doors suddenly jolted outward with a boom. The men roared and shoved them closed again.

Evliit ran toward them. "Make a hole!" someone shouted, and the men parted.

"Amphileph ordered us to hold this door," a soldier said. "But many of us can still fight. Let us come with you!"

"No," Evliit said sharply. "Only the Watchers and Spellmakers went forward?"

"And a small group of Rion Guard."

"Hold your post. I'll sort this out. Open the doors!"

The spearmen obeyed. Evliit slipped through, and the doors slammed behind him.

Chanting, moans, and cries of pain echoed through the chamber. As his eyes adjusted, he saw the battle was over. Blood covered the floor. Dead and wounded soldiers and Camonra lay everywhere.

A group of Watchers spotted him. "Praise the Creator's holy name!" Hiadhlian cried. "Come quickly!"

Amphileph met him on the far side. "It's good you remain among the living!" he said, embracing Evliit. "I feared the worst."

Evliit looked past him. A semicircular alcove lay ahead, its raised tile floor patterned in a broken circle. Shattered stained-glass windows ringed the space, beams of colored light cutting through the smoky air. At the circle's edge lay amulets, herbs, stones, bowls of salt and water.

At its center knelt a massive older man — twice Evliit's size — bound to the broken shaft of a halberd. His robes hung in bloody tatters.

Amphileph stepped back.

"The Creator has spared me," Evliit said. "What of Praedhos?"

Amphileph's face fell. "I'm sorry. Praedhos destroyed the monster — but he gave his life doing it."

"Praedhos…" Evliit whispered. "No."

Amphileph gestured around the room. "Many soldiers and militia fell with him. The Watchers insisted on taking Broeden alive, to stand trial before the Elders. I warned them this would happen. The old wizard fought savagely. Our numbers prevailed — but the cost was terrible."

"This chant — this binding spell — we can't keep that up forever," Evliit said.

"It is *I* who bind him," Amphileph replied. "My brothers pray for my protection, but I hold him. He is not going anywhere."

"Do not be deceived," Evliit warned. "To be deceived by this one is to invite your own ruin." He raised his voice. "Everyone, move back! His words are poison!"

"Everyone back!" Amphileph echoed.

The Spellmakers and the few remaining warriors retreated as far as the chamber allowed.

"What more do you command, sword bearer?" Amphileph asked.

"I'll speak with him," Evliit said. "Broeden is my burden. The Creator and this sword will be my strength."

"Of course." Amphileph bowed and gestured toward the prisoner, then stepped down the short ramp, ready to intervene.

Evliit approached the old wizard with caution.

Broeden was nothing like the legend Evliit had imagined. His face was swollen and beaten. His bloodshot eyes glared through the narrow slits formed by bruised lids. His mouth was clenched so tightly that a split opened in his upper lip, blood dripping down his chin.

Evliit circled behind him. Jenna's face filled his mind. The weight of every life Broeden had destroyed pressed on him. *But first — he needed Ebert.*

"Where is Ebert?" Evliit demanded. "The monk your Huntress stole from the monastery. Where is he kept?"

Broeden lowered his gaze, but defiance radiated from him. "What makes you think I concern myself with the names of captives? Or that I would lower myself to speak with you? End it. Use your own sword, if you've the stones."

He stared at Evliit — a stare so intense Evliit involuntarily stepped back. It felt as though Broeden's eyes were burning through him.

Amphileph strode up the ramp and struck Broeden in the throat. "Do not dare speak to him that way!"

Broeden gasped, then glared at Amphileph. "You are cursed among men," he hissed — but not in the speech of the living.

Evliit froze.

Broeden was speaking in the tongue of the dead — the language that had haunted Evliit since the day he opened the dark portal.

Broeden continued in the ancient tongue: "You will rue the day you struck—"

Amphileph backhanded him, knocking him sideways until the halberd staff stopped his fall. His bound arm dangled like a puppet.

"Do you think that's the first time I've heard the dark speech?" Amphileph shouted. "Spellmakers live in the shadows! We've lost everything because of the filth you unleashed!"

"Enough!" Evliit commanded. "Answer me. Where is Ebert?"

Broeden righted himself and looked at Evliit, eyes narrowing. "You understand the speech of the dead, don't you?" he asked in that tongue, smiling through bloodied teeth.

Evliit said nothing.

Broeden's smile widened. "You do. It pains your ears, but you understand."

Evliit drew his sword. "Hold your tongue."

"Hear it," Broeden said, "or hear nothing more of your precious monk."

He straightened, grimacing. "Ah, the monk. That I did not foresee. Well played, sword bearer. Such a hex I never imagined — destroying my champion. To think I believed taking the monks would lure the sword to me."

Destroy his champion? Evliit didn't understand.

Broeden saw the confusion. Realization dawned. "You hadn't planned it?" He gave a broken laugh. "Then it's worse than I thought. She left of her own accord — and took him with her. And he went willingly, lured by a woman's scent."

A woman's scent.

Jenna's hair flashed through Evliit's mind — the night they hid in the markets of Rion.

A scream tore from him. He struck Broeden across the jaw with the hilt of his sword. The wizard's head snapped sideways like a spindle.

"Ebert is pure of heart!" Evliit shouted. "I will not permit you to slander him!"

His hand went numb. He glanced at it — for a moment, his skin looked gray, as though some of his life force had drained away with the blow.

Broeden slumped, then lifted his head. A cut opened on his cheek. He spat a molar onto the floor and cackled.

"Pure, yes. I saw it in his eyes. The fool truly loved her."

"Loved… the Huntress?" Evliit forced himself to stay calm. *Broeden was toying with him.*

"My servants saw her carry him into the sky, far to the west," Broeden said. "She wasn't dragging him."

"You've lost your mind," Evliit snapped. "Ebert would never go willingly with that murderous witch!"

"Believe what you will," Broeden said. "But my Huntress will come to her senses. And when she does, she'll kill him — just as I taught her — and then she'll return and kill all of you."

He planted one foot, testing his strength. "How long do you think these charms will bind me?"

"As long as it takes!" Amphileph shouted.

"Stay down, Broeden!" Evliit warned. "Do not test me!"

"He should be brought to justice before all Rion!" Ardidhus cried. "If we bind him together, we can take him—"

"You'd best kill me now!" Broeden roared. "You will never drag me before those bastards! I'll kill you all first!"

"Your tongue is too loose, Ardidhus!" Hiadhlian snapped.

Broeden tried to rise. Amphileph stepped forward. "Back on your knees! You're not going anywhere!"

Broeden's strength surged. He pulled downward — the halberd staff splintered over his shoulders.

"Can you hold him?" Evliit shouted.

Amphileph didn't answer.

"Amphileph! Can you hold him?"

"I have him!" Amphileph cried. His palms glowed red — but he was straining.

The halberd snapped. The crystals in the binding ring shattered. Shards struck Evliit's face. He ducked, brushing fragments from his skin.

"No!" Amphileph screamed.

He advanced, hands blazing like twin fires.

Broeden rose to his full height. He cast off the broken halberd and screamed — the windows shattered.

"Come to me!" Broeden roared.

He reached out. An unseen force extinguished the flames in Amphileph's hands. The Spellmaker flew into Broeden's grasp.

"Die!" Evliit shouted.

He raised his sword — but Broeden flicked his head. Evliit slammed into the wall, dropping his weapon.

Amphileph screamed as Broeden pulled him close. The wizard's eyes rolled back. He opened his mouth and vomited a stream of thick black liquid into Amphileph's face.

The scream cut off. Amphileph gagged, convulsed, and then went limp. Black fluid bubbled from his mouth. His head lolled.

Evliit scrambled for his sword. The Watchers' chanting rose, forming a wall of plasma around Broeden.

"Enough!" Broeden thundered.

The wall vanished. The Watchers flew backward as if struck by a gale.

Broeden held Amphileph's corpse in one hand and reached toward Evliit with the other.

"Come to me, sword bearer!"

Evliit resisted, but his feet slid toward him.

"I am the sword bearer," Evliit growled. "I am your end of days."

His sword blazed brighter as his feet locked against the platform steps.

Broeden laughed. "Delay this no further!"

"In memory of all the innocents you've slaughtered," Evliit said, "I will cast you to the Underworld!"

He stood alone against the great wizard.

Evliit raised his sword — but Broeden seized his free hand. Evliit felt his life force draining. His skin shriveled. The sword grew impossibly heavy.

The room shook. Oversized millipedes poured from every crack.

"The sword is heavy," Broeden whispered. "Let me release you from your burden."

He dropped Amphileph's body and reached for the sword. Evliit was powerless to stop him. The blade's light dimmed.

"My reign will never end!" Broeden screamed.

Evliit's vision dimmed, and time seemed to freeze. In the stillness, a quiet voice reached him.

"Evliit?"

A familiar fragrance drifted through the darkness — the sweet scent of Jenna's hair.

"Evliit, my love… awaken."

"Jenna?"

Her face appeared before him, gentle and radiant. Her smile filled him with a joy so sharp it hurt.

"Awaken, my love."

Evliit's sight snapped back into focus. Broeden's hand was inches from the sword when its edge flared with blinding light. Evliit thrust with the last of his strength, driving the blade into Broeden's chest just above the heart.

Broeden stared at him in disbelief, grabbing the blade with his free hand as the glowing steel burned his flesh. Evliit wrenched the sword free. Black blood sprayed from the wound, gurgling down Broeden's chest with each fading heartbeat.

Broeden released him. Evliit dropped the sword and collapsed.

The wizard's eyes turned black as coal. "My vengeance will consume you and yours!" he boomed, his voice echoing through the chamber. "I… I will—"

Black blood choked his words. His skin paled. He shuddered and fell.

Evliit drifted in and out of consciousness. When he opened his eyes again, Sardhor was kneeling over him. With the Watcher's help, Evliit sat upright.

"Help me!" Sardhor called, and battered Watchers gathered around Evliit, laying hands on him. Strength seeped back into his limbs. He rose with their support.

Others tended to Amphileph.

"Amphileph?" Evliit asked.

"He's alive," Sardhor said. "A miracle."

The Watchers stepped back. Amphileph's eyes fluttered open. They helped him stand.

"Master!" Clogren said. "Do you remember what happened?"

"I had a vision," Amphileph murmured. "I was flying over Etharath… then descending into a great wood. I landed in a clearing. A man and a woman walked along a path."

"A vision!" Olidan exclaimed. "What more?"

"I followed them to a cabin. We sat by the fire." Amphileph shuddered. "Then a knock at the door. The woman answered. Lightning. Rain. Thunder. A dark minion held up Broeden's shredded banner. He pointed at me."

"The woman is the Huntress," Olidan said.

"Yes. She seized me by the neck, lifted me off the ground, took a sword from the minion's side, and ran me through. I felt it. I tasted my own blood."

Clogren spat. "A curse upon the Huntress! Broeden is no more." He pointed to the corpse. "Do you see, Master?"

Sardhor snorted. "Where's Mategaladh and his wine when you need him?"

Nervous laughter rippled through the group.

"Mategaladh!" Evliit gasped. "I must check on him — and Tophian!"

As the Spellmakers surrounded Amphileph, Evliit staggered toward the door. Hiadhlian sat slumped against the wall and reached for him.

"Evliit… where are you going?"

"Mategaladh is injured. I left him with Tophian. I must go. Prepare Broeden's body for transport to Rion. All will want proof of his death."

"Yes, sword bearer."

"And tell the others — I leave to find Ebert."

"Now?" Hiadhlian asked, tension in his voice.

"As soon as I know Mategaladh's condition."

"But you must lead us in this new peace, as you led us in war."

"Amphileph will rise to leadership. He has proven himself."

Hiadhlian nodded. "He will relish that role."

"You have my gratitude, Hiadhlian. May the Creator watch over you."

Evliit stepped through the steel doors.

"Evliit!" soldiers cried. "What of Broeden?"

"Broeden is dead," Evliit said, pushing past them.

The news rippled outward. A roar erupted from the troops, echoing through the halls. Soldiers poured from the castle, shouting the victory to the sky.

Evliit crossed the drawbridge onto the battlefield.

"Evliit!" Tophian called. "Come! Hurry!"

Evliit ran to him. Mategaladh lay limp across Tophian's lap.

"He said he couldn't breathe," Tophian said, voice breaking. "I can't revive him. Help him!"

Evliit examined the burned skin where Mategaladh had sealed his wound. "Roll him over."

Tophian gently turned him. A second wound gaped in his back, still bleeding.

Evliit prayed and pressed his hands to it. Mategaladh gasped and moaned.

Evliit swayed, light-headed. He steadied himself on Tophian's shoulder. "He must rest. Take him home."

"Thank you," Tophian whispered, a tear sliding down his cheek. "I don't know what I'd do without this old coot."

"I must go," Evliit said.

"What happened inside? What of Ebert?"

"Broeden is dead," Evliit said flatly. "As for Ebert…" He shook his head. "The Huntress has taken him west. I don't know where — but I will find him."

"Alone?" Tophian asked. "How can you face her alone?"

Evliit scanned the battlefield. "She didn't fight for Broeden today. When he needed her most, she failed him. Something else is at work."

"But where will you begin? The western frontier is vast."

Evliit smiled faintly. "Take care of him, Tophian."

He whistled — a sharp, rising call. Angwen appeared, galloping across the field. Evliit stroked his neck, relieved to see him unharmed, and mounted.

"She won't hide in the Black Mountains — too close to Rion," Evliit said. "And she's known little but the icy north. No… she'll choose the far western woods, or whatever lies beyond."

He clasped Tophian's shoulder. "Take Mategaladh to Moonledge Peak. I'll find you when this is done."

"Be safe, my friend," Tophian said.

Evliit nodded, turned Angwen westward, and spurred him toward the distant forests.

CHAPTER 14

THE PRICE OF SECRETS

"He did what?" Ardidhus asked.

"He left! He left to find this monk — Ebert!" Amphileph snapped. Fury radiated from him. "I returned to check on the preparations for Broeden's body, and Evliit was gone. Hiadhlian told me he'd gone in search of the monk. I went outside, found Tophian preparing to take Mategaladh home, and he told me the same. Evliit is gone."

He paced, hands clenched. "And now it falls to me to clean up this mess? Someone must lead!"

He didn't wait for Ardidhus's reply. He strode to the Watchers wrapping Broeden's corpse.

"It is time to deal with the spoils of this war," Amphileph said. "Evliit has gone to find Ebert, and only the Creator knows how long his quest will keep him from us."

"And you will take Evliit's place?" Hiadhlian asked.

"As I did when he first abandoned us for a woman," Amphileph replied.

"That is uncalled for!" Olidan exclaimed.

Clogren stepped forward. "Was it not Amphileph who commanded the dead so brave Praedhos could strike the monster's skull?" Murmurs and nods followed. "It was Praedhos's blade — not Evliit's — that felled the creature."

"And was it not Evliit's blade that slew the dark one?" Hiadhlian countered. "Praedhos swore allegiance to Evliit, as should we all."

Sardhor spoke. "He is the sword bearer, yes — and his deeds fulfilled prophecy. But prophecy says nothing of what comes after Broeden's fall. A new day is upon us. We must adapt."

"Adapt how?" Hiadhlian asked. "What are you implying?"

"The prophecies end here," Sardhor said. "We are on our own now. We need a leader who is present."

"I say put it to a vote," Clogren declared.

"Odhramorus and Hrast have succumbed to their wounds," Sardhor said. "But I speak for them — and I side with Clogren."

"Of course," Hiadhlian muttered. "The men of the Northern Plains stick together."

"As Tophian and Mategaladh would with you," Clogren replied. "What of it?"

Rorindan, Olidan, and Faldhian — the Watchers of the western forests — conferred quietly. Then Olidan spoke.

"Let Amphileph and the Spellmakers handle this. Many of them are of these lands. We will take Broeden's body to Rion."

"Very well," Amphileph said. "It is decided. I will deal with matters here — with the Camonra and the wounded."

The group dispersed. Amphileph stepped onto the balcony for air. Sardhor joined him.

"Yesterday, from this very balcony, Broeden screamed his vengeance," Sardhor said. "Now the men of Rion celebrate his death on his own lawn. What a difference a day makes."

Amphileph stared west, toward the hazy forests of Etharath. The thought of Evliit somewhere out there rekindled his anger.

"He should not have left," Amphileph said.

"I understand your frustration," Sardhor replied. "But we have no time for it. Evliit has made his choice. We must deal with what remains."

Amphileph looked down at the tents of wounded. "Food and water will soon become a crisis. Many cannot be moved. Their fate grows grimmer by the minute."

He turned to reenter the chamber — and a stabbing pain shot behind his right eye. His nose began to bleed. His right ear rang sharply.

Sardhor saw him wince. "Amphileph... are you well?"

Amphileph wiped the blood away. "It's nothing."

They crossed the room to Broeden's wrapped body.

After a moment, Sardhor asked quietly, "Do you remember anything of

Broeden's last moments? Anything he said when he held you?"

Amphileph bristled. *Sardhor is weak.*

"What are you implying? Did you let the old wizard rattle you? I am fine." The ringing faded. "He was babbling — a coward at the point of a blade. He would have said anything."

Sardhor held his gaze. "I know enough of the dark tongue to understand some of it."

"So he cursed me. What did you expect? Gratitude?"

Amphileph's tone made Sardhor step back. "No… I suppose not."

Hiadhlian approached. "A fitting end for one so evil."

Olidan examined the wrappings. "Do you need anything more from me?"

"No," Olidan said. "The preparations are complete."

"Then, if Amphileph permits, I will take my leave," Hiadhlian said.

"Not yet," Sardhor said. "First we must conjure a dark place for Broeden's spirit — to bind him even in death."

"I cannot join that conjure," Hiadhlian said. "I will tend to the wounded."

"To each his own," Sardhor replied.

Hiadhlian nodded and left. Those remaining formed a circle around Broeden's body.

As Sardhor and the Spellmakers conjured, the Watchers prayed. Their prayers stabbed at Amphileph's ears like needles.

When the vigil ended, they wrapped Broeden's body and carried it outside. Amphileph led the procession.

Soldiers burned the remains of Praedhos's monster nearby, its guts popping in the flames. The Watchers hurried across the ruined drawbridge, warriors lining the path to glimpse the corpse.

Hiadhlian emerged from the healers' tents, wiping blood from his hands. His attendants placed Broeden's body in a wagon as a crowd gathered.

Amphileph met him. "The wounded — will they survive?"

"Their injuries vary," Hiadhlian said. "Some will not last the night. Others, like you, bear no wounds — but what they've seen haunts them. Broeden's curse lingers."

"There is no curse!" Amphileph shouted.

His attendants turned. Hiadhlian pulled him aside.

"Lower your voice," he said. He nodded to his attendants. "Be about your work."

They obeyed.

"You doubt Broeden's ability to curse?" Hiadhlian asked. "The Elders must hear what transpired. I leave for Rion at once."

"To do what?" Amphileph demanded. "Give the Elders the excuse they've always wanted? To hunt Spellmakers like dogs?"

Hiadhlian stepped close. "You are changed, brother. I pray you do not rue the day you pitted yourself against that wizard — for all our sakes."

Amphileph did not flinch. "You spiritual types — with your lofty ideals — leaving the killing to men like Praedhos and me. Go, then. The day is won. We have no need of you."

Sadness clouded Hiadhlian's face. He mounted his horse.

"You judge your brothers wrongly," he said. "We do not seek death. Your hubris has opened your door to wickedness."

He rode west. The remaining Watchers followed the wagon bearing Broeden's body. Only Amphileph and the Spellmakers remained.

Clogren stepped beside him. "The Watchers are blind. For the Elders, we have given everything. We mixed with filth for them — all because Evliit left us leaderless. It was *your* hand that enabled Praedhos to kill the darkest creature ever seen. *Your* hand that allowed Evliit to slay the wizard. Only you are fit to lead."

He pointed to Amphileph's arm. A pulse of black moved through the veins.

"The dark magic flows in you," Clogren said.

Amphileph met his gaze.

"The Spellmakers will follow you," Clogren continued. "We are not like the Watchers or the Rionese. We are conjurers. We joined monks and Elder-lovers only to destroy Broeden. That goal is achieved. Now we move on. We will command both the living and the dead."

Amphileph's voice was low. "What has the wizard done to me?"

"You have stolen Broeden's power," Clogren said. "A momentous gift."

"And his curse?"

"Sardhor is a pessimist. I see conquest ahead. With this power, all will fear you — and the Creator who sent you."

Amphileph breathed deeply. Power thrummed through him like a second heartbeat.

"Walk with me," he said.

Clogren followed eagerly.

Amphileph looked toward the castle. "Gather every man here," he said. "And release the Camonra."

Clogren froze. "The Camonra, master?"

Amphileph continued walking, glancing back with a cold smile.

"They will do my bidding now."

When Clogren finally emptied Broeden's castle of all remaining Rionese troops and captives, night had fallen. Soldiers bearing torches crowded the castle lawn, their flames flickering against the ruined stone.

Clogren released the Camonra from the dungeons. They emerged blinking and confused, filing past the Rion Guard and militia. A murmur rippled through the ranks. Some guards mounted their horses and fled; others simply ran.

"Today marks the end of the time of Broeden!" Amphileph cried. "Now I command the Camonra!"

At his words, the Camonra dropped to one knee. A surge of power coursed through Amphileph, intoxicating and absolute.

"Let the name of Broeden be forgotten!" he shouted. "Let the name of Amphileph rise anew!"

He turned his back to them and faced the castle. Raising his arms, he called to the heavens. The sky churned above them.

"Gone is the name of Broeden!"

Lightning struck the highest peak of the castle. Stone exploded outward. The structure buckled inward. More lightning fell, hammering the grounds. Within seconds, the entire fortress collapsed into a burning heap. No wall remained standing.

"Let us prepare a new day!" Amphileph roared. "Let us go into the valley of the Black Mountain and multiply!"

The Camonra leapt to their feet, roaring their approval.

Clogren leaned close, shouting over the jubilation. "Your powers are great, my lord! Long live Amphileph! Our loyalties lie with you!"

Amphileph watched the chaos with a grim, calculating expression. "Then I will test your loyalties first. Send Sardhor after Odhramorus and Hrast. I want all our brother Spellmakers gathered. Together we are invincible."

He pointed to the kneeling Camonra. "Bring me the fiercest among them. There is still one who might topple my plans. I have seen Rendaya in my visions. If Broeden could not control her, I will not try. The Huntress must be hunted down and destroyed."

"Yes, of course, master," Clogren said. "It will be done."

"But first," Amphileph shouted, "we must rid ourselves of the weak and useless!"

He pointed toward the tents of the wounded.

The tents erupted into flames.

Screams rose, then fell silent as the fire consumed them. Smoke from the charred bodies drifted through the ranks, curling around the Spellmakers and Camonra like a dark benediction.

Amphileph's new army — Spellmakers and Camonra alike — marched southwest toward the Black Mountains, leaving the smoldering ruin of Broeden's castle behind them.

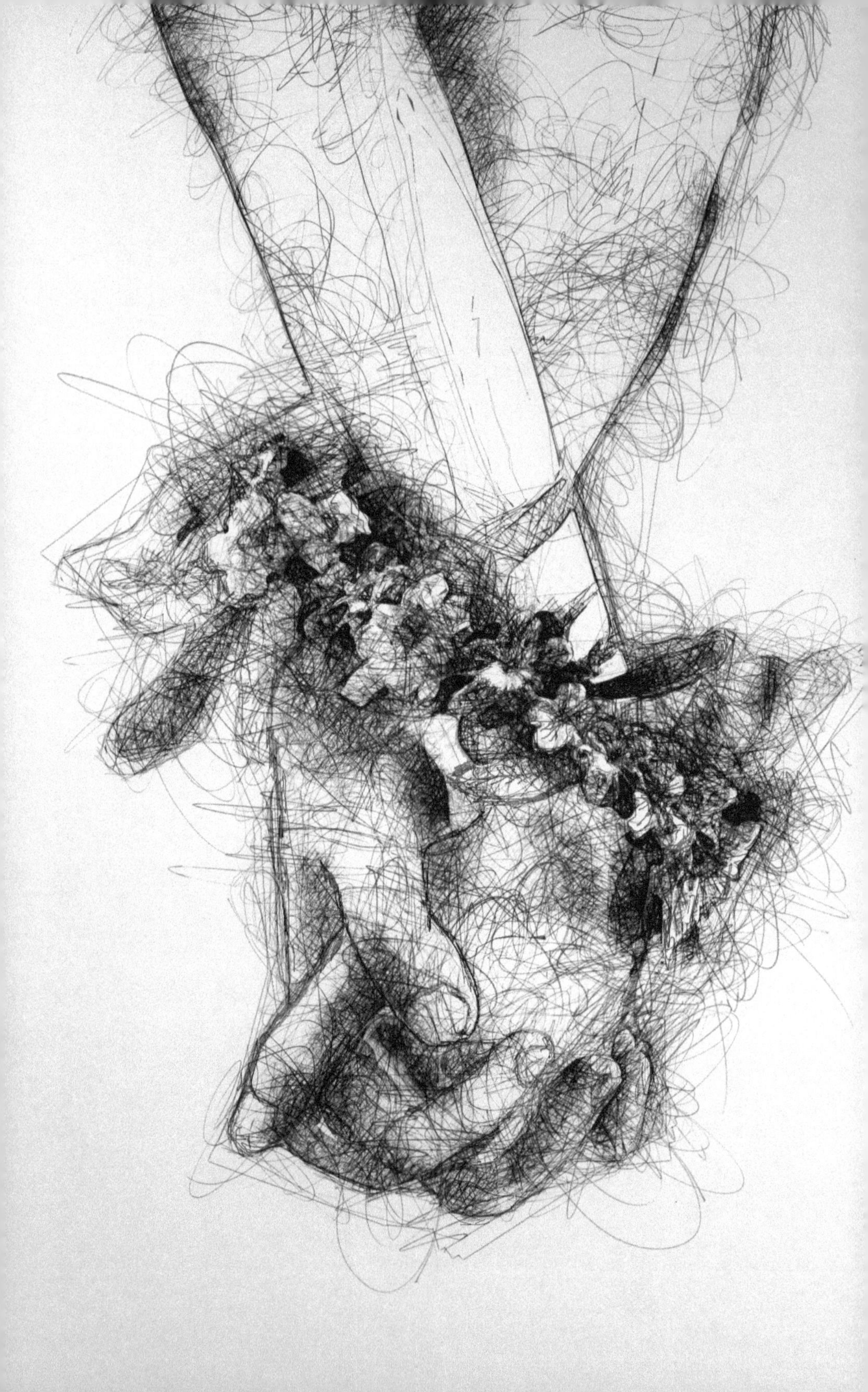

CHAPTER 15

A Seaside Forest

Ebert pressed the final glass pane into place and smoothed a line of cement along the frame with his fingertip. More than two months had passed since he and Rendaya fled Broeden's castle, and autumn was beginning to creep into Southwood.

Distance had given them comfort, but not peace. Every morning Ebert woke wondering if today would be the day Broeden found them. Etharath was vast, and Southwood's forests stretched for thousands of miles — finding them would be like finding a needle in a haystack. But the fear lingered all the same.

Rendaya stepped into the cabin. Gone were the shadows that once clung to her — the worry lines, the haunted look.

"That's coming along beautifully," she said, running her fingers over the smooth glass. Her smile lit the room. "I told you I could make a good trade. I didn't even have to go into Rion. There's a glassmaker in the servants' shanties south of the city."

Ebert huffed. "You know you make me nervous going anywhere near Rion. Did you stay near the cliffs?" He stepped off the folding ladder and crossed his arms, tilting his head at the window. "Is that straight?"

Rendaya laughed softly. "Yes, it's straight. You worry too much." She glanced at him, then at her nails. "And yes, I mostly stayed near the cliffs. I watched the ocean while the glassmaker worked."

He turned toward her, arms still crossed. "You went into Rion, didn't you?"

She looked up with wide brown eyes. "Yes. But there was a great commotion in the city, and I wanted to know why."

"Rendaya, we talked about this—"

"I know, but there were celebrations in the streets! I had to see what was happening!"

That caught his attention. "Celebrations? Did you find out why?"

"Not at first. So I went down and walked among the Rionese."

"You did what? Rendaya, you know I—" He stopped when he saw her expression shift. Her eyes glistened. "What happened?"

"They were celebrating the defeat of Broeden." Her voice cracked. Tears welled.

Ebert wrapped his arms around her. She pressed her face to his chest. "Oh, Rendaya… Broeden brought these things upon himself. He would have sacrificed you without hesitation."

"I know," she whispered. "I shouldn't feel this way, but I do." She wiped a tear from her cheek. "I knew he would die if I didn't fight for him. I knew it the moment we leapt into the air. But hearing it… it's difficult." She forced a small laugh. "We should be celebrating our freedom, and here I am crying."

"Come here," he murmured, holding her again. She squeezed him tightly, sniffled, then pulled back and took his hand.

"The sea was beautiful, though," she said, smiling faintly.

He gazed into her eyes. "Do you realize we can stop living in fear now? I know it's not that simple, but this is good news."

She looked down. "I know, Ebert."

He chose his next words carefully. "I remember the first time you showed me the cliffs. I loved them — but the western shores… that first sight of the ocean from the forest's edge, the long slope to the water, the white sands…"

A spark lit her eyes. "That was the first time we kissed."

"Yes," he said softly. "We should go again. Soon. Forget Rion and everything else."

"I like the window," she said suddenly, pointing.

"Oh — yes." He laughed. "The shutters were quaint, and I know how you love watching the rain, but winter's coming. Now you can see out without freezing, and I won't have to build a fire so big it frightens me."

"You don't like how the stove glows red around the flue pipe?" she teased.

"I'd prefer not to wake up to the house burning down."

She wiped his brow. "You're working up quite a sweat. Why didn't you use the skills I've taught you? I don't understand you sometimes."

"I could have done it by conjure," Ebert said. He lifted his hand, and a burst of light flared above the table before he dismissed it. "But a gift for you should be the product of harder work — a deeper commitment than a wave of my hand."

Her eyes softened, and he felt his heart swell. As a monk, he had always tried to love everyone — but this was different. She was the rhythm of his days, the warmth of his nights.

She turned back to the window, running her fingers along the frame. Ebert thought she blushed.

"You romance me still?" she asked.

"How could I not?" he said. "You've shown me places untouched by man — mountains, plains, seas, cliffs that shape the wind itself. You've taught me to shape the world in ways I never imagined." He couldn't look away from her. "How could I not love you?"

"And you've made tea," she said, smiling.

"Yes — earlier. Probably cold now. But I brought fresh water."

She checked the pot. "Warm enough for me."

She poured a cup and sipped. "This tastes like the tea you brought me the first time we talked."

He blinked, surprised. She rarely spoke of the past. Maybe — just maybe — they were moving beyond the shadows that haunted her.

"It's delicious," she said.

"Hey — I've been cramped up in here all day. How about a walk in the garden?"

"Absolutely charming." She offered her arm, and he eagerly took it.

Outside, the late-summer breeze swayed the branches overhead.

"I love this little path," she said. "A path to our secluded garden. What could be better?"

For a moment, Ebert thought of the Garden of Huergol — of Evliit — and wondered where his friend was now.

They stepped through the brush into the garden, where Ebert had laid stone paths around the vegetables and flowers he'd planted.

"It's like a ship's wheel," Rendaya said. "Does it mean something?"

"It's traditional among my people," Ebert said. "The many paths of life leading to one Creator — the resting place at the center. Beauty surrounds you no matter which path you take."

Rendaya rolled her eyes — barely — but fondly. She challenged him, always, and in answering her, he had grown.

"I especially love my little stone bench," she said, sitting. He joined her, drawn again to her quiet wonder.

"I love you," he said.

"You know I know nothing of love," she replied. "But if you ask whether my heart quickens when I'm with you... whether I look forward to hearing your voice each day—"

"That's enough," he said gently.

She kissed him — and the world fell away. Overcome, Ebert dropped to one knee and took her hand.

"Will you fasten hands with me?" he asked. "Will you be my wife?"

"Oh, Ebert..." She sighed. "We don't need any of that."

His heart clenched. He began to rise, but she caught his shoulder.

"No — that's not what I meant." She cupped his face. "I've never been happier. And you are the reason. I want to be with you."

"You want to be with me?"

"Now and forever."

Ebert grinned, sprang up, and hurried to a patch of flowers. He wove a small ring of stems and blossoms, returned, and placed it around their joined hands.

He looked to the sky. "Creator, I declare my love for this woman, Rendaya. I swear I will care for her all my days."

"We're doing this now?" she asked, nervous.

He lowered his gaze to hers and squeezed her hand.

"Yes," he said softly. "We're doing this now."

She blinked in surprise, then smiled. "Now, then... do I say something?"

"Yes, of course," Ebert said. "If it's truly in your heart, declare your love for me."

Rendaya looked upward as he had. "Creator, I declare my love for this man, Ebert."

She paused and glanced sideways. "Do I say the second part?"

"Yes."

"I swear to you that I will care for him all my days."

"Now together," Ebert said, "we say, 'Bind us together, oh Creator of all.' Ready?"

She nodded.

"Bind us together, oh Creator of all!" they said in unison — and then they kissed.

Ebert laughed, breathless with joy. "It can be much more formal than that, but see? That wasn't so bad. We are one, you and I — and you've made me the happiest man in the world."

"Well, that makes me happy as well," she said. "But I don't feel any different. How does this spell work?"

"It's no spell!" he said — then caught her sarcastic look. "Oh, you're the funny one." He nudged her shoulder playfully. "What do you say to making us some of that stew of yours in celebration? I'll see how many fresh carrots I can find."

"Deal," she said. She gave him a sly sideways glance, then turned and headed down the path toward the cottage.

A Promise Kept

Evliit had ridden south across the Northern Plains, following the valley that led west toward the edge of the continent. With Angwen's speed, the long highlands eventually gave way to the sea. Finding no sign of Ebert along the shoreline, he turned his attention to a mountain farther south, wanting to search it before winter set in. Two months had passed since he began his search, and the temperature was falling.

From the mountaintop, he surveyed the land and decided to backtrack east. A river flowed from the mountain's eastern ridge, winding southward — and if Ebert and Rendaya were anywhere nearby, they would likely be near water.

The next day, he descended beside a waterfall, washing away months of travel in the pool below. He watered Angwen, refilled his flask, and followed the river as it cut through the valley and into the dense tree line he had marked from above. A stroke of good fortune, he thought.

He entered a tall stand of live oaks beside the river. As he knelt to drink from the cold mountain stream, a distant booming sound echoed across the valley.

Evliit froze.

He mounted Angwen at once and rode toward the noise, alert and wary.

That night, more sounds drifted through the forest — one unmistakably a war horn.

By dawn, he reached the eastern edge of the woods. He tied Angwen and climbed a tall oak to survey the valley leading south toward Rion. This far north, the land was untouched. No Rion Guard patrolled here.

A rustle below caught his attention. Leaves shifted. Something moved closer.

A Camonra war dog emerged from the brush, its black coat gleaming. It sniffed the ground, weaving back and forth, then stopped directly beneath Evliit's tree and looked up.

Evliit held his breath. *Did it see me?*

Before he could decide whether to strike or flee, a Camonra war horn sounded behind the beast. The dog snapped its head toward the sound and bolted, barking furiously.

Far to the south, bright flashes lit the second stand of trees. Moments later, a roaring boom shook the oak, nearly knocking Evliit from its branches. The shockwave rippled through the forest.

There was only one person he knew who could unleash such power.

Rendaya.

He climbed down and ran for Angwen.

He moved south cautiously, avoiding open ground. The forest was eerily silent.

Under cover of night, he crossed the field between the northern and southern woods, reaching the shelter of the southern trees by daybreak.

Half a mile in, he noticed the trees leaning — all of them — in the direction he had come. The farther he went, the more extreme the angle became, until he reached a clearing littered with fallen trunks. The devastation was immense.

He climbed an upturned tree to gain a better vantage.

At the far end of the destruction stood a small cottage — untouched.

Dead Camonra and war dogs lay scattered around it.

A smaller body lay near the cabin door. Female. *The Huntress.*

Why would they kill her?

And where was Ebert?

Evliit shifted for a better view — and saw one more body.

Crucified against a standing tree with several spears.

"Oh no…" His voice broke. "Creator, no…"

He scrambled through the wreckage, tearing through branches and debris until he reached the tree.

It was Ebert.

Long dead.

Evliit bowed his head, tears falling freely. His chest heaved with grief.

Why, Ebert? Why were you here with her?

Nothing made sense.

When he could bear no more, he turned toward Rendaya. She lay pinned to the ground by two spears, her body torn and bloodied.

All his anger drained away. Shock prickled across his skin.

The cottage door stood ajar. Inside, everything was untouched. No cages. No restraints. Nothing to suggest captivity.

Did Ebert truly come willingly?

Morning light streamed through the window, illuminating a Soru flower in a tin vase. A note lay beside it.

"Dearest Ebert,
Your love is more rare than this Soru flower.
It has changed my life.
Where once I saw only darkness,
now I see beauty and know true happiness.
I will cherish fastening your hand to mine
in this life and the next.
All my love,
Rendaya."

Evliit set the note down slowly.

Somehow, impossibly, these two — as different as night and day — had found *love*. He remembered Ebert's radiant spirit and understood: Ebert had conquered what warriors and wizards could not.

There was nothing left but to bury them.

He found a shovel and returned to Rendaya's body first. He could not yet face unpinning Ebert from the tree.

But when he pulled the first spear from her leg, Rendaya groaned.

Evliit's breath caught.

He looked heavenward. "If it pleases you, holy one… pour out your healing power."

He placed his hands on the deep wound in her chest. Golden light surged through her. Her eyes flew open. Her body arched as life poured back into her.

As the wound closed, she relaxed and turned her head toward him.

"Ebert! Where's Ebert?" She reached for the spear pinning her shoulder, but her strength failed.

"Hold still," Evliit said. "You're badly hurt."

He removed her hands and pulled the spear free. She screamed, writhing, trying to see past him — and then her eyes found the tree.

She went still.

A quiet sob escaped her.

"I'm sorry you had to see that," Evliit said softly.

She turned her face away.

"Let me take you inside."

"No!" she cried. "He'll not hang there another second!"

She pushed him aside and tried to stand — but collapsed face-first. Evliit rushed to her. She tried again, but her body failed her. She broke, sobbing openly.

"Ebert..." she whispered.

"Let me take you inside," he said gently. "I will tend to Ebert."

Defeated, she nodded.

He carried her inside and set her at the table. She stared blankly out the window while he healed her shoulder and calf.

Evliit moved the vase and note aside, placing the Soru flower in the window's light where she could see it. She said nothing.

"I'm going to get Ebert now," he said.

She didn't respond.

"I'm—"

"Very well," she whispered.

He steeled himself and went outside.

When he brought Ebert's broken body inside, he laid him on the table. A bucket and towel sat near the stove. As Evliit reached for them, Rendaya rose.

"Ebert always brought me fresh water," she said quietly.

She reached for the towel. Evliit hesitated, then handed it to her.

"I want to do it," she said.

She looked at Ebert's body. Tears filled her eyes, but she wiped them away and mouthed the words again: *I want to do it.*

She undressed him gently, laying his bloodstained clothes on the floor. Evliit took them outside.

When he returned, she stood frozen, water dripping from the towel onto her skirt.

"I can help," Evliit said.

"No… please." She wrung out the cloth. "Can you get me the needle and thread from beside the bed?"

"Of course."

He retrieved them and set them on the table.

She took the towel and began washing the dried blood from Ebert's body. When she finished, she threaded the needle and began stitching his wounds.

"His face is so swollen," she whispered. "It almost doesn't look like him."

Evliit covered his mouth, lowered his head, and wept. When he finally caught his breath, he said, "He was my friend."

Rendaya didn't answer. She only nodded and returned to her work.

When she had cleaned him, she dressed Ebert in fresh linens. Evliit lifted his friend and carried him into the garden Ebert had tended with such love. Rendaya watched silently as Evliit buried him there.

"Rendaya," he said softly. "May I call you that?"

"Yes."

"Go inside and rest." He looked at the scattered dead. "I'll deal with this."

"Thank you," she murmured, her brow furrowed. She never lifted her eyes from Ebert's grave.

Evliit worked the rest of the day burning the bodies of the Camonra, their Azrodh mounts, and their war dogs. Halfway through, Rendaya brought a chair outside and sat near the cottage, elbows on her knees, staring into the distance. At times, he thought she was speaking to herself.

He approached her and turned to watch the dark smoke rising.

"Broeden's savagery is unmatched," he said.

Her expression shifted. "You think Broeden did this?"

Evliit turned to her. "Is this not your father's vengeance for leaving him at the battle for Durageim?"

"No," she said. "This is the work of one called Amphileph. He sent the Camonra to kill Ebert and me."

Evliit stared at her. That couldn't be true. Amphileph would never have ordered Ebert's death. "How do you know this?"

Rendaya pointed toward the pyre. "Do you see that one? The body with the captain's helm?"

Evliit stepped closer, shielding his face from the heat. "No."

She joined him and pointed. "The dyed crest burns bright orange."

Evliit nodded. "Yes. I see it."

"He told Ebert as much while they killed him." She looked at Evliit. "The dark spirit of Broeden infects the one called Amphileph. Do you know this name?"

Evliit hesitated. He would not lie. "Yes. He was under my charge. Leader of the Spellmakers."

"You'll command him no more," Rendaya said. "He has become the embodiment of the darkness that once dwelled in Broeden."

She looked again at the burning plume. "Ebert told me of you and your brethren. He loved you dearly."

"Ebert was innately good," Evliit said. "I loved him as well."

"Then heed my warning, Evliit. Ready your Watchers. Amphileph will grow mighty in his wickedness. With Broeden's powers, he will conjure many Camonra to carry his banner."

"The Watchers are scattered," Evliit said. "Injured or worse."

"Then I hope you renew their strength before Amphileph raises an army of his own," Rendaya said. "I tell you truly — the Camonra will follow him."

Evliit squared his shoulders. "And what of you, Rendaya? Won't you stand with us?"

"I will not," she said. "To cross paths with that darkness again would be my undoing. It might carry me away once and for all." She looked down. "You've done right by me. You are as Ebert described you — a decent man. His sword bearer. I'll not forget what you did today."

"Can I not convince you? You need not fight. Just come — be among friends, not alone here."

"You suppose too much," she said. "I would never feel welcome among the Watchers. Southwood is my home." A faint smile touched her lips. "And what warrior wants to hear the grieving of women?" The smile faded. "Let them respect this forest as Ebert's resting place. They will enter it otherwise at their own peril."

Tears welled in her eyes. Evliit had never seen such sorrow.

"Leave me now," she said. "And do not return to this forest."

She turned to go, then looked back. "And have no doubts — I'll have my revenge on Amphileph."

Her tears vanished, replaced by cold resolve. Before Evliit could speak, she leapt into the air and flew west toward the sea.

Evliit looked around. The pyres were collapsing into soft ash.

He turned to the tree where Ebert had hung. Already the red stains were fading into the bark. Evliit closed his eyes and replaced the horror with the memory of Ebert smiling, releasing birds into the sky.

Then he left the forest and rode north toward the Faceless Mountains.

EPILOGUE

On the sixth day after Ebert's burial, Evliit approached Tophian's home in the Faceless Mountains. But before he reached the stone steps, he saw them—an ocean of people stretching across the Northern Plains. Men, women, and children covered the land as far as he could see, all moving westward from the direction of the Black Mountains.

Evliit pulled Angwen's reins. "What's happening here?"

"A conjurer called Amphileph has taken the lands east of the Black Mountains," a man said. "We've been cast out of our homeland."

"He gathers slaves to build a great temple to the Creator," another added, "in honor of Broeden's defeat."

"We've traded one tyrant for another," a woman said bitterly. "The boot on our neck feels the same no matter who wears it."

More refugees gathered around Angwen.

"We've seen the Camonra encamped with Amphileph's forces—the ones who call themselves Spellmakers. What man joins with the very monsters who terrorized us for generations?" Several murmured their agreement. "We're going to Rion to beg the Elders for protection."

It is as Rendaya said, Evliit thought. *Amphileph has succumbed to darkness.*

He had no answers for them. He rode through the crowd and up the mountainside to the entrance of Moonledge Peak's great library. As he dismounted, Hiadhlian emerged from within.

"Evliit, brother!" Hiadhlian cried, embracing him in a crushing hug.

Evliit stepped back. "You're here? What of Broeden's castle?"

"Gone," Hiadhlian said. "All of it."

"I must know more… but first—how is Mategaladh?"

"Better. Much better indeed!" Hiadhlian said. "Praise the Creator."

"As do I," Evliit replied. "Tell me—what madness possesses Amphileph?"

"The Amphileph you knew is gone," Hiadhlian said grimly. "Broeden's curse has claimed him. The Spellmakers have joined with the Camonra in the valley beyond the Black Mountains."

"Rion will know soon enough," Evliit said. "His conquest is driving refugees toward them."

Hiadhlian pointed to Evliit's sword. "It won't be long before the Spellmakers insist that Amphileph—not you—should bear that blade."

Evliit placed a hand on his shoulder. "Walk with me. I want to see Mategaladh."

They descended into the mountain's halls and entered the sleeping quarters, where Tophian and Mategaladh sat talking.

"My friends!" Evliit exclaimed.

"It's truly good to see you!" Mategaladh said, beaming.

"You're looking much better," Evliit said, embracing them both.

More Watchers filed in, greeting the sword bearer. Tophian's home had become their refuge. When the welcomes quieted, Evliit sat beside his friends.

Mategaladh's expression hardened. "What news of Ebert?"

Evliit lowered his head. "Ebert is dead," he said quietly. "At Amphileph's order."

Gasps filled the room.

Tophian raised a hand. "Then it's true. Amphileph has turned on us."

"Yes," Hiadhlian said. "He's declared himself our leader."

"The leader of the Spellmakers," Tophian corrected. "But who leads the remaining Watchers?"

Silence fell. All eyes turned to Evliit.

Evliit rose. "I will," he said. "For Ebert—and for the innocents."

They raised their cups.

"For Ebert and the innocents!"

They drank, and the room fell solemn again. Then Tophian spoke.

"It's a frail new world. The people will flock to the Elders in Rion.

Amphileph will seek to crush the southern threat."

"He won't move quickly," Evliit said. "Amphileph is patient. He'll grow his armies before he marches."

Mategaladh looked around the room. "Far fewer of us remain than answered the calling."

"Then let us gather our strength," Evliit said, "and prepare for the darkness to come."

They planned long into the night, drinking long-saved casks of wine. When at last the others retired, Evliit wandered alone into the library hall. The prophetic painting of the sword bearer loomed above him. A faint scent of Soru drifted through the air.

He followed it outside.

The stars were brilliant. Far to the south, the last torches of the refugees flickered toward Rion. The Northern Plains lay quiet.

Tophian stood on his balcony, pipe in hand. He nodded to Evliit, then turned back to the eastern horizon.

Evliit joined him.

They said nothing.

For over an hour, they watched the dark clouds swirling above the Black Mountains.

Author's Note

When I first began shaping the world of Erathe, I didn't yet know the cost its heroes would bear. Stories have a way of revealing themselves slowly, and sometimes painfully, and this one demanded its price. The Watchers' War is a tale of loyalty, sacrifice, and the fragile line between light and darkness — not only in wizards and warriors, but in all of us.

Evliit, Rendaya, Ebert, Amphileph, Praedhos, and the others walked with me far longer than I expected. Their choices surprised me. Their losses weighed on me. Their victories felt earned. If you felt any of that along the way, then I am grateful, because it means these characters lived for you as they lived for me.

This book closes one age and opens another. The continent of Etharath is changing — its alliances, its faith, its balance of power. The Watchers are scattered. The Spellmakers are corrupted. The Camonra march under a new banner. And somewhere in the western forests, grief has given birth to a new kind of resolve in a formidable foe.

The next chapter of this saga is already stirring. I hope you'll walk with me into the darkness that follows, and into whatever light may rise beyond it.

Thank you for reading, and for giving these characters a place to live beyond my own imagination.

— John Montgomery

Mimir na Stydhra
(The Well of Kings)
Collected and preserved by Jaros

Editor's Note on the Following Text

The pages that follow are drawn from the Moonledge Peak Recension, a reconstruction compiled by the scribes of Rion from fragments preserved after the fall of the Monastery of Ardidhus. Though incomplete, these writings represent the most faithful surviving account of the ancient orders and the lost Well of Kings. They are presented here in their restored form for the benefit of the reader.

I. The Ages of the World

The Ages of Etharath are preserved through fragments of Watcher-era inscriptions, oral traditions, and the surviving chronicles of the early kingdoms. These records trace the shaping of the lands, the rise and fall of realms, and the long arc of history that culminated in the tyranny of Broeden and the prophecy that would lead to the founding of Rion.

II. The Prophecy and Martyrdom of Janus (626 B.F.)

Janus, a prophet of the Creator, foretold a free land far to the south and west—a place of abundance where the people could live unshackled. He named this land Rion, "the Free Land," describing mead in plenty, fertile soil for bread, and wild game in abundance.

Janus also prophesied that the Fortress of Durageim was doomed, warning that Broeden's tyranny would one day be swallowed by the very forces he sought to command.

Broeden, fearing the hope Janus inspired, sent assassins to silence him. Janus was murdered in his sleep, struck down in the quiet of his own home. His death became the catalyst for a movement that would reshape the world.

The Creator's Sorrow

When Janus died, the Creator was filled with great sorrow, and tears rained upon the lands for two moons. The storms did not break. The skies did not clear. The world lay beneath unending rain, as if the heavens themselves mourned the fallen prophet.

The Creator's Wrath

As the Creator's tears fell, His grief turned to righteous anger.

He released three mighty winds—from the north, the east, and the west—and they swept across the world with terrible force.

The Creator's tears, carried aloft by the winds, froze into snow and ice.

Sheets of frozen rain fell from the skies.

The northern lands were buried, entombed beneath the weight of divine sorrow turned to judgment.

This event, remembered as the *Sorrow of the Creator*, marked the moment when Janus's death reshaped not only the hearts of men, but the very face of the world.

III. The Exodus from Durageim

In the days following Janus's murder, thousands abandoned Durageim. Entire families, clans, and villages departed in a vast migration, guided by the prophet's final vision.

Their path led south along the Black Mountains, through the open reaches of the Western Frontier, and into the coastal forests and plains near the southern shores of Blue Water. The people carried Janus's memory with them, believing the Light would guide their steps.

IV. The Founding of Rion

Upon reaching the land Janus had foretold, the exiles built the first structure of their new settlement: the Temple of the Creator, raised upon *Bern na Stydhra*, the Hill of Kings.

This act marked the beginning of a new era. The Foundation of Rion became Year Zero, the start of the modern calendar. Around the hill, the first halls and hearths of Rion were built, forming the heart of a free people.

V. The Celestial Order

Jaros records the structure of the heavens as understood in the early years after the Foundation:

- The Light — the central star

- Denf — the swift inner world
- Sapath — the temperate world of balance
- La, The Dark Planet — pale and light-drinking, tied to endings and transitions
- Erathe — the world of Etharath
- The Moon — keeper of cycles and covenants
- Hrast — the red star of binding, transformation, and forbidden rites
- Thasyria — the white-gold star of truth, fortune, and blessing

These celestial bodies shape the rites, miracles, and destinies of mortals.

VI. The Stars Hrast and Thasyria

Hrast is a red, ominous star associated with binding, transformation, and the Alignment required for the creation of an Angrodha.

Thasyria is a brilliant star of good fortune. Its sighting is considered a blessing, and many of the younger generation swear oaths by its light.

VII. *The Rite of the Twin Stars*

A marriage performed when Hrast and Thasyria appear together is considered profoundly blessed. This rare celestial pairing symbolizes endurance, truth, and harmony.

Rion has hosted great ceremonies during this phenomenon, where many couples wed beneath the twin lights in celebrations remembered for generations.

VIII. The Erathian Calendar

The year consists of 372 days, divided into:

- ten months of thirty-seven days
- one month of thirty-nine days (Falingsor)

The calendar begins with the Foundation of Rion, marking the first year of freedom.

IX. The Lands of Etharath

A survey of the major regions:

- Candra Mountain
- Candra Valley

- Upland Plains
- Calarph
- The Faceless Mountains
- Durageim
- The Northern Plains
- Highwood and the Highborne River
- The Western Frontier
- The Black Mountains
- Rion and the Eastern Realm
- Southwood

Each region holds its own customs, histories, and celestial interpretations.

X. Prayers, Sacred Rites, and Invocations

Rites of Light

Healing, protection, clarity, and the sanctification of oaths.

Rites of the Moon

Transitions, births, funerals, and the sealing of covenants.

Rites of the Stars

Thasyria for truth and fortune; Hrast for binding and transformation; La for endings and remembrance.

Invocations of the Watchers

Ancient words of seeing, binding, remembrance, and severance—fragments preserved from the earliest Ages.

Miracles

Interventions of Light, Moon, or Stars, occurring when the natural and sacred align.

Common Prayers

The Prayer of the Light, the Oath of Thasyria, the Vigil of the Moon, the Quieting, and other daily devotions.

XI. Forbidden Rites

The Aramandhi

The sacrificial rite that creates an Angrodha, requiring:
- the Alignment of the planets and moons with Hrast

- the black blood of the Arcula-Naroom
- the destruction of a Camon host

A violation of the natural order, preserved only as a warning.

XII. The Bestiary of Etharath

A catalog of known creatures, natural and unnatural, including those shaped by the Watchers, the Inferiors, and the forbidden sciences. Each entry records origins, behaviors, and the dangers they pose.

XIII. Notes on the Watchers

The Well of Kings
From the Moonledge Peak Recension

The Structure of the Well

The ancient *Well of Kings* was the great archive of the Watchers and Spellmakers, containing the collected wisdom of the earliest Ages. Though the original tomes no longer survive, their structure is known through fragments and later reconstructions.

The Well consisted of:

- Seven white-bound tomes — visions, laws, rites of the Creator, and the ancient tongue of the Watchers
- Nine red-bound tomes — alchemy, mathematics, sciences, and shaping-formulae of the Spellmakers

These volumes were once housed in the Monastery of Ardidhus, tended by the Elders and by Jaros, whose writings form the oldest surviving witness to the ancient orders.

The Fall of Ardidhus

During the raids that preceded the fall of the monastery, the tomes were believed lost—scattered, destroyed, or carried away into darkness. Jaros perished in these events, leaving behind only fragments of his work. The completion of the Wall and the later construction of the Great Library at Moonledge Peak occurred long after his death.

The surviving fragments passed into the hands of Tophian, who gathered, translated, and stabilized what remained. Recognizing the fragility of the knowledge, he commissioned the scribes of Rion to create faithful copies and commentaries. Their work formed the basis of the recension later preserved within the mountain fortress of Moonledge Peak.

The Schism of the Scribes

The portions of the Well attributed to the Watchers were preserved openly, regarded as sacred and sanctioned knowledge. The fragments of the Spellmakers, however, were met with fear and suspicion. Some scribes who uncovered such writings brought them before the Elders of Rion, only to see the messenger silenced and the message destroyed, as the Elders sought to extinguish even the memory of such arts.

Yet not all scribes obeyed. Quietly, and at great personal risk, a few began transferring these forbidden fragments into the early archives that would one day form the Great Library of Moonledge Peak, ensuring their survival despite the efforts to erase them.

The Enigma of Jaros

Jaros appears throughout the surviving records across multiple centuries, always in service to the Creator as preserver and safe keeper of sacred knowledge. Whether this continuity reflects an extraordinary lifespan, a title passed from keeper to keeper, or mysteries now forgotten is unknown. His presence simply endures—quiet, constant, and unwavering—across the Ages.

The Legacy of the Well of Kings

Though the tomes of the Watchers and Spellmakers survive now only in fragments, their legacy endures. The ancient orders taught that knowledge was never truly lost so long as there remained those willing to seek it. The Moonledge Library, founded in later Ages, became the refuge of this belief, gathering remnants, translations, and interpretations of the surviving works.

Those who follow in the footsteps of the Watchers or the Spellmakers continue this tradition. Through study, discipline, and the shaping of glyph-strings, they labor to reconstruct the Well of Kings, piece by piece. These modern glyph-strings, though far removed from the original tomes, echo the same principles of creation, balance, and transformation.

In the hands of the devoted, such strings can be woven with remarkable potency, preserving the ancient art in forms both practical and perilous. Thus the *Well of Kings* lives on—not as a single place or archive, but as a living work, renewed by each generation that dares to take up the craft.